MURDER AT SWANN'S LAKE

MURDER AT SWANN'S LAKE

A Chief Inspector Woodend Mystery

Sally Spencer

severn
House

First published in Great Britain and the USA 1999 by
SEVERN HOUSE PUBLISHERS LTD of
19 Cedar Road, Sutton, Surrey, England, SM2 5DA.

Trade paperback edition first published in
Great Britain and the USA 2017 by
SEVERN HOUSE PUBLISHERS LTD.

British Library Cataloguing in Publication Data
A CIP catalogue record for this title is available from the British
Library.

ISBN-13: 978-0-7278-2285-7 (cased)
ISBN-13: 978-1-84751-814-9 (trade paper)
ISBN-13: 978-1-4483-0049-5 (e-book)

Typeset by Palimpsest Book Production Ltd.,
Falkirk, Stirlingshire, Scotland.

For Connie, Spudder and Smoke, without whose constant interest and affection during the course of my working day, this book would have been completed much sooner.

One

It was a pleasant evening in late August, one of the busiest times of year for the village of Swann's Lake. The fairground had all but closed down for the night, and the social clubs had just begun to start livening up. Anyone who knew the place well could have predicted that there would soon be a great deal of drinking, some harmless flirting and possibly a few fights in which both participants would urge their mates to hold them back. No one, however knowledgeable, could have guessed that within an hour there would be the village's first ever murder.

Robbie Peterson swung round on his bar stool and surveyed The Hideaway – the club which was the centre of his small business empire. It was an almost square wooden building. The walls were covered with red-flock paper, and at each side of the windows purple mock-velvet curtains hung from ceiling to floor. At one end was the bar, at the other a small stage – with just enough space for a compere and electric organ – and a slightly larger dance floor around which a few couples had already begun to shuffle. The rest of the room was taken up by tables, most of which were already reassuringly occupied.

Robbie lit a cigarette. You've come a very long way in a very short time, he told himself. Five years ago, you were nothin' but a common criminal, doin' Sid Dowd's biddin' and runnin' the risk of landin' up in gaol every time you went out on a job. Now you've got a club, half a fairground, a caravan site an' three holiday bungalows. Yes, you're doin' very nicely indeed.

His mood of well-being was shattered by the arrival of a young couple. Unlike most of the women in the club, who were wearing loose-fitting floral dresses and cardigans, the girl was dressed in a tight leather skirt which revealed her knees, and a blouse with a plunging neckline which declared quite openly that she possessed a splendid pair of breasts. And then there was her make-up! The way she'd applied it, she might as well have written, "Does anybody want to sleep with me?" across her forehead.

The girl looked over at Peterson, tossed her head contemptuously, and then turned to the man who was accompanying her. *He* looked out of place, too. Most of the club's customers were working men – fitters and bricklayers, dockers and carpenters – but this young man had never got his hands dirty in his life. The suit he was wearing must have cost more than anybody else in the room earned in a fortnight, and the haughty disdain on his face said more clearly than words that he considered The Hideaway below him.

So if you don't like it, why don't you just bugger off! Robbie thought angrily.

But the man wouldn't, because that was not part of Annabel's plan. She had come to the club to humiliate her father, and she would not leave until she had achieved her objective.

Annabel nodded curtly to her mother, Doris, who was talking to her cronies, then led her escort to an empty table near the stage. She'd deliberately chosen to sit there so she could get a proper look at him once he was behind the mike, Peterson thought. So she could show her boyfriend what a coarse, common lout her father really was. For a few moments, he actually toyed with the idea of not going on stage at all that night. Then he decided, sod it! He hadn't backed down from gangland fights in the old days, and he certainly wasn't going to retreat now from his own daughter.

The organist was coming to the end of his number. Robbie signalled that he should not start another one, and wove his way in between the tables to the stage. He mounted the steps, and turned to face his audience. Several of the women smiled warmly at him. And why shouldn't they? He was pushing fifty, and, at five feet seven could not have been called tall, but he still had the body of the hard young man he'd once been. And

2

whilst he couldn't exactly have been called handsome, there was a certain attractiveness in his dark eyes, large nose and square jaw.

"Welcome once again to The Hideaway, ladies and gentlemen," he said. "I know there's some real talent out there, an' later on you'll get your chance to show what you can do, but in the meantime I thought I'd kick us off with a little song made famous by the lovely Doris Day an' called, 'Que Sera Sera'."

The organist struck up the first few chords, and Robbie began to sing. He had a rich tenor voice, and even if his phrasing wasn't all it might have been, the people listening to him didn't seem to mind.

The words came automatically, and Robbie found his eyes roving around the club. Annabel was saying something to the man she'd brought with her, and he could tell from the twist of her lip that it was both about him and probably rather unpleasant. Doris was still chattering away to her friends and ignoring him completely, but there was nothing new about that – on or off the stage. Jenny was listening to him, though. His elder daughter always listened. She was his pride and joy. She was five years older than her sister, and whilst Annabel had inherited her mother's blond hair, there was a dark beauty about Jenny which could have come only from him.

The song came to its end and there was some applause. Robbie bowed. "I'd like to follow that with an old favourite originally sung by Dickie Henderson," he said. He searched around the audience, then raised his arm and indicated a middle-aged woman who he knew, from past experience, blushed easily. "It's called 'The Finger of Suspicion Points at *You*'."

The woman's friends giggled and Robbie launched into the song. His son-in-law, Terry Clough, was standing at the back of the club, he noticed. And he was not alone. Next to him was a slightly younger man dressed in a brown corduroy jacket – Michael Clough, Terry's schoolteacher brother.

Robbie had always liked Terry. He'd never been much in the brains department, but he was a good kid with a big heart

3

– which was why he'd been allowed to marry Jenny. Except that recently, Robbie reminded himself, Terry hadn't been such a good kid. In fact, if he'd done in Liverpool what he'd obviously been doing in Swann's Lake, he'd probably have ended up in concrete wellies, talking to the fishes at the bottom of the Mersey. But this wasn't Liverpool and, when all was said and done, Terry was part of the family. Robbie was confident he could sort out the mess without too much damage being done.

He turned his thoughts to Michael Clough. He was a strange one, all right – a bit of a do-gooder, always championing some cause which he thought would change the world. And when it became obvious – even to him – that the world was still in the same state as it had been when he'd started, he'd find himself another cause and fling himself into it with just as much energy as he'd devoted to the last one. Still, Michael had been very useful recently, there was no disputing that.

The two brothers seemed to be having a very deep conversation for a Friday night, and Robbie wondered what they could possibly be talking about. Terry made an agitated gesture with his hands. Michael shook his head. Then the two of them headed for the door. Strange, Robbie thought. Strange – and very unusual.

The final notes of the song faded away. Robbie bowed once more, then turned to look at Annabel. She held his gaze, and her expression seemed to be challenging him to get on with the show – to let her boyfriend see for himself what her father was *really* like.

"Did you hear the one about the honeymoon couple?" Robbie asked his audience. "Well, just before they tied the knot, he got talkin' to his mates, and she got talkin' to hers. You know what it's like yourselves, don't you?"

Some of the audience were already tittering in anticipation. Robbie winked at them.

"Anyway, her mates say, 'You've got a big shock comin' to you on Saturday night, Enid,' an' Enid says, 'I don't know what yer talkin' about.' So one of her mates says, 'You know when you have big fat pork sausages for your tea?' And she says . . . she says . . .''

The sight of the new arrival at the doorway stopped Robbie in his tracks. He was a young man wearing a smart blue suit and a hard expression. His name was Phil, and he worked for Sid Dowd. It was a bad sign he was there at all, but it was worse that Wally, the chief bar-steward – the chief bar *idiot* – was blocking the young man's path and holding out his hand. Asking for his membership card, for God's sake! As if any of Dowd's people needed membership cards for *anything*. Bloody hell, when you worked for Sid, that was a membership card in its own right.

Robbie felt his palms start to sweat. He raised a hand and waved wildly in Wally's direction, but the bloody fool was still looking down at his *own* hand, as if he really did expect the hard young man would suddenly produce a card from out of nowhere.

Robbie's mouth was dry, and he suddenly realised, from the puzzled faces which were looking up at him, that he must have stopped his joke mid-sentence. He had to say something, he told himself. He had to say bloody *something*.

"Wally," he croaked into the microphone. "Why don't you take that young feller over to the bar and give him a drink on the house."

"Drink on the house!" someone from one of the tables called out with mock amazement. "Has the age of bloody miracles finally come to pass?"

That was better, Robbie thought. Something normal was happening. Something he felt confident he could handle. He located the heckler, a middle-aged man with a red face and a flat cap. "The age of miracles?" he repeated. "No, George. But when it does arrive you'll soon know it – 'cos that'll be the night you'll be able to sup ten pints an' still do what's right by your Mabel when you get home."

The audience roared. Mabel gave her husband a furious glance, then forced herself to join in with the joke. And Wally had finally led the hard young man in the sharp suit over to the bar and was pouring him a drink.

"Anyway, these two Irishmen I was talkin' about . . ." Robbie continued.

"You weren't talkin' about no Irishmen," George said, despite receiving a dig in the ribs from his wife. "You were talkin' about a honeymoon couple."

"So I was," Robbie agreed. "Well, like I was sayin', Enid's friend tells her about the sausage, an' then she says, 'That's what you've got to look forward to.' But Enid's a bit thick, you see, and *she* says, 'You mean he'll bring me breakfast in bed?'"

He was back in his stride, the jokes rolling automatically off his tongue, but his mind was in turmoil. He'd thought he'd made it clear to Sid Dowd that he wasn't interested in doing any business with him. Yet he couldn't have done or Sid would never have sent one of his lads down to the club like this. Unless the lad was doing a bit of freelancing! But nobody freelanced on Sid Dowd – not unless they'd got tired of having their heads attached to the rest of their bodies.

It seemed to have got very hot in the club – almost stifling – and though Robbie had intended to be on the stage for another five minutes, he suddenly decided he'd had enough.

"'. . . yes, but I've never seen one come out of the fly in your trousers and eat a pork pie before'," he said, concluding the joke about the stolen goose. "And now, ladies and gentlemen, it's time to get back to the dancin'."

He walked off the stage to friendly applause and made his way towards the door. He didn't look at the bar to see if the young man in the blue suit was still there. If he was honest with himself, he'd really rather not know.

The club was separated from the rest of the buildings – the house, the adjoining outhouse and the garage – by a cinder yard, and as Robbie crossed it, he could hear some of the larger cinders crunching under the heels of his shoes.

Crunch . . . crunch . . . crunch . . .

He was a fool to let Sid Dowd's lad worry him, he told himself. Things had changed since they'd worked together in Liverpool. It would soon be the 1960s, for God's sake, and the sort of jobs they'd pulled together now seemed so old-fashioned they could have come out of the Ark. Yet did a leopard ever change its spots, especially when it was as *big* a leopard as Sid?

Robbie unlocked the outhouse door, switched on the light and experienced the vague mixture of disappointment and disgust he always felt when entering the room. It had started out simply as a workshop, a place where he could potter around doing the little jobs which he could just as easily have paid someone else to do. There was still evidence of the outhouse's original purpose – the carpenter's bench against the far wall, the tool rack hanging above it – but now, thanks to his wife's insistence, the place had lost the air of a retreat which it had once had.

'We need a proper office,' Doris had told him.

'What's wrong with working on the kitchen table?' he'd asked.

Doris had sighed, exasperatedly. 'There's no wonder you never can never get on in society however much you try,' she'd told him. 'You've absolutely no idea of the right way to do things, have you?'

And so the workshop had been converted into the office which Doris had felt they needed. A desk had been her first purchase – solid mahogany with brass handles. That had been followed by an oak filing cabinet – mostly still empty – and a black leather three-piece suite. Finally, only the day before, Doris had added a coffee table, a heavy one with a mosaic top. Robbie hated it.

'And when we've got rid of that workbench, there'll be room for a bookcase,' Doris had threatened.

'But we haven't got enough books to fill one,' Robbie had protested.

'Then we'll buy them as well,' his wife had told him.

Robbie walked across the room, past the window which looked out onto the yard and the club, and came to a halt in front of the workbench.

It stays, he decided. Whatever she says, it bloody well stays.

He removed the hammer from the tool rack and tapped the edge of the bench with it a couple of times. It was a very reassuring sound. He'd always been useful with his hands and often reflected that if he'd had a different upbringing, he might have made a good craftsman. But it was pointless to think like that, he told himself angrily – if he'd been a craftsman, he'd never have been able to afford what he had now.

He replaced the hammer in the rack, walked over to his desk and sat down. From this position he could see the club door and noticed how many times it swung open as new people arrived or customers made their way across the yard to the lavatory. It was a good business he had, he thought. Perhaps too good – if he'd just been ticking over, maybe Sid Dowd would have left him alone.

He was getting things out of proportion, he told himself. Not that that was at all surprising the way things were piling up – Sid Dowd bothering him, Doris always on at him, his younger daughter forever doing her best to humiliate him. And now this thing with Terry. What he needed was a break.

"Perhaps I'll go an' see how Alex Conway's getting on," he said aloud. "Old Alex always appreciates a visit from me."

He laughed at his own private joke, and wished he could tell it to Annabel – just to prove that his sense of humour didn't consist solely of stories about the things which dangled between men's legs. But, of course, he couldn't tell her. Even if she'd listen.

The light bulb overhead began to flicker and then went out completely. Apart from the small amount of light which filtered in from the club, the office was plunged into darkness.

"Shit!" Robbie said aloud.

The replacement bulbs were in the house, and he didn't feel like getting up to go and fetch one. Not at that moment, anyway. It had been a long day and the sight of Phil – the young man in the blue suit – had first made him nervous and now exhausted. He folded his arms on the desk, rested his head on them and went to sleep.

Detective Sergeant Gower stood in the shadow of The Hideaway's garage and looked longingly at Robbie Peterson's office. It was in darkness, which meant that Robbie wasn't there. But he could also clearly see that the door was open an inch or two. It wasn't like Peterson to be so careless – to present him with such an unprecedented opportunity. He wished he had a search warrant, but he didn't have enough evidence to obtain one – and anyway, he was not officially on duty.

His colleagues called Gower 'The Toad', and though it might not have been a very kind title, it was certainly accurate enough. He was squat and only just met police height requirements. In addition, he was cursed with bulging eyes and a skin which could have been a 'before' advertisement for any of the well-known brands of acne cream. But there was nothing toad-like in his attitude to his work. There, he was more of a fox terrier – pursuing his investigations with dogged determination, and never, ever, letting go once he'd got his teeth into something. And he'd got his teeth into the Peterson family. True, Annabel was his main target for the moment, but Robbie had always been his ultimate objective, and the open door just might provide him with a short cut.

Gower looked across the yard at the club. He wondered whether Robbie Peterson was inside The Hideaway at that very moment, and *if* he was, how long he was likely to stay there. It wouldn't do for a policeman to be discovered – unauthorised – on private property, even if the property in question was well-known to belong to a notorious villain. No, getting caught would do his career no good at all. On the other hand, since fate had clearly given him his chance . . .

It was two short strides to the window. Gower pressed his nose against it. He could see the workbench which was catching the small amount of light that shone from the club, but the rest of the office was in total darkness. Which meant that once he was inside – and as long as he stayed away from the bench – he would be completely invisible to anyone coming out of The Hideaway.

He rapidly formulated a plan. He would go over to Robbie's desk, from where he should get a good view of the yard, and when there was no one out there, he would quickly draw the heavy curtains. Once he had done that, he could switch on his torch with impunity and get down to some serious investigating.

Gower pushed the door open, stepped inside and closed the door softly again behind him. Phase One completed entirely satisfactorily.

The sergeant set off in the general direction of the desk. In the darkness, he should have walked slowly and cautiously, but caution had never been Gower's way, especially when he had the scent of his quarry in his nostrils.

It was his speed which was his downfall. If he hadn't been going so fast, the collision between his right shin and the coffee table would not have hurt half so much as it did. If he hadn't been going so fast, he might have stayed upright instead of lurching forward into the blackness.

Gower put his hands out in front of him for protection. His knees hit the floor with a sickening crunch. His torso landed heavily against the edge of Robbie's desk, knocking the wind out of him. But it was the thing his right hand made contact with which alarmed him most. He was touching a head – a brylcreamed head – which was lying on the desk.

Fighting for breath, Gower struggled to his feet. There was a man asleep at the desk! But could he *really* be asleep? Could he have received that jolt from the sergeant's hand without waking up?

Still gasping, Gower reached into his jacket pocket for his torch and switched it on. The beam fell on the hammer first – a perfectly ordinary woodworking hammer which was lying there on the desk. He moved the beam a little higher and it settled on the head which his outstretched hand had touched, and which undoubtedly belonged to Robbie Peterson. If anything could actually be said to belong to a corpse. And a corpse was definitely what Robbie was – because nobody, not even a hard case like him, could have survived having a six-inch nail driven deep into his temple.

Two

The old lady was sitting on her usual bench by the Serpentine and was studying the people who passed by with the eye of a connoisseur. So far that day she had seen no one who really interested her, but the couple approaching, hand-in-hand, looked very promising.

The man was perhaps twenty-five years old, and nearly six feet tall. His brown hair was neatly cut and his clothes showed that he took pride in his appearance. His features were perhaps a little *too* regular to earn him the title of handsome, the old lady thought, but by any standards he was certainly attractive. The woman was smaller and a little younger – probably no more than twenty-two or twenty-three. She had jet black hair, flashing dark eyes, a wide, passionate mouth and an oval chin. She looked foreign – possibly southern European.

The old lady allowed herself to indulge in her favourite game of imagining their histories. The man, she decided, had probably gone to a good school and was now something in the City. The woman was more difficult, but it was possible to believe that she was some kind of exiled aristocrat.

The couple had almost drawn level with her. The exiled aristocrat gave the old lady a warm smile. "Isn't a beautiful day?" she said with a slight accent.

"Very nice indeed for the time of year," the old lady agreed.

The couple walked on, and the old lady watched them with a sigh of regret. Separately, each of them would have been enough to gain her approval, she thought. Together, they looked like a fairytale come true.

"You made that old dear's day," Bob Rutter said, as he and Maria passed the boathouses.

"You think so?" Maria replied. "I only smiled at her."

Rutter squeezed her hand. "A smile from you is enough to make *anybody's* day."

He meant it. He thought her smile lit up a room, and he was sure he'd still have considered that true even if he hadn't been totally, helplessly in love with her.

A uniformed constable was on duty near the edge of the park. He recognised Rutter, and saluted.

Maria giggled. "You really are an important man, aren't you?" she said mischievously.

"No, I'm not," Rutter contradicted her. "But I'm going to be."

Maria's hand tensed. "In Spain, that policeman would not have saluted," she said.

"Because I'm only a detective sergeant?"

"Because we have no chaperone with us, and are holding hands in a public place. He would not have saluted because he would have been too scandalised even to raise his arm."

"Then it's a good job we're here, and not in Spain."

"Perhaps," Maria said wistfully.

Rutter felt instantly ashamed of being so insensitive. "You really miss your homeland, don't you?" he asked.

"Yes, I do," Maria admitted. "I know it's foolish – I was only a tiny child when my parents became refugees, and I haven't been able to go back since – but I *feel* Spanish, and until the Dictatorship is finally toppled, I'll never really be whole. That's why I will be going to the demonstration tomorrow."

Ah yes, the demonstration. Rutter had been trying to force his worries about it to the back of his mind, but they simply wouldn't stay there. "Do you really have to go?" he asked. "It's not as if General Franco himself was coming to London."

"No, but the man who *is* coming is one of his closest advisors."

"I know that, but—"

"Someone has to make the protest," Maria said passionately. "Someone has to show him that the barbarities of Franco's regime are not forgotten in the rest of Europe."

"There'll be police on duty outside the embassy," Rutter warned her. "Probably a large number of them."

Maria shrugged. "Of course there'll be police. Now that your government is on good terms with the Dictatorship, it feels obliged to do its utmost to protect Franco's lackeys."

"Things may get out of hand."

"You mean your British bobbies, of whom you are all so proud, might suddenly become as vicious as the General's *guardia civil*?"

"Of course not," Rutter said. "But we're not used to protests in London. We're not trained to handle them."

"There was the march by the Campaign for Nuclear Disarmament a few months ago," Maria replied.

"The CND march was entirely different," Rutter pointed out.

"Because all the marchers were British?" Maria asked, an edge of anger in her voice.

Rutter sighed. "No, not because they were British," he said. "Because they held their meeting in Trafalgar Square, which is a public space. Because they didn't threaten private property."

"We will not be threatening private property. It will be a peaceful demonstration."

"I'm sure it will," Rutter agreed. "But put anybody – including policemen – in a difficult situation they're not used to handling, and there's always a chance there'll be trouble."

"Then that's a risk I'll have to run," Maria told him. "Listen, Bob, my parents and I have a good life here. My father is a professor and when I get my doctorate, I will probably teach at the university too. Very nice for us. But there are other members of my family back in Spain who are not having such an easy time of it. I have an uncle who lives in poverty because all his property was confiscated. I have a cousin who is in gaol for no other crime than calling for democracy. I will be marching for them."

"If you must go, then I'm coming with you," Rutter said.

Maria laughed, alleviating the tension which had been

building up inside her. "If you did march with us, you wouldn't be working at Scotland Yard very much longer."

"I don't care about the Yard. I just want to know that you'll be safe."

"You *do* care," Maria said, turning serious again. "You know you do. Your work is desperately important to you, just as my protest is to me. We both have to do what we have to do, Bob."

She was right, he thought. However depressing her insight might be, it was undoubtedly completely on target.

They had reached Hyde Park Corner where a newspaper vendor, wearing a muffler despite the warm weather, was bawling at the top of his voice about an ''orrible murder' in Cheshire. Rutter reached in his pocket for some small change.

"You're off-duty, Bob," Maria said. "Leave it."

"I can't," Rutter told her, handing the vendor the coins. "If it's important enough to make the London papers, then it'll be important enough to make the Chief Constable call in the Yard."

"You see what I mean about your job?" Maria asked accusing, though she was secretly glad of anything which steered them away from another fractious discussion about the demonstration. "There has been a murder and you automatically assume that you will be involved in solving it."

"I will," Rutter told her. "In case you've forgotten, I work for Chief Inspector 'Cloggin' it Charlie' Woodend, who—"

"Who you worship," Maria said, with a smile playing on her lips.

"Who can be both bloody brilliant and bloody impossible – often at the same time – and is the best bobby I've met," Rutter answered. "But that wasn't what I was going to say."

Maria forced her face into an expression of mock humility. "I'm sorry I interrupted," she said.

"What I *was* going to say is as far as the top brass are concerned, 'Cloggin' it Charlie' is the Yard's expert on 'Up North'." Rutter permitted himself a grin. "Besides, if the truth be told, I think they'll jump on the excuse to get him out of London. He can be a real thorn in their sides when he wants to be."

Rutter opened the paper and scanned the story. Social-club boss with criminal past found murdered in his office. Nail driven into his skull. It sounded interesting. But it couldn't have come at a worse time. The murder meant that when Maria was demonstrating outside the Spanish Embassy, he would already be in Cheshire. And he couldn't banish from his mind the thought that without him in London, something terrible was going to happen to her.

Detective Sergeant Gower stood to attention in front of his chief superintendent's desk. It was not a position his toad-like body felt comfortable with, but given the trouble he was in, he thought it the best stance to take.

"You were off-duty last night, weren't you, Gower?" the Chief Superintendent asked.

"Yes, sir."

"So why did you go to the social club?"

"Because I wanted a drink?" Gower suggested hopefully.

The Chief Superintendent frowned. "Are you a member of the club, Mr Gower?"

"No, sir."

"Do you know any members of the club who might have been willing to sign you in?"

"I know a few of them," Gower admitted, though he doubted whether any of the petty criminals who were members of the club would ever willingly have done a favour for him.

"Did you go into the club to see if they'd serve you, even though you were not a member?"

"No, sir."

"But you did go into the office, didn't you?"

"Yes, sir."

"An office which was in total darkness?"

Well, of course it was, Gower thought. I wouldn't have gone in if there'd been bloody lights on, now would I? "That's correct," he said.

"And what made you do that?"

15

"I thought something was wrong."

The Chief Superintendent shook his head almost despairingly. "Based on what?" he asked.

Gower shrugged. "Professional instinct."

"And once inside, you discovered the body of Robbie Peterson."

That's when I made my mistake, Gower told himself. I should never have reported it. I should just have got the hell out of there and left it to some other daft bugger to find the stiff. But aloud he said, "Yes, sir. That's correct."

The Chief Superintendent frowned again, and looked down at the folder which was spread in front of him. "You've had a very chequered career, Sergeant Gower," he said. "You can be a very good detective. You've managed to solve some cases the rest of us had all but given up on. But that's only one side of the story, isn't it?" He pointed his index finger squarely at Gower's chest. "The other side is that you've been disciplined several times for breaking with official procedure."

"The villains I deal with don't follow official procedure," Gower said, almost to himself.

"No, but we do," the Chief Superintendent retorted sharply. "Shall I tell you what I think? I think that you were down at the club looking for just such an opportunity as the one you found. Isn't that the case?"

"I did not go to the club with any thought of entering the office," Gower said. And for once he was telling one of his superiors the truth – it had been Annabel Peterson, not Robbie, who'd been the focus of his interest the night before.

"Was Mr Peterson the subject of any official investigation?" the Chief Superintendent asked.

"No, sir."

"Yet you *were* investigating him? *Unofficially?*"

"Yes, sir," Gower lied, considering that he'd been truthful enough for one day.

"And might I ask why?"

"Robbie was a villain from way back. He hadn't changed."

"Do you have any proof of this?"

"No, sir."

16

The Chief Superintendent sighed. "You really leave me very little choice of what action to take in this matter, Sergeant. You will be suspended pending an investigation into your conduct."

It was unfair, Gower thought, but then that was only to be expected in this life. It wasn't fair that his wife had run off with a bloody milkman. It wasn't fair that he had to stand there now, listening to this prat who wouldn't know real police work if it hit him in the eye. But that was just the way things were.

Once out in the corridor, Gower quickly reviewed the meeting in his mind. He'd have been suspended whatever he'd said, he decided. So he'd played it just right – because the Chief Superintendent still had no idea that he was on to Robbie Peterson's daughter.

Doris Peterson replaced the hall telephone on its cradle, lit a cigarette and walked into the kitchen where her elder daughter was on her knees scouring the oven. "Well, that's settled," she said.

Jenny Clough, who had been cleaning and polishing relentlessly all day, looked up from her work. "What's settled?" she asked.

"I've just been talking to Wally on the blower. He thinks he can get me extra staff for tonight."

"Extra staff!" Jenny repeated incredulously. "You're never thinking of opening tonight, are you? Not with Dad hardly cold?"

"You can't afford sentimentality in this business," her mother replied practically. "Customers expect you to be open, and if you're not, they just go somewhere else. And there's a danger that might become a habit with them."

"It's not right," Jenny protested.

"People who work hard for a living are entitled to their bit of fun when they're on their holidays," her mother pointed out. "The world doesn't stop for them just because Robbie's gone."

Jenny bit her lower lip. "It shows a lack of respect," she said.

17

Doris sighed. "It's not as if I'll be behind the bar myself," she said. "Anyway, I've not noticed that your dad's death has stopped *you* workin'."

Jenny stood up and slammed her scouring pad down on top of the cooker. "That's not fair!" she said, almost shouting the words. "I'm only doin' this to take my mind off things."

"So maybe I'm doin' the same."

"You!" Jenny screamed. "You didn't give tuppence for him!"

"Well, I'm certainly too old to go around pretendin' I'm devastated by his death," Doris admitted.

"Did you *ever* love him?" Jenny demanded. "Was there a time when you really did care? Or has he never been more than a meal ticket to you?"

"Did you ever love *your* husband?" her mother countered. "Or did you just marry him because it was what your wonderful dad wanted?"

"Dad was good to you," Jenny said fiercely. "He was good to all of us. And what did he get in return? You treated him like dirt, and Annabel did everything she possibly could to embarrass him."

"Well, at least he still had you, didn't he? *You* were always his good little girl."

Jenny ran her hand agitatedly through her dark hair. "Somebody had to show him affection. Somebody had to let him know that he was appreciated."

"Who do you think killed him, Jenny?" Doris asked, surprisingly gently.

The question seemed to catch her daughter off-guard, as if, up to that point, she had still not come to terms with the death, let alone the manner of it.

"Well?" Doris repeated. "Who *do* you think killed him?"

"I don't know."

"Of course you don't," Doris agreed. "But I'll put money on it that if you sat down and tried to make a list, you could come up with nine or ten names in no time. Now that's true, isn't it?"

"I suppose so," Jenny admitted reluctantly.

"So let me ask you this," Doris said. "If your dad was so bloody marvellous, how is that there are so many people who'll be really chuffed to see him dead?"

Chief Inspector Charlie Woodend mopped up the last of his gravy with a piece of bread, popped the bread into his mouth and leant back in his chair.

"You've excelled yourself with that meal, lass," he told his wife.

Joan Woodend smiled, so that dimples formed in her plump cheeks. "You always say that," she pointed out.

"An' it's always true," Woodend said. "You could hardly cook when I married you. An' now look at what you serve up."

Joan shook her head. "Don't try that line on me, Charlie Woodend," she said playfully. "If I hadn't been able to cook, you'd have ended up takin' somebody else to the altar."

It wasn't true, but Woodend still somehow managed to look guilty. "Do you want a hand with the plates?" he asked.

Joan stood up. "No, I'll do it. You get yourself back to that book of yours."

Woodend walked over to his favourite armchair and picked up his copy of *Pride and Prejudice*. Soon he was completely enveloped in Jane Austen's world – a closed world where newcomers were treated with both anticipation and suspicion. It was like that for him, he thought. His job meant that he was always the newcomer, stepping into a society which had its own rules and ways of doing things. That was why, unlike most other officers of his rank, he didn't send his subordinates to do his footwork for him. He liked to get about himself, to absorb the atmosphere of the area and listen to the gossip in the local pubs. He was aware of his nickname – 'Cloggin'-it Charlie' – and though the man who'd thought it up had probably intended it to be insulting, he himself preferred to think of it as a badge of honour.

The phone rang in the hallway. "Can you get that, Charlie?" his wife called from the kitchen. "It's probably our Annie, callin' from camp."

She was wrong about that, Woodend thought, as he padded across the fitted carpet. It wouldn't be their daughter, wanting to tell them how she was getting on with the other girl guides. This would be the call he'd been expecting ever since he glanced at the newspaper headlines that morning.

He lifted the receiver. "Kilburn 2492," he said.

"Is that you, Charlie?"

"It's me, sir."

"There's been a murder in Cheshire and it seems to me it's right up your street."

Aye, an' it'll get me out of your hair for a while, thought Woodend, who appreciated just as keenly as Bob Rutter did that the Brass were not always comfortable in his presence. In a way, he supposed, that was not surprising. He was, as had often been pointed out, not like other men – or at least not like other *policemen* of his rank. Other chief inspectors, with one eye on the commissioner's job, usually wore smart lounge suits. Woodend favoured baggy sports coats from the pockets of which he would sometimes produce a volume of Dickens, sometimes a corned-beef sandwich, with the bread cut in thick, door-step slices, just as he liked it.

He knew he would never rise above the rank of chief inspector and he accepted the fact philosophically, because although a salary well in excess of a thousand pounds a year sometimes seemed appealing, he already earned enough to meet his simple needs and didn't like the thought of giving up the kind of work his present job brought him.

"Are you still there, Charlie?" asked the voice on the other end of the line.

"Yes, sir."

"I'd like you up there as soon as possible. Take a sleeper, if there's one available."

"An' can I take my lad, Rutter, with me?"

"Rutter?" the Chief Superintendent repeated. "You've still got him with you? You haven't you worn him out yet – like you seem to have worn out every other sergeant you've been assigned?"

"No, sir."

20

"Then he must be a remarkable young man."

"He's a good lad," Woodend agreed.

He said his goodbyes and put the phone down. Bob Rutter *was* a good lad, he thought as he walked back into the living room. And that girlfriend of his, young Maria, was a crackin' little lass who it was always the greatest pleasure to have round for tea. Joan thought the world of her too, and despite the difference in their ages, they seemed to have struck up a real friendship.

He ambled over to the kitchen door. Joan was still at the sink, cleaning out a large saucepan. "That was the Super," he announced. "A new case has come up, an' he wants me to handle it. I'll probably be leavin' tonight."

Joan dried her hands on the tea towel. "Well, your bag's packed an' ready like it always is," she said. "Would you like me to make some butties to take with you?"

"Champion," Woodend replied. "But don't make enough of them to fill a suitcase like you did the last time. This murder's not in Essex. It's up North – an' you can still get decent grub there."

Three

Inspector Chatterton of the Mid-Cheshire Police stood on the platform at Crewe railway station and watched the London train pull in. When the carriage doors opened, a number of passengers got off, but only one was wearing a hairy sports jacket and carrying the sort of bag in which a plumber might keep his tools. Chatterton, well briefed as to what to expect by colleagues who'd worked with the Chief Inspector before, stepped forward and introduced himself.

Woodend shook the Inspector's hand. "Nice of you to meet us, Mr Chatterton," he said. "Last time we were up here, they sent a DI to keep his beady eye on us." He turned to the man next to him, who was carrying a smart tartan suitcase. 'What was his name, Sergeant?"

"DI Holland, sir," Rutter supplied.

"That's right," Woodend agreed. "Why isn't it him this time? Won't his constitution stand the excitement of another encounter with us?"

"Mr Holland's been promoted and transferred back to Manchester, sir," Chatterton explained.

"I'm not surprised," Woodend said. "I always thought he was a bit of a pillock myself, but that doesn't seem much of an obstacle to gettin' on in the modern police force, does it, Inspector?"

Chatterton glanced at Rutter for guidance, and finding no more than an amused expression on the Sergeant's face, decided that his wisest course might be to change the subject. "The car's just across the road, sir," he said.

"Oh aye?" Woodend replied, sounding genuinely interested. "An' what make would it be?"

"It's er . . . a Wolsey."

Woodend turned to Rutter again. "A Wolsey? Isn't that what the powers that be gave us the last time we were here?"

"Yes, sir."

The Chief Inspector shook his head as if were a truly disappointed man. "After the way we pulled them out of the shit in Salton, you'd have thought they'd have made an effort an' stretched to a Rolls this time," he said.

"I'm afraid the Cheshire Constabulary doesn't have any Rolls Royces," Chatterton said apologetically.

Woodend rolled his eyes. Just what he needed, he thought – a liaison officer with no sense of humour. "Lead on, Inspector," he said. "Lead on."

The route from Crewe to Swann's Lake took the Wolsey along country roads wide enough to allow two lorries to pass each other – but only just. Woodend looked out of the window, enjoying the sight of the lush green fields and the contented, grazing cows. It wouldn't be like that on the new-fangled motorway they were about to open between Luton and Dunchurch, he thought sourly. With three lanes in either direction, cars would be able to go so fast that the countryside would just whizz by. And it wouldn't stop with the M1 – they'd never have called it that if they didn't intend to build any more. The whole of England would soon be criss-crossed with the bloody things. Huge scars cut onto the countryside, just so people could get to where they were going a little quicker.

He turned to Inspector Chatterton who was sitting next to him. "Tell me about Swann's Lake," he said.

"What exactly would you like to know, sir?"

"Well, we could start with who Swann was," Woodend suggested.

"As I understand it, he owned most of the land around the lake about two hundred years ago," Chatterton said. "But no one called Swann has lived in the area for a long, long time."

Woodend nodded. "It's a sort of holiday spot, isn't it?"

"That's right, sir. There are several caravan sites and a fair number of wooden bungalows which are rented out during the summer season."

"So what's the attraction of the place?"

"Well, there's the lake itself – people like to go boating – then there's the funfair and, of course, five or six social clubs like The Hideaway."

"And where do the visitors come from?"

"All over. Liverpool, Manchester – even as far north as Bolton."

"For your information, that's nearly thirty miles," Woodend said to Rutter. He turned his attention back to Chatterton. "My sergeant's knowledge of geography doesn't stretch any further north than Watford," he explained. "So tell me, Inspector, what sort of people are these visitors? Lawyers? Architects? Chief Inspectors from Scotland Yard?"

"No, nothing like that. They're mainly ordinary working people – taxi drivers, bricklayers and pipe fitters. Not that they seem too badly off, by any means. Most of them manage to run a little motor car, and you can't say *that* about everybody."

"They come from all over the place," Woodend repeated thoughtful. "In other words, you're tellin' me that in addition to the locals, there could be several thousand outsiders in the village at any one time."

"I suppose so," Chatterton admitted.

"Grand," Woodend said. "That makes my job *a lot* easier."

Woodend stood in the cinder yard, looking first at The Hideaway, then across at the outhouse/office where Robbie Peterson had been murdered. "How much time passed between this Peterson feller last bein' seen, an' his body bein' found?" he asked Inspector Chatterton.

"Roughly half an hour, sir."

"Roughly?" Woodend repeated,

Chatterton nodded. "We know what time Detective Sergeant Gower found him – the man's a trained bobby, and the first thing he did was check his watch. What we're not exactly sure about is when Robbie Peterson left the club and went to his office. We can pin it down to somewhere around a quarter to ten, but no one we've talked to is prepared to be more specific than that."

Woodend nodded understandingly. Folk out for a good time didn't keep looking at their watches – at least, not until it was getting close to calling for 'last orders'.

"An' how many people would have gone in and out of the club durin' that time?" the Chief Inspector asked.

"There were around a couple of hundred people in the club on Friday night," Chatterton said, "and about fifty of them have volunteered the information that during that crucial half-hour they either went home or paid a visit to the toilet block, which is located on the far side of the garage."

"An' did any of them notice anythin' unusual?" Woodend asked.

The Inspector shook his head. "There were a few who couldn't say for sure whether or not there was a light in the office, but most of them are definite that it was in darkness."

"Tell me what you've been able to find out about the murdered man."

"He came here about five years ago," Chatterton said. "Bought the club outright, as well as the caravan site, a few fairground attractions like the ghost train, and several holiday bungalows."

Woodend whistled softly. "Must have had plenty of money behind him, then. And what exactly did our Robbie do *before* he moved to Swann's Lake?"

"You'll already have read most of what we know in the papers," Chatterton said.

"No, I won't," Woodend said. He turned to Rutter. "And you can stop grinnin', Sergeant."

Rutter looked down at the ground. "Sorry, sir."

"What's amusin' my sergeant," Woodend said to Chatterton, "is that he knows I don't go much by reports, whether they're in the papers or on official police stationery. So while I might have read the headlines on this case, I've not gone much beyond that. All of which means that if I'm ever to find out what's goin' on, someone will have to tell me."

"I see, sir," Chatterton said – though it was clear that he didn't. "Well, it seems that Robbie Peterson comes originally from Liverpool, and from what the Merseyside force have been able to tell us, he was involved in all kinds of nasty work."

"An' what exactly does that mean?"

"Robbery, fencing, protection. He worked for a feller called Sid Dowd, who seems to run most of the underworld activity there. And he worked *with* a lad called Terry Clough, who eventually became his son-in-law, and moved here at the same time as he did."

"But Peterson's been straight ever since he left Liverpool?"

"Not according to one of the sergeants down at the station – Gower, his name is. He's convinced Robbie was still as bent as a nine-bob note."

"I see," Woodend said thoughtfully. "What do you make of it, Bob?"

"Make of what, sir?"

"The method chosen to dispatch our Mr Peterson to his final restin' place."

"Unusual," Rutter said.

"In what way?"

"It's rather gruesome. It's almost as if there was something ritualistic about it."

Woodend beamed with pleasure at his star pupil, then turned to Inspector Chatterton. "Hear that, Inspector? Ritualistic! My sergeant's a grammar-school boy. You want to go any further with that, Bob?"

"It's as if it was a murder to set an example," Rutter said.

"You mean like hanging, drawing and quartering?"

Rutter smiled. "I was thinking more of knee-capping."

"So was I," Woodend told him. "And that would suggest—"

"That the murder was carried out by someone in the criminal fraternity."

"Aye, it would," the Chief Inspector agreed.

And that's not going to make things any easier, he thought, because the person who'd wanted Robbie Peterson dead was probably not the one who carried out the act. Worse than that, whoever the man was, he probably had a watertight alibi for the time Peterson died.

26

"What do you want to do now, sir?" Chatterton asked.

"We may as well go and look at the scene of the crime," Woodend said.

The three policemen stood in the doorway of Robbie Peterson's office. Woodend's quick eyes ran over the desk, the three-piece suite and the heavy coffee table which had caused Detective Sergeant Gower to go arse over tip.

"Impressions, Sergeant?" he said to Rutter.

"Some money's been spent on this place," the Sergeant replied.

"But?"

"But the effect isn't quite right. It's not enough to buy expensive things. You have to buy expensive things which harmonise."

"I'd never have noticed that myself," Woodend admitted. "There's no wonder Joan won't let me go shoppin' for furniture with her." He walked across the office to the workbench and looked down at the box of six-inch nails. "It's one of these that was used, is it, Inspector?"

"That's right, sir."

"An' what about the hammer which drove it in?"

Chatterton pointed to the tool rack hanging on the wall. There was one gap in it. "The hammer which hung in that slot was lying on the desk," he said. "It's a fair assumption it was used to drive the nail in, but we can't say for certain. The lab's checked it over. It's been wiped clean of prints."

Woodend frowned. If the killer had been a professional hit-man, as he suspected, then surely he would have brought his own murder weapon with him. Or perhaps not. A gun could be traced. Even a knife might leave a trail. But by using Robbie Peterson's own hammer and nail, the murderer had left them absolutely no line of investigation to follow.

"I'd like you to get hold of hammer for me," Woodend said to Inspector Chatterton.

"A hammer, sir? What kind of a hammer?"

Woodend sighed. The problem of workin' with new people all the time was that you were forever havin' to get them into your way of seein' things. Young Rutter wouldn't have needed to ask what kind of hammer – he would already have known. "I want a hammer as near as possible to the one which was used to kill Robbie Peterson," he said patiently.

"Oh, all right, sir. Understood," Chatterton said.

But he didn't understand, Woodend thought. He had no idea of how sometimes just holding the murder weapon could actually give you some kind of feeling about the person who had wielded it.

"We'll need somewhere to operate from," he said.

"Yes, sir. We've cleared some office space for you in Maltham."

"Have you now?" Woodend said. "And how far away might that be from Swann's Lake?"

"Only about six miles."

"Then that makes it six miles away from the scene of the crime," Woodend said. "I'm sorry, lad, that won't do at all."

"I suppose we could get you a room in the nearest police house," Chatterton suggested.

"An' how close is that?"

"A couple of miles."

Woodend shook his head. "You're not getting' the point, are you? When I investigate a crime, I like to be on top of it eighteen hours a day."

"Well, I really can't think anywhere closer than—" Chatterton began.

"Have forensics finished with this office?" Woodend interrupted.

"Yes, sir."

"Right, then. Get somebody to clear out all this posh stuff and have it replaced with the battered rubbish I'm used to, and we'll have what my sergeant here likes to call a nerve centre for our operation."

"You want to use this place?" Chatterton asked incredulously.

"Aye. Any objections?"

The Inspector shrugged. "Not really. It just seems a bit macabre, that's all."

"Murder tends to be a macabre business," Woodend said. "It's funny that way. Now, about accommodation. Where are we supposed to be stayin'?"

"In Maltham, sir. There's a new hotel opened since the last time you were here, and I've been told it's very nice indeed."

"I need to feel the pulse of a place, even when I'm sleepin'," Woodend said. "Get me somethin' closer."

"Well, there's always the Red Lion pub," Chatterton said dubiously.

"Where's that?"

"About half a mile up the road. I believe they do have a couple of rooms for bed and breakfast, but I'm not sure it's exactly—"

"It'll do fine," Woodend said. "An' if the rooms are already occupied, fit up whoever's in them on some trumped-up charge and throw the buggers in the clink for a couple of days."

Chatterton paled. "I don't think I could do that, sir. There are certain rules and reg—" He saw the look of exasperation in Woodend's eyes. "You're joking again, aren't you?" he said with some relief.

"I'd better be, or I'll soon end up behind bars myself," Woodend said. He checked his watch. "You've been a great help so far, Inspector. Now, if you wouldn't mind, I'd like you to get this furniture removal underway."

"I'll get one of my sergeant's to organise it right away," Chatterton said.

"I'd rather you supervised it yourself," Woodend told him.

"But I've . . . er—"

"You've had orders to stick to me like glue, so you can report back to your bosses on exactly what I'm up to?" Woodend asked.

"I wouldn't put it quite like that, sir," Chatterton replied, though his expression suggested that what the Chief Inspector had said wasn't far from the truth.

"Tell your Chief Super I can't work that way," Woodend said. "I need freedom to move about without constantly feelin' the local flatfeet breathin' down my neck. Understood?"

"I'll pass your message on, sir," Chatterton said dubiously.

"Good. Now get crackin' on shiftin' this furniture. But don't take that filin' cabinet – my sergeant, with all the enthusiasm of youth, is just itchin' to take a look at all of Master Robbie's correspondence. Isn't that true, Sergeant?"

"Itching," Rutter said, deadpan.

"And once you've got the office up and runnin', I'd like you to arrange for me to see a few of the people connected with the case – starting with Peterson's ever-lovin' family," Woodend told the Inspector.

"And what will you be doing, sir?" Chatterton asked. "I mean, just in case I need to contact you," he added hastily.

"What will I be doin'?" Woodend repeated. "Well, since it's such a nice day, I thought I might take my sergeant here for a little walk round the lake."

The hum of the diesel engines merged with the tinny sound of the steam organ and the blare of the latest Elvis Presley record pumping out of the speakers around the dodgem track. There were children everywhere. Children eating candy floss and toffee apples. Children proudly and carefully carrying goldfish in plastic bags full of water. Children begging for one more ride, and children crying because their requests had been turned down. The funfair was as cheerfully brash and as gaudy as only funfairs can be.

Woodend, his jacket draped over his arm, strolled through the crowd with the easy nonchalance of a man who has nothing more on his mind than wondering what he's going to be served up for his tea. There was a time when the pose would have fooled Bob Rutter, but that time was long since past. He knew that though the Chief Inspector might appear relaxed, his eyes were constantly alert, fixing firmly the various strands of life which co-existed around the lake. At some point in the case, something he had seen that afternoon would prove useful – perhaps even a key point in the investigation – and God help his sergeant if he hadn't noticed it too!

Woodend came to halt in front of the ghost train, and looked up at the lurid paintings of phantoms, corpses and executioners which festooned its walls. "Didn't Inspector Chatterton say that Robbie Peterson owned this, Sergeant?" he asked.

"Yes, sir, he did," Rutter confirmed.

"Very interestin'," the Chief Inspector muttered, turning his attention to the two men who were running the train.

Both were in their middle twenties and had black hair which hung unfashionably over their collars. Their shirtsleeves were rolled up above the elbows, displaying purple and red tattoos at least as garish as the signs advertising the attraction. They looked like hard men and had such similar features that they had to be brothers.

The Chief Inspector took out his packet of Capstan Full Strength cigarettes, and offered one to his sergeant, who, as usual, shook his head and reached for his own packet of cork tipped.

"What do you make of them two lads?" Woodend asked, as he held a match in his cupped hands for Rutter to light his cigarette.

Rutter considered the matter. "It wouldn't surprise me if they'd been in trouble with the law at some time," he said.

"And what makes you think that?"

"The way they're both looking at us."

A smile began to form on Woodend's lips. "Oh aye?" he said. "And how might that be?"

"As if they'd like to catch us alone in a dark alley."

"Perhaps because we've got no family with us, they think we're a couple of queers," Woodend suggested. "An' maybe they just don't like bum boys."

Rutter shook his head. "They've spotted us as bobbies. You can tell that," he said. "And it's not something everyone could do."

Woodend chuckled. "Looks like I might make a detective out of you yet. But if you're right and they do have criminal records, it raises a couple of interestin' questions, doesn't it?"

"Like what?" Rutter asked.

"Like why did Robbie Peterson hire a couple of ex-gaolbirds to work in a cash business where it would be as easy as anythin' for them to cream off half the profits?"

"Maybe he believed in giving people a second chance," Rutter said.

"That's one possibility," Woodend admitted. "But it's hardly likely, is it?"

"Or maybe Peterson thought that with the reputation he'd got, they'd be too scared to try and cheat him."

"An' what's the third possibility?"

Rutter examined the glowing end of his cigarette. "This job is just a front," he said. "An excuse for having them around. It was entirely another kind of work that Peterson needed them for."

"Just what I was thinkin'." Woodend put his hand in his trouser pocket, and when he withdrew it again, it was holding two sixpenny pieces. "Come on," he said. "Let's take a ride."

"On the ghost train?" Rutter asked, incredulously.

"Aye. Why not? We're on expenses – let's live it up for once."

"But it's kids' stuff, sir."

"We're all kids deep inside ourselves," Woodend said. "Come on, Bob. You might actually enjoy yourself if you could learn to let your hair down."

Woodend stepped forward and handed his money over to one of the unsmiling brothers, then climbed into one of the small open carriages just behind a couple of young girls who were already giggling hysterically. Rutter hesitated for a second, then squeezed himself in next to his boss.

The carriage was soon full and the second unsmiling brother pulled the lever. The carriage clanked clumsily forward, picking up speed as it hit the double doors which heralded the start of the ride. For a second, the passengers were plunged into complete darkness, then a glowing, headless corpse appeared out of the gloom and a piercing mechanical shriek filled the air. Collision with the spectre seemed inevitable, but at the last moment the track made a sharp turn and the carriage rattled away in another direction.

The girls just in front of the two detectives were screaming in earnest now, and as more ghouls appeared before them, most of the rest of the carriage joined in.

"Aren't you glad you came?" Woodend bellowed into his sergeant's ear.

"Wouldn't have missed it for the world!" Rutter shouted back, wondering why it seemed impossible to be both loud and sarcastic at the same time.

The carriage took three or four more unexpected twists, then once again it battered against a pair of wooden doors and re-emerged into the bright sunlight of a Swann's Lake Sunday afternoon.

Woodend climbed out of his seat, nodded pleasantly to the two scowling men in charge and stepped clear of the ghost train. "It's a bit like the human mind, is that ride," he said to his sergeant.

Rutter smiled. "In what way, sir?"

"Well, for a start, it doesn't seem very big from the outside, but once you get in it, you find there's a hell of a lot goin' on," Woodend said seriously. "Then there's all them twists and turns, so you never know quite where it's going to lead you. An' lastly, I suppose, if you're not careful, you'll soon start mistaking what's fake for what's real."

Rutter shook his head in wonder. "Getting a bit philosophical today, aren't we, sir?"

Woodend grinned ruefully. "Aye, you're right," he said. "Let's get back to the club and do some of that detective work we're gettin' paid for."

Four

In the time Woodend and Rutter had been down at the funfair, Robbie Peterson's office had undergone a transformation. The filing cabinet was still there, as per Woodend's instructions, but the rest of the furniture had been removed and in its place were two gun-metal desks, four folding chairs and a large blackboard.

"Champion," Woodend pronounced after examining it. "Still a bit tidy, but we'll soon rectify that, an' then I'll feel right at home."

"The tool rack's still here," Rutter pointed out.

"Aye, I noticed that, bein' a detective," Woodend replied.

"Sorry we haven't got round to taking it down yet, sir," Inspector Chatterton said. "My lads are shifting Robbie's furniture at Maltham police station at the moment, but the second they get back here, I'll put one of them on the job."

"Call through an' tell them to stay where they are," Woodend said. "They'd just be wastin' petrol comin' back."

"Won't you be needing them, sir?"

Woodend shook his head. "Until I've got my bearin's, even my sergeant's little more than a liability."

"But the tool rack, sir?"

"Leave it where it is. Some of them chisels might come in handy when I'm interrogatin' witnesses."

Chatterton gave a half-hearted laugh which was only a second or two late. "Interrogating witnesses," he repeated. "Very good, sir. Would you like talk to the family now?"

"Aye, I think it's about time I did."

"Who would you like to see first?"

34

"I might as well start with the grieving widow," Woodend decided.

Doris Peterson, Woodend discovered, was a brassy blonde who might once have seemed very soft and feminine, but had definitely hardened with age. Without waiting for an invitation, she sat down on the folding chair opposite him and crossed her legs in a way which revealed more of her calves than might have been considered seemly. But it was an act of defiance rather than one of exhibitionism, Woodend thought – more designed to show her contempt for the police than to titillate them. Not that Doris had bad legs for a woman her age.

The Chief Inspector leaned forward across the desk. "I'm sorry to be questionin' you at a time like this, Mrs Peterson," he said.

Doris snorted. "Let's start as we mean to go on, shall we?" she said. "I was married to Robbie Peterson for twenty-seven years, and I can count on the fingers of one hand the number of times I've been happy about the fact. So if you're expectin' tears and sighs of regret, you've come to the wrong place."

"Was he a bad husband?" Woodend asked.

"He was a *man*," Doris told him, "and he did what all men do – drink too much, act bone idle when they think they can get away with it, an' chase anythin' wearin' a skirt."

"You're sayin' your husband was unfaithful to you?"

"Well, of course he was." Doris paused, as if she'd realised she was not quite telling him the whole truth. "Or at least, he used to be when we lived in Liverpool. When we moved down to Swann's Lake, he seemed to have lost the urge."

"An' why do you think that was?"

Doris shrugged. "Age catchin' up with him, I expect."

"Let's talk about his background," Woodend suggested.

"Why would we want to do that?" Doris asked belligerently.

Woodend sighed. "The only reason I'm askin' questions is because I think they might help me to find your husband's killer. You do *want* him caught, I take it."

"Yes," Doris admitted, almost reluctantly. "Robbie was a

bit of a bugger, but when all's said and done, I wouldn't like to see whoever did him in gettin' away with it."

"Very commendable of you, I'm sure," Woodend said drily. "I was askin' you about his background."

Doris laughed. "Robbie was what you might call the family success story," she said. "His dad an' his uncles never got beyond petty theft, but Robbie made it to the big time."

"Was he in the rackets when you met him?"

A look of caution came to Doris' face. "None of this is goin' on the record, is it?"

"Do you see my sergeant writin' anythin' down?" Woodend countered.

"Yes, he was in the rackets. An' doin' very well – big car, money to burn."

"And that's what attracted you to him?"

"I'd be lyin' if I said the money didn't play a part in it, but there was more to it than that. Robbie had somethin' about him. A spark, I suppose you'd call it. An' he had guts. He wasn't a big feller, but he'd take on anybody who got in his way, whatever their size."

"Who had the idea of givin' it all up and movin' to Swann's Lake?" Woodend asked.

"Robbie."

"Did he give you any reason for the decision?"

"He said he wanted a new start, somewhere he wasn't known. Said it was time for him to go straight."

"*Did* he go straight?"

The widow hesitated for a second. "As far as I know."

"And what exactly do you mean by that?"

"I mean that I was careful not to look too closely at what Robbie was doin'. If he got caught, *I* wasn't goin' inside as his accomplice."

"But you did have your suspicions?" Woodend pressed.

"He used to go away, sometimes for as long as a week or two at a time. When I'd ask him where he'd been, all he'd tell me was it had been a business trip. Well, there's only one kind of business Robbie ever knew anythin' about – the crooked kind."

"Do you know if he's seen any of his friends from the old days recently?" Woodend asked.

"Funny you should say that," Doris told him. "Sid Dowd was down here just the other week. Robbie used to work for him in Liverpool."

"An' why did he come? Was it a social visit?"

Doris laughed with the rasp of a heavy smoker. "You don't know Sid, do you? He wouldn't cross the street if there wasn't some money in it for him."

"And what kind of money was he hopin' to make in Swann's Lake?"

"He wanted Robbie to let him buy into the club."

"And what did you husband say to that?"

"He said no. What did he need a partner for? We own this business outright – why would he want to see part of the profits goin' to somebody else?"

Maybe because it was safer that way, Woodend thought, though he kept the idea to himself. "Thanks for your help, Mrs Peterson," he said. "No doubt I'll be wantin' to talk to you again."

Doris stood up. "No doubt," she repeated.

Annabel Peterson carried herself with the same air of defiance as her mother did, but she managed to do it with more class. She was a pretty girl, Woodend thought, and it was a pity that she had chosen to apply her make-up in a way which implied such crude sexuality.

"I've just a few questions to ask you," he said as she sat down. "I'll try to make them as painless as possible."

"Painless!" Annabel repeated, as if the term held no meaning for her – and Woodend noticed, even in that one word, that her accent was much more refined than her mother's.

"Your father's death must have come as quite a shock to you," he said.

Annabel opened her handbag and took out a packet of cigarettes. When Woodend struck a match and reached across the desk, she shook her head and produced an expensive gold lighter. Taking her time, she flicked the lighter open, lit the

37

cigarette, and inhaled deeply. "Robbie was a criminal," she said, blowing smoke through her nostrils. "So it wasn't a shock at all. I'm not the least bit surprised he came to a bad end."

Woodend tried to imagine his own daughter talking about him in these tones. It was almost too painful to contemplate. What in God's name had Peterson done to this girl to merit such contempt?

"I was part of Robbie's experiment," Annabel said, as if she could read the Chief Inspector's mind.

"His experiment? His experiment in *what?*"

Annabel laughed bitterly. "In social climbing. I didn't used to be 'Annabel' when I was a little kid, you know. 'Annie' was good enough for me then. *And it is now.*"

"Unlike the rest of the family, you don't live here, do you, Miss Peterson?" Woodend asked.

"No, I certainly bloody don't," Annabel said viciously. "I've got a flat in Maltham."

"And what do you do for a living?"

Annabel sneered. "I do just what my expensive private education has equipped me to do," she said. "I live on the dole."

So much bitterness, Woodend thought. "But you do come home now an' again," he said. "You were in the club on Friday night."

"Oh yes, I was there," Annie agreed. "I like to bring my 'boyfriends' here occassionally. It was much more fun watching Robbie making a fool of himself in company."

Why had she felt the need to squeeze so much contempt into the word 'boyfriends'? Woodend wondered. But now was not the time to ask – he had other fish to fry. "Did you notice anythin' unusual while you were in the club?" he asked.

"Like what?"

"Did you happen to see any suspicious strangers?"

Annabel shook her head. "Only the usual riffraff who get in there on a Friday night."

"What about your father? Was he behavin' strangely in any way? Did he seem worried at all?"

"He forgot his lines in the middle of his act – if that's what

you want to call it – but that was only because there was some
trouble at the door with a non-member. After he'd sorted that
out, he was back to being his normal vulgar self." She clicked
her fingers as if she'd suddenly remembered something. "But
I'll tell you who was acting a bit off – Jenny's husband Terry
and that schoolteacher brother of his."

"Actin' a bit off? In what way?"

Annabel lit a new cigarette from the stub of her old one, then
threw the stub on the floor and ground it with the sole of her
shoe. "They were arguing about something. And if you knew
Michael Clough, you'd realise how uncharacteristic that is."

"Tell me more," Woodend said with growing interest.

"Michael's a little saint. A perpetual do-gooder. He doesn't
argue with people. He reasons. Reasons and reasons and
reasons until you're sick to your guts with it."

"He's tried that with you, I take it."

"Pull yourself together," Annabel said, her voice imitating
a tenor's, her tone whining. "You're a pretty girl. A beautiful
girl. And so intelligent. There's nothing you couldn't achieve
if you put your mind to it." She took another drag of her
cigarette. "That's the kind of thing you have to put up with
from Michael Clough," she continued in her normal voice.

"But you're sure that him and his brother were arguin' in
the club on Friday night?"

"Positive. And then they went outside together. They were
gone for quite a while."

Was there a touch of malice in her last statement? Woodend
wondered. Was she trying to point the finger of suspicion at
the Clough brothers? And if she was, *why* was she doing it?

"When they left the club, was your father still inside?"
he asked.

"Yes. He was still on the stage, telling his dirty jokes."

"And when they returned?"

"He'd left by then. In fact, if you want to pin it down, I'd
say that they didn't come back until just before the alarm was
raised by that swine Detective Sergeant Gower."

Woodend played a scene quickly through his mind. The
Clough boys have a real problem with Robbie Peterson.

Perhaps he has some kind of hold over one of them. Michael – the teacher, the reasonable one – wants to try talking their way out of the situation, but Terry – who was part of Robbie's criminal network in Liverpool – says that will never work with a man like Peterson. There's only one solution, he insists. They have to kill Robbie while they have the chance. But even discounting the fact that Robbie was Terry Clough's father-in-law, would they be stupid enough to kill him when there were witnesses who could place them near the scene of the crime? Wouldn't it have been wiser to wait for a better moment? Unless, of course, Robbie Peterson was planning to do something that very night which could ruin them both.

"You don't like your family very much, do you, Miss Peterson?" Woodend asked the girl.

"I don't like *anybody* very much," Annabel replied dully. "And that includes myself."

Gerry Fairbright rested his hands, hardened by years of work as a fitter and turner, on the waist-high fence which separated the caravan site from The Hideaway's yard. From where he was standing he had a clear view of the office. Those policemen from London were in there now, and with them – as he knew because he'd been watching for some time – was Annie Peterson. He wasn't worried about Annie. She could do nothing to hurt him. There had been only two people with the power to do that. One of them was now dead, and the other was useless without him. No, people weren't the problem. *People* weren't what would point the finger at him.

He turned round and looked back at his caravan. It was a cream Alpine Sprite, which he'd bought on the never-never for £280. It had seemed such a good idea at the time.

'Think of the money we'll save on boardin' houses,' his wife had said. 'An' it'll be there for us every weekend, not just for a couple of weeks a year.'

Oh yes, it had seemed a fine idea all right. How could he have known that it would lead him into such trouble, that it would be like the forbidden fruit in the Garden of Eden? He hated the caravan now. He hated Swann's Lake. But most importantly, he hated himself – hated the cowardice he had shown when it really mattered. He could have gone back into Robbie Peterson's office the night after the murder, but he hadn't dared. Now the Scotland Yard men were there, and it would be much more difficult. But difficult or not, he was going to have to break in. There really wasn't any choice.

"Can I help you, sir?" said a voice from behind him.

Gerry jumped, then turned around. One of the policemen – the older one, who wore the big hairy sports jacket – was standing just the other side of the fence. "Help me?" Gerry asked stupidly.

"Yes," Woodend replied. "I couldn't help noticin' that you've been standin' there for some time, and I was wonderin' if perhaps it was because there was somethin' you wanted to tell me."

Gerry shook his head, more violently than he'd intended. "N . . . no," he stuttered, "there's nothin'."

"You've got a right to be here, have you, sir?" Woodend asked.

"A right?" Gerry gasped.

"What I'm askin' you, in my roundabout way, is do you own one of the caravans on this site."

"Yes. Yes I do."

Woodend smiled. "Must be very pleasant to come down here for your holidays." His eyes narrowed. "I expect your wife's enjoyin' it, too."

"I . . . no . . . she's—" Gerry said.

"She's *what*, sir?"

"She's not here at the moment. She . . . she had to go back to Oldham. That's where we're from. Her mother's been taken proper poorly."

"Oh, I'm sorry to hear that," Woodend said. "Are you expectin' her back soon?"

"I'm not sure. It depends."

Woodend nodded sympathetically. "Well, enjoy your holiday as best you can, sir. And now, if you'll excuse me, I'll have to get back to my work."

He turned and walked away, leaving Gerry Fairbright standing there in a cold sweat. He was no fool, that bobby, Gerry decided. No fool at all. And now they'd spoken, things were even worse than they'd been before. Oh God, what was he going to do?

Standing in Trafalgar Square, surrounded by so many of her fellow countrymen, Maria was engulfed with a nostalgia for a Spain she'd never really known. How many people were there, she wondered. Five hundred? A thousand? It was difficult to say.

She looked up at the base of Nelson's Column, on which one of the march's organisers was standing. "This will a peaceful demonstration," the man was shouting through his megaphone. "I repeat – peaceful. When we reach the embassy, we will form lines in front of it, and then I will step forward and present our letter of protest."

"They won't accept it!" someone called angrily from the crowd.

"If they refuse to accept it, I shall offer it a second time," the organiser said with dignity.

"And if they *ignore* you a second time?" the same heckler called back.

"Even if they use refuse to acknowledge it, we will still have made our point. I will step back into the ranks, and together we will march away up Chapel Street."

"Let us act like men!" the heckler bellowed. "Let us fight fire with fire."

The organiser shook his head. "We will not stoop to their level," he said. "We will show them the true meaning of dignity. Brothers and sisters, it is time to go and face the enemy."

Perhaps the heckler said more, but if he did, his words were lost in the general groundswell of noise as the demonstrators formed a column. Maria, finding herself at the front of the column, felt a sudden burst of exhilaration. It was true what they said, she thought – strength did come from unity. She lifted her placard high in the air, and when the whistle blew she took a decisive step forward.

There were only a few policemen in evidence as they marched down Whitehall, but by the time they had reached Victoria Street there was one every fifty yards, and the closer they got to Belgrave Square, the more the officers there seemed to be. Standing silently. Watching them.

"They must have cancelled all leave today," Maria said to the girl who was marching next to her.

"Do you think there'll be policemen in front of the embassy?" the girl asked nervously.

"There's bound to be," Maria said. "But don't worry, as long as we behave in a civilised manner, there'll be no trouble."

But she couldn't help remembering that Bob had been worried – and Bob *knew* about these things!

They entered the square from Belgrave Place, and Maria let out an involuntary gasp as she saw the embassy. Yes, she been expecting a police presence – but not like this! Not this wall of blue serge which hid the embassy railings from view. Not so many badges on pointed helmets reflecting the rays of the afternoon sun at the oncoming marchers. And even more threatening, six policemen on horses towered over their colleagues at each end of the cordon. Though she tried to tell herself she was a fool to be concerned, Maria could feel a tiny knot of fear start to form itself in the pit of her stomach.

There was a low, angry murmuring from further back in the column. This is how the British authorities treat us, the murmur seemed to saying. We are not even to be allowed to get near our own embassy.

"Fan out," one of the organisers was shouting through his megaphone. "Form a line to face the police. But make sure you are at least ten feet away from them."

Ten feet! Maria thought. That was no distance at all! But if that was what was necessary, then that was what they would have to do.

The protestors' line, though more ragged than the one maintained by the police, was soon in place. Maria ran her eyes over the policemen's faces. Some of the officers had their expressions set in grim concentration, others – mostly the younger ones – seemed a little frightened.

'We're not used to protests in London,' Bob had said. *'We're not trained to handle them. And that could spell trouble.'*

She could feel the people behind pressing against her – not aggressively, but relentlessly – and it took all her effort to hold her position. It had been agreed they would stand in silence, but from further back she could hear ugly taunts being shouted. She wished the organisers would get it over with quickly. Wished they would try to deliver their letter, then everyone could go home.

One of the policemen suddenly lifted his hands in front of his face. At first, Maria couldn't understand why. And then – with sudden horrified realisation – she did. A brick! Someone in the crowd had had the criminal stupidity to throw a brick!

As if it had been the signal for a general outbreak, bricks and bottles were suddenly raining down on the police line from all directions.

"No!" Maria shouted. "No! It wasn't meant to be like this!"

The policemen had had their arms linked, but now they broke free of each other. Some held their hands up to protect themselves – others were already drawing their truncheons.

It was the clatter of the horses' hooves which started the panic. The huge animals edged their way into the crowd, and immediately people began to scream, to push – to lose all control. Some of the demonstrators stumbled and fell. Then others tripped over them, landing in a heap of struggling arms and legs which didn't look like people at all.

Maria no longer had her placard, though she'd no idea where she'd lost it. She heard the girl next to her call out to God for help, and knew that would do no good – they could only help themselves. She saw a young policeman, his truncheon drawn and his face ablaze with hatred, heading towards her particular section of the chaos. She somehow managed to pull herself free, so that she was standing right in front of him.

"Leave us alone!" she begged. "Please!"

With one hand the constable grabbed her roughly by the hair. With the other, he swung his truncheon. Maria had a split second of absolute terror – and then everything went black.

Sid Dowd was sitting at a table in the members' bar of a golf club which wouldn't even have taken him on as a caddy twenty years earlier. A newspaper was spread out in front of him, and he didn't look pleased.

"There's not as much about Robbie's murder in today's paper as there was in yesterday's, Phil," he said to the hard young man in the smart blue suit who had been waiting patiently to be addressed, "but it's still not good."

"No, Mr Dowd," the young man admitted. "It's still not good."

"I made a mistake sendin' you up to the club on Saturday night," Dowd said. "I should have been playin' things much more cautiously. But how was I to know the way things would turn out?"

"No way in the world, Mr Dowd," Phil assured him.

"Do you think many people will have noticed you?"

"Most of the club," Phil confessed. "You see, the steward didn't want to let me in without a membership card, then Robbie Peterson – who was on the stage at the time – told him to buy me a drink. Well, he was speakin' into the microphone, so most of the punters turned round to see who he was talkin' to."

"Not good," Dowd repeated, signalling the steward for another round of drinks. "I've come too far and taken too many risks to have this sort of cloud hangin' over me."

Phil nodded. "So what do you intend to do about it, Mr Dowd?"

Dowd thought for a moment. "Get onto one of the coppers who belong to my lodge," he said finally. "DI Roberts is probably your best bet. Ask him to find out what he can about this Chief Inspector Woodend feller."

Five

J enny Clough sat with her hands folded demurely on top of her pinafore, almost like a nun in quiet contemplation. She was a pretty woman, Woodend thought. Not pretty like her sister was pretty. Not pretty so she'd turn every head in the street. Hers was a prettiness it would be good to come home to after a hard day at work – a prettiness that offered a great deal of consolation for the right man.

"I expect you've heard some quite horrible things about my dad," she said across the desk.

"Now why would you think that?" Woodend asked.

Jenny laughed bitterly. "Because you've already spoken to my mum and sister. Why else?"

"Why don't you tell me how you saw him?" Woodend suggested.

"He wasn't perfect – nobody ever is – but he always tried to do his best for his family."

"Like sendin' your sister Annabel to an expensive boardin' school?"

Jenny nodded. "That's right. He wanted her to get the best education money could buy."

That was not how Annie Peterson saw it, Woodend thought. As far as she was concerned, Robbie had merely been using her as a ladder to climb out of the gutter. "Why didn't he send you to private school as well?" he asked.

"He told me recently that he would have done if he'd had the money at the time."

There was something evasive in her answer, Woodend thought – something which didn't ring quite true in her words.

"Did you believe him?" he asked.

Jenny Clough shook her head again. "No."

"So what was the real reason?"

"He couldn't bear the thought of me being away from home."

"But he didn't mind Annabel goin'?"

"All parents have their favourites among their children," Jenny said, adopting a fiercely defensive tone. "They shouldn't – but they do. Annie's always been Mum's favourite. I was always Dad's. But that doesn't mean that he didn't treat her right. She could have had anythin' she wanted. She could have gone to university. And what did she do instead?"

"I don't know," Woodend said. "You tell me."

"She did everythin' she could to humiliate him and embarrass him. How could he ever expect to get on in Swann's Lake when his own daughter behaves like a common tart?"

"Behaves? Or merely dresses?" Woodend asked.

"Behaves!" Jenny answered emphatically. "The men she knocks around with might drive sports cars and wear expensive clothes, but they're all still only after one thing – and she gives it to them. I've seen her."

"Where?"

"There's a copse of trees just beyond the caravan site," Jenny said. "Sutton's Copse, they call it round here. I don't know why. Anyway, a lot of courtin' couples go there. An' couples that are . . . well, you know."

"Havin' a bit on the side?"

"That's right. Well, after Annabel an' her latest feller had finished laughin' at Dad, that's where they usually went. They didn't have to, of course. Her men always had enough money to pay for a nice hotel somewhere. But she liked doin' it there – because it was just another way of rubbin' Dad's nose in it."

She stopped speaking, flushed and exhausted by her outburst.

"You don't like your sister very much, do you?" Woodend asked quietly.

"I love her," Jenny said. "But that doesn't mean that I'm

blind to how she's been carryin' on, and what an effect it's had on Dad."

"If it's not too painful, I'd like you to tell me about the night your dad died," Woodend said. "You were all in the club, weren't you? The whole family?"

"That's right."

"Is that normal?"

"Well, Terry's always there. He's the sort of assistant manager. Mum and Dad usually looked in at the weekends. Dad liked to do a bit of entertainin', and Mum likes a natter with her friends. You never know when Annabel's goin' to turn up. It's just as the mood takes her."

"What about your brother-in-law, Michael?"

"He doesn't come very often."

"So it was just a coincidence he and Annabel were there on the same night?"

"I suppose so."

"Your husband and Michael got into a bit of an argument, didn't they?" Woodend asked.

"I saw them talkin' by the door," Jenny admitted, "but I wouldn't say they were arguin'."

"Oh, so you were close enough to hear what they sayin'?"

"No," Jenny confessed. "It just didn't *look* serious, that's all."

"Do they often spend a lot of time talkin'?"

Jenny twisted the hem of her pinafore. "You've got to understand, Michael's very different from the rest of us," she said. "He's educated. Been to teacher trainin' college. Him and Terry don't have much in common any more."

"They had enough in common to carry on their conversation outside," Woodend said.

"Annabel!" Jenny hissed. "She's the one who told you that!"

"Well, it's the truth, isn't it?"

"Yes, it's the truth. But they weren't gone long."

"Accordin' to your sister – and I'm sure I can get other witnesses to confirm it if I really try – they left while your dad was still on stage, an' they didn't come back until about the time the body was found."

The implications of where this line of questioning was leading finally hit her. "You're . . . you're not sayin' that you think Terry an' Michael killed Dad, are you?" she gasped.

"I'm investigatin' every possibility," Woodend said evenly.

"But they couldn't. They just couldn't. I mean, Terry's a bit of a rough diamond, but he got on really well with Dad. An' as for Michael, if you'd met him—"

"Which I intend to do very shortly."

". . . you'd know there's not a violent bone in his body."

"All right, let's assume for the time bein' that they didn't kill your dad," Woodend said. "We're still left with an interestin' question, aren't we? Just what were two brothers – who you've admitted have absolutely nothin' in common – doin' outside all that time?"

"I have absolutely no idea," Jenny said – and Woodend knew for sure that she was lying.

Maria groaned and opened her eyes. A series of pink blobs were floating around in front of her, blobs which gradually solidified and became faces.

"Are you all right?" asked a voice which she recognised as belonging to Javier, one of her friends from the university.

"I've got a splitting headache," Maria said. "What happened?"

"You were knocked unconscious," Javier said. "I dragged you away from all the trouble. I know you're not supposed to do that when a person's been injured, but you'd have been trampled if I'd left you where you were."

Away from all *what* trouble? Maria asked herself. And then it all came back to her – the demonstration, the bricks and bottles, the policeman with his truncheon – and she felt such a fool for not remembering it earlier.

"Is it . . . ? Is there . . . ?" she asked, wishing she could think clearly enough to frame her questions properly.

"It's calmed down again," Javier said, anticipating what she'd wanted to know. "The police have let us pull back to other end of the square. Nobody's been seriously hurt unless . . . unless you—"

"I'm fine," Maria told him. "If you could just help me get up."

Two willing pairs of hands lifted her to her feet. It felt funny at first, almost if she were standing on top of a large rubber ball, but she soon got used to it.

"I think we should call you an ambulance," Javier said.

"I'm all right now," Maria insisted.

"You don't look all right."

"It's just this headache."

"I could ring your parents," Javier suggested.

Maria shook her head. It hurt. "They're away," she said. "In South America. Raising money for Spanish refugees. Just get me a taxi. I'll go straight home, have a warm bath and tomorrow it'll be like this never happened."

"If you're sure," Javier said, dubiously.

"I'm sure," Maria replied

The man standing at the bar of The Green Dragon, a pub just off Lime Street, was around forty-five years old and carried a warrant card in his pocket which proved he was a detective inspector in the Liverpool police force. The man who sidled up to him and ordered a tonic water was considerably younger, and obtained his power not from any document but simply by virtue of who he worked for.

"Evenin' Mr Roberts," said the younger man.

"Evenin' Phil," the policeman replied. "I heard through the grapevine that you're lookin' for a favour."

Phil smiled. "Not exactly a favour. More in the line of a bit of information."

"Information can be expensive, too," DI Roberts pointed out, taking a sip of whisky. "Especially given the shockin' price of good Scotch these days."

"We'll see you all right," Phil told him. "We always have before, haven't we?"

"True," Roberts agreed. "So what do you need to know?"

"Tell me about Chief Inspector Woodend."

The Inspector almost choked. "Charlie Woodend?" he gasped "'Cloggin' it Charlie'? From the Yard?"

"That's the man," Phil agreed.

Roberts whistled softly. "Don't mess with him."

"You know him, do you? Done a bit of work with him?"

"Let's just say I've come into contact with him – a murder case in Grange-over-Sands a couple of years ago."

"And . . . ?"

"He's got the dedication of a missionary, the obstinacy of a mule and the balls of a bull. He can't be bought, an' he can't be threatened. An' if he was workin' in Liverpool, I'd be a very different bobby to what I am today."

"What do you mean by that?" Phil asked.

Roberts took another sip of his whisky. "Well, for a start, if he was here, I'd have more sense than to be seen talkin' to you right now," he said.

"That bad?" Phil said.

"Or that good, dependin' on which side of the fence you're lookin' at it from," Roberts said. "I know a few fellers in the force who'd love to have him cleaning up some of the messes we've got on our hands at the moment. But if you're a bobby like me, who wants to put a little bit aside for his retirement, then Chief Inspector Charlie-Bloody-Woodend is definitely bad news."

"Suppose somebody I knew was havin' a little trouble—" Phil said.

"What's this 'somebody' business," Roberts interrupted. "We both known you're talkin' about Sid Dowd."

"*Somebody*," Phil repeated firmly. "It has to be *somebody*, because at the moment we're skatin' on very thin ice."

"Understood," Roberts said.

"Let's suppose this somebody was on the fringe of an investigation that this Woodend bloke was lookin' into. What would you advise him to do?"

"You can warn Sid – sorry, this 'somebody' you're workin' for – that there are only two ways to handle Charlie Woodend," Roberts said. "Either you tell him everythin' he wants to know, or you stand clear of him – an' I mean *well* clear."

Phil slipped the brown envelope into Roberts' pocket so skilfully that even the Detective Inspector didn't realise it was happening. "Thanks for your time, Mr Roberts," he said. "It's been very interestin' talkin' to you."

Woodend had not expected to see Jenny Clough again so soon, nor had he expected the two plates of beans on toast which she laid on the desk in front of him. "This is a nice surprise," he told her.

Jenny shrugged. "I just thought the two of you might fancy a bite to eat," she said.

"An" you weren't wrong," Woodend replied. "Thank you, lass."

"If there's anythin' else you want, I'll be in the kitchen." Jenny smoothed down her dark hair with her left hand. "I'm doin' a bit of cleanin', you see."

Woodend gave her a friendly smile. "Yes," he said sympathetically. "I think I do."

"Well, I'll be off then," Jenny said, stepping into the yard and closing the door behind her.

Woodend picked up his knife and fork and cut into the thick sliced toasted bread on which the beans tantalisingly rested. "Aren't you goin' to have yours before it goes cold, Bob?" he asked.

Rutter, who was working his way through the contents of the top drawer of Robbie Peterson's filing cabinet, shook his head. "I'd rather get this job done now I've started it," he said.

"Please yourself. I'll see your share doesn't go to waste," Woodend told him, then added, almost under his breath, "Keen young bugger."

The beans were probably the same brand as he could have bought in London, yet they seemed to taste better up north. Must be something to do with the air, Woodend decided. Either that or he was prejudiced – and he knew that couldn't possibly be the case.

He turned his mind to Jenny Clough. She was a nice lass. There weren't many women who would have thought to make a snack for a man who'd as near as dammit accused her husband of killing her dad. Yes, she was a *really* nice lass. But that didn't mean he'd forgotten that she'd lied to him when she'd said she didn't know what the Clough brothers were doing outside the club the previous Friday.

"Found anythin' interestin' yet?" he asked Rutter.

"Just invoices and bills."

Woodend pushed one plate aside and attacked the second. "Well, if you come up with anythin' unsavoury, like say, a used french letter, don't feel under any obligation to tell me about it till I've finished eatin'," he said.

Rutter grinned. "From what Doris told us, Robbie hasn't felt much of a need for one of those for quite a while."

"Wouldn't surprise me if she'd been puttin' somethin' in his tea to cool his ardour," Woodend opined. "Well, it would have been cheaper than takin' him to the vet's, don't you think?"

When there was no reply, he turned to look at his sergeant. Rutter was closely examining a brown paper envelope. "Have you found somethin', lad?" the Chief Inspector asked.

"I'm not sure," Rutter said, laying it on the desk. "You take a look at it."

Woodend shovelled the last few beans into his mouth – no point in wasting them – and picked the envelope up. He'd never seen one quite like it before. It wasn't square, but it was squarer than most office envelopes tended to be. And it was made of stronger paper, too – so strong it was almost cardboard.

"Interestin'," he said. He looked at the address. "Mr Alexander Conway, 7 Hatton Gardens, Doncaster. Who the bloody hell's Mr Alexander Conway when he's at home?"

"Look on the other side, sir," Rutter advised him.

Woodend turned the envelope over. A crude sketch map been pencilled in on the reverse. It showed a road, marked as the A628, and a town labelled Peniston. Just before the town, an arrow was pointing to the side of the road, and below that were the words, 'Lay-by, 3.00 a.m., Mon 26, 50,000 cartons'.

"What do you make of it?" Woodend asked his sergeant.

"Well, it's obviously a map of somewhere, sir."

"It's a map of one of the main roads into Yorkshire, you ignorant southern bugger," Woodend said. "What else?"

"It seems fairly obvious. Whoever sketched out the map . . ."

"Probably this Conway bloke."

". . . did it because he wanted to arrange a meeting with someone else—"

"Probably Robbie Peterson. Or somebody who was workin' for him."

"Agreed. Wanted to arrange a meeting in a lay-by outside Peniston at three o'clock in the morning, on the 26ᵗʰ of last month."

"Or next month," Woodend pointed out. "Or the month before. But whatever month we're talkin' about, it's a funny time to have a meetin', wouldn't you think?"

"Yes, sir."

"Funny place, too. Hardly congenial. So why arrange it then and there?"

"Because they didn't want to be seen?" Rutter suggested.

"Go to the top of the class," Woodend said. "What about the last two words – '50,000 cartons'?"

"I don't know," Rutter confessed.

"That's because you're not thinkin', lad," Woodend told him. "We're agreed that whatever they were shiftin' was probably illegal, aren't we?"

"Yes."

"An' when you're dealin' in stolen goods, what are you lookin' for? Well, the first thing is as little weight per item as possible. That's why people steal televisions rather than washin' machines. An' the second thing you want is the highest possible resale value. So what would fit the bill in this case?"

"Diamonds?" Rutter suggested.

Woodend smacked his own forehead. "50,000 cartons of *diamonds*? Are there enough diamonds in the whole bloody world to fill 50,000 cartons?"

"Sorry, sir, that was stupid," Rutter said. He thought again. "Cigarettes!" he exclaimed.

"Exactly," Woodend agreed. "An' I'm bettin' on *cork tipped* cigarettes."

"You've lost me," Rutter admitted.

"Most of the fags made in this country don't have cork

54

tips," Woodend explained. "But because poncy buggers like you can't handle a real fag, we have to import them, thereby seriously damagin' our balance of payments account. And where do we import them from?"

"Mostly from America."

"And how do they get here? By carrier pigeon?"

"No," Rutter said. "I imagine most of them come by boat."

"And a lot of the boats will dock in . . . ?"

"Liverpool!"

"Precisely, my dear Watson. Liverpool – where Robbie Peterson used to be the cock o' the walk. The way it probably works is that somewhere between the docks an' the bonded warehouse, the fags go missin'. But there's a score of other ways it could be done. They might be unloaded onto another boat in the river or even on the open sea. The details don't matter. What's important is that the next time they see the light of day, it's in Swann's Lake."

"And from here, they're taken across to Yorkshire," Rutter said.

"Yorkshire, Lancashire, Derbyshire, probably as far as Northumberland," Woodend speculated. "Think about it, Bob. Isn't this just the perfect place for the centre of an operation like that? For a start, there's the local police. I mean, that Inspector Chatteron might be a dab hand at movin' furniture, but when it comes to crime prevention, he couldn't catch a cold. Then there's the fact that this is a holiday resort."

"How does that help?" Rutter wondered aloud.

"Some of the people Peterson's been dealin' with must have come here from time to time, mustn't they?"

"Probably," Rutter conceded.

"Almost definitely," Woodend said.

Rutter tried to hide his grin. What he was being subjected to at that moment was what he'd come to think of as Woodend's Minefield Mood. When this mood struck him the Chief Inspector would plough a straight course, ignoring all the objections and questions exploding all around him, intent only on reaching the other side. Sometimes, it would take him only half an hour sheepishly to admit he'd got it all completely wrong. But there were other times – admittedly fewer – when, despite the objections and the questions, he'd turn out to have it completely – brilliantly – right.

"OK, say they've almost definitely been here," Rutter said. "Why is Swann's Lake better than anywhere else?"

"Oh, it's not better than *anywhere* else," Woodend said dismissively. "Manchester would be better – except there, like I said before, you'd have a smarter police force to deal with. No, what Swann's Lake is, is better than anywhere else of *its size*. Think about it. If a couple of shady characters appear in most communities as big as Swann's Lake, they'd be noticed immediately. But here there's so many new faces comin' in an' out every day that they'd be practically invisible."

"And you're sure Peterson was involved?"

"Certainly I am. The map wouldn't have been in his filin' cabinet otherwise. And then there's his Liverpool connections. Who would be in a better position to get the fags nicked in the first place?"

"But even if he was involved in a smuggling racket, does that get us any closer to finding out who murdered him?" Rutter asked.

"Of course it does," Woodend said. "Look, right from the start we've thought this was a gangland killin', and now we have a suspect. Peterson and this Conway character had a sweet little Trans-Pennine number goin' for them. But then somethin' went wrong. Maybe they argued over how to split the money. Maybe Conway decided he just couldn't trust Peterson any more. Whatever the reason, Conway decided to have his partner killed."

"A couple of hours ago, you were saying the Clough boys were behind it," Rutter pointed out reasonably.

"I was *suggestin'* the Clough boys *might* be behind it," Woodend said defensively. "And they still could be. For all I know, Doris could have done her old man in 'cos she was sick of him whistlin' in the lavatory. I'm not sayin' we should abandon our other lines of inquiry. All I *am* sayin' is that this Conway character is the best suspect we've come up with so far. So it looks to me like one of us will have to go to Doncaster and follow it up." He leant back in his chair. "I know that road," he continued. "It's a long pull, an' if you get stuck behind a lorry goin' over the Pennines, it can take for-bloody-ever."

With his boss still high on his Minefield Mood, Rutter decided it might be wisest to play along with the game. "So which one of us will be going, sir?" he asked.

A huge grin spread across Woodend's face. "I haven't really decided yet," he said. "But I think it might well end up bein' you."

Six

W oodend reached across the desk and offered his opened packet of Capstan Full Strength to Michael Clough. "Fancy a weed, son?"

Clough shook his head. "No, thank you."

"Oh, you're one of the cork-tipped brigade, are you?" Woodend said. "I might have guessed." He turned to the other desk where Rutter was sitting. "Throw your fags over, Sergeant."

"I don't want one of those, either," Clough said. "I don't smoke. And neither should you."

"I beg your pardon?" Woodend said, taken aback.

"Whatever the tobacco companies claim, smoking's bad for your health. People like us – people with some standing in the community – should be setting a good example for the youngsters, not leading them into bad habits."

"Well, bugger me," Woodend said.

He examined the man sitting opposite him more closely. Michael Clough looked every inch the dedicated, liberal teacher who was used to fighting a continuous battle with narrow-minded authority and was, therefore, making it clear from the start that he was not the least intimidated to find himself in the presence of the two Scotland Yard men. Yes, Woodend thought, he had it all down pat – the slightly unruly hair, the cord jacket with leather patches on the elbows, the knitted tie, the CND badge in his buttonhole. The only thing which spoiled the effect was the slight discoloration around his right eye which told the Chief Inspector that, sometime in the last few days, Clough had probably been in a fight.

Woodend leant back in his chair. He couldn't ask straight-forward questions to Clough, as he had with Doris Peterson. If he was going to get anywhere with this cocky young bugger, he was going to have to go round the houses. "Tell me about Robbie Peterson," he said.

"What do you want to know?"

Woodend shook his head. "It doesn't work like that, lad. I'd rather hear what *you* want to *tell* me."

Michael Clough placed his hands on the desk and looked around him as if he were about to make a speech. "You have to put things in context," he said. "You need to understand what it was like living in certain parts of Liverpool before the War. There was a great deal of poverty, a great deal of injustice and a great deal of ignorance."

He *was* making a speech, Woodend thought, and probably one he'd made many times before. But there was no doubting the young man's sincerity. "Go on," he said.

"Robbie Peterson was brought up in the kind of environment in which you had to be tough to survive, and where the only way to break free from the grind seemed to be to turn to crime."

"He was in the protection racket, wasn't he?" Woodend said.

"Among other things," Michael admitted.

"Which means that he wasn't some kind of modern-day Robin Hood," Woodend pointed out. "He wasn't robbin' from the rich to give to the poor – he was creamin' off some of the hard-earned money of other poor buggers who were trying to claw their way out of poverty and despera-tion."

Michael Clough sighed. "I'm not saying that what he did was right, but I am saying that until you've been in that situation yourself, you've no right to sit in judgement."

"No, I haven't," Woodend agreed. "I leave that to the courts. You can see the good side to everybody, can't you, lad?"

"Isn't that better than seeing only the bad side?" Michael Clough countered.

"Then answer me this. If Robbie was merely a victim of circumstance, why did he continue with his life of crime long after he'd made enough money to go straight?"

"I don't know what you're talking about."

Woodend spread his hands out in front of him. "Come on, son. You're part of the family – even if you're only on the fringes. You must know that Robbie was usin' this club as a base to run his rackets from."

"I don't believe it," Michael Clough said firmly. "I didn't always get on with Robbie – which was probably my fault as much as it was his. But I do know that he moved to Swann's Lake because he wanted a chance to make a new start – a chance to leave the past behind. Why would he risk that chance by doing anything illegal?"

"Maybe because that new start wasn't everythin' he hoped it would be?" Woodend suggested.

"I can't accept any of what you're saying," Michael Clough told him. "I *won't* accept it."

No, he bloody wouldn't, Woodend thought – not even if the evidence was staring him right in the face – because it didn't conform to the world as seen through the eyes of Michael Clough. "All right," the Chief Inspector said. "Let's move on to the night of the murder. You were in The Hideaway, weren't you?"

"Yes, I was."

"Is that normally how you spend your Friday nights? Surrounded by smokers in a tatty club?"

"No. I belong to several voluntary organisations. I'm usually in committee meetings on Friday nights."

"So why not last Friday? Weren't there any committee meetings then?"

"Yes, there were," Clough admitted. "But I thought that just for once, I'd give myself a night off."

Woodend's eyes narrowed. Michael Clough didn't look like the kind of man who would shirk his duty, even occasionally. "I still don't see why you chose The Hideaway," he said. "Were you meetin' someone there?"

"No."

"Or perhaps 'meetin' someone' is puttin' it too strongly. Perhaps you were just hopin' to run into someone."

"No."

"Not even the Peterson girl?"

For a couple of seconds, the effect of the words on Michael Clough was startling. The young man's eyes flickered and his jaw wavered. Then he regained control of himself. "Why should you think I'd want to see *her*?" he asked.

"Annabel Peterson's an attractive girl," Woodend said. "Why *wouldn't* you want to see her? Besides, she seems to me like a lass who's got more than her share of troubles – and you're just the sort of lad who'd want to try and sort it out, aren't you?"

"Annabel has had a very difficult life," Clough said, side-stepping the question.

"How'd you reach that conclusion?" Woodend asked, giving him a little more rope.

"Sending her away to a posh school was a mistake," Clough explained. "She never really fitted in there, but at the same time it put a distance between her and the family. As a direct consequence of that she lives on the edge of two worlds, but doesn't really belong to either of them. The result is that she's confused, she's unhappy, and she's throwing her life away."

Apart from that last bit, you could be talking about yourself, Woodend thought, but aloud he said, "So you *were* in the club hoping to see her?"

Michael Clough shook his head. "I've tried to help her before, and she's turned me down flat. But she knows I'm always willing, and when she's ready, *she'll* come to *me*."

"You got into what witnesses described as 'quite a serious discussion' with your brother Terry," Woodend said, changing tack again.

"We talked," Michael said guardedly.

"And was Robbie the subject of your serious conversation? Were you perhaps trying to persuade your brother to stop playing a part in his father-in-law's racketeering?"

Michael Clough put his hands to his head, as if he despaired of Woodend ever understanding anything. "Terry works –

worked – for Robbie in the club, and sometimes on the fairground. He's not involved in any rackets."

"He used to be, though – back in the good old days in Liverpool."

"He gave that up when he married Jenny. Said he couldn't run the risk of getting caught now that he had a wife to take care of."

"But no children."

"What?"

"They've been married for five years, and they don't have any children yet. Why do you think that is?"

"You'll have to ask him," Michael Clough said, suddenly sullen.

"You still haven't told me what your 'serious' conversation with your brother was about," Woodend said.

"It was about personal matters. Family matters. It had nothing to do with the murder."

"You can't be sure of that," Woodend pointed out. "Not unless you actually know who killed Robbie Peterson and *why* he killed him. Do you know that, Mr Clough?"

"Well, of course I don't," Michael Clough said angrily. "But I'm equally sure that what we had to say to each other had no bearing on it."

"You and your brother went outside for some quite con- siderable time, didn't you? Why was that?"

"It was hot in the club. We both felt the need for some fresh air."

"So you would have been in the yard at the time Robbie Peterson crossed it to go to his office?"

Clough shook his head. "No, we went for a walk down to the lake."

"So the office was in darkness when you left?"

"Yes."

"And when you came back?"

"Yes."

"But in the time it took you to walk down to the lake and back, somebody did Robbie Peterson in."

"So it would seem." Michael Clough glanced at his watch.

"Is this going to take much longer, Chief Inspector?" he asked. "Because I have an appointment in Manchester in just over two hours time."

"An appointment?" Woodend repeated questioningly.

"Yes, I'm giving a talk to a group of prisoners at Strangeways Gaol."

"And what's the subject?"

"Characters from Nineteenth-Century Literature," Clough said. "I don't expect you—"

"So there'll be a lot of Dickens in it," Woodend interrupted.

"That's right," Clough agreed, surprised.

"And let me guess what your theme will be," Woodend said. "It'll have to be something along the lines that the likes of Bill Sykes and the Artful Dodger aren't really bad in themselves, but are more victims of their upbringin'."

Michael Clough's eyebrows rose. "It seems I've underestimated you, Chief Inspector," he said.

"Don't worry about it, lad," Woodend advised him. "It happens all the time. Well, if you don't want to be late for that lecture of yours, you'd better get going now."

Clough, looking a little relieved, stood up and walked towards the door. Woodend waited until he actually had his hand on the latch, then said, "There is just one more question I'd like to ask, sir."

Clough reluctantly turned round. "And what might that be?"

"That black eye of yours. It's a real shiner. Who gave it to you?"

"I walked into something," Michael Clough told him.

"Aye," Woodend replied. "I thought you'd say that."

Annie Peterson's high-heeled shoes made a sharp clicking noise as she walked rapidly down Cardigan Street. This was always the dangerous part – the part where some busybody from the Ministry of Labour could spot her and start to wonder what someone who lived in a one-roomed rat-trap the other side of town was doing in a posh area like this.

By the time she was passing Number 44 Cardigan Street, she was already opening her handbag and taking out a packet of cigarettes. As she drew level with the front gate of Number 46, she stopped, put a cigarette in her mouth, and lit it. Then she turned, as if she'd thought she'd heard someone calling her. The street was deserted.

Annabel pulled a set of keys out of her bag, walked quickly down the path of Number 46, inserted one of the keys into the front-door lock and turned it. After another quick glance over her shoulder to make sure she wasn't being observed, she pushed the door open.

Only once she was inside the pleasantly decorated hallway did she feel safe. And even there, the feeling was not as strong as it used to be. The two detectives from London – especially the older one – had ensured that.

Annabel opened a second door, the one which led to her flat. Yes, that Woodend man had definitely got her rattled, she thought. And not without cause. Being interviewed by him had been a gruelling experience. It had felt as if he'd found a chink in the screen she'd erected between herself and the world, and looking through it could see her as she really was – naked and vulnerable. And if he could do that, it wouldn't be much of a trick to find out about this flat. Then the trouble would start.

She flopped down in one of her armchairs, already playing out the almost inevitable interview in her mind.

'*Why do you pay the rent on two flats, Annabel?*'

'*It's a free country, isn't it?*'

'*More to the point, how can you afford to pay the rent on two flats? What's the dole pay out these days?*'

'*Two pounds a week.*'

'*The flat in Cardigan Street must cost nearly that. So where's the money been coming from, Annabel? Your dad?*'

'*I wouldn't touch a penny of Robbie's money.*'

'*Your mum, then?*'

'*It'd still be Robbie's money.*'

'*You're not on the game, are you?*'

'*No. Haven't you heard? I give that out for free.*'

'Then where's the extra money comin' from, Annie? You must be getting' it from somewhere!'
She needed help. Needed it badly. She picked up the phone, which was sitting on a small table beside her, and dialled.
"Can I help you?" asked a crisp, efficient voice.
Annabel gave the operator the number, then listened with growing desperation to the ringing tone. *Where are you, Michael?* her mind screamed. *Where the hell are you?*
"I'm afraid there's no answer," the operator said. "Please try again later."
The line went dead. Annabel slammed the receiver onto its cradle, stood up and began to pace the room. Bloody, bloody Michael Clough. Always there when she didn't want him, not answering his bloody phone when she really did.
She stopped in front of the sideboard, and slid open the top drawer. Lying in it was a photograph which she'd long ago torn in two, and yet had never been able to bring herself to throw away completely.
She held the two halves together now, so that they formed a complete picture. A man and a girl were standing together in front of what had once been a Victorian cotton magnate's mansion, but since just after the First World War had functioned as a very expensive girls' boarding school. The man was dressed in a suit which proclaimed that while he probably had a great deal of money to spend, he had very little taste. He had his arm resting on the girl's shoulder and was smiling proudly. The girl herself, dressed in her school uniform, wore an expression which was a mixture of dismay and anxiety.
"How they all laughed after you'd left, Robbie," she told the photograph. "You thought you'd cut a fine figure, didn't you? But you hadn't. They teased me about it for months. You were a joke they never got tired of." She looked into the distressed eyes of the girl she'd once been, then back at the smiling face of the proud father. "You knew I was unhappy there, didn't you? But you refused to take me away, because you wanted to make me into a lady. Well, look at me now!"
But he couldn't look at her now – because he was dead.
The two pieces of the photograph were still in her hands. It

would have been easy for her to damage it further – to rip and rip in a frenzy of destruction until only pieces of glossy black and white paper were left. But she didn't do that. Instead, she placed the two halves back in the drawer, and, wiping a tear from her cheek, returned to her chair.

Detective Sergeant 'Toad' Gower drummed his fingers impatiently on the steering wheel of his old Morris Oxford, which was parked in front of Number 20 Cardigan Road, just up the street from Annabel Peterson's secret flat.

"When's the bitch going to come out again?" he asked his dashboard.

He should have had a full team on a case like this, he thought. Six or seven men, so that he could run a proper round-the-clock surveillance operation. With resources like that, he'd probably already have all he needed to make his case. But he didn't have a team. Hell, ever since he'd been suspended the day before, he didn't even have official status.

He thought about the board of inquiry he was soon to appear before. He'd beat the charge of illegal entry, just as he'd beaten the charges at all the other inquiries, for one simple reason – because the pencil pushers who sat in judgement of him knew that nobody else could get the results he could. And if additional proof of his indispensability were necessary, he'd give them Annie Peterson's head on a platter. True, he didn't exactly know what she was up to yet – but he was sure she was up to something.

Terry Clough had none of his brother's self-assurance, Woodend thought. While Michael was an independent thinker and a rebel, Terry was nothing more than Robbie Peterson's lieutenant, his right-hand man, and now that Peterson was gone, Clough looked completely at sea.

"Tell me an' my sergeant here about the night of the murder," the Chief Inspector said.

"There's not much I can say," Clough replied. "I was down at the lake with my brother when Robbie was killed."

"Talkin' about personal matters?"

66

"That's right."

"An' I'm willin' to bet you're not prepared to go into more detail about them than that."

"Why should I? What me an' our Michael talked about don't have nothin' to do with the murder inquiry."

His brother had briefed him well, Woodend decided. "All right," he said. "If you won't tell me what you an' Michael were arguin' about, at least fill me in on those two lads who work on the ghost train."

"The Green brothers. What about them?"

"Have they got criminal records?"

"I don't know."

"Come on, son," Woodend said. "One quick call to Maltham nick an' I'll have the information anyway. All I want you to do is save me a little time. Is that too much to ask?"

Clough shrugged. "Yes, they've both got form," he said sullenly.

"Have they done any time inside?"

"Eighteen months apiece."

"What had they done to earn that?"

"I think Robbie said they'd been handlin' stolen property."

"So knowing that about them, why did he give them jobs?"

Michael Clough would have come up with some guff about Robbie wishing to rehabilitate them just as he'd supposedly rehabilitated himself. His brother merely said, "I don't know."

"It couldn't have been because he was usin' them in one of his rackets, could it?" Woodend asked.

"I don't know what you're talkin' about," Clough replied.

"You're sayin' that Robbie wasn't involved in any rackets?"

"I'm sayin' that if he was, I didn't know anythin' about it. Look, I might have been a bit bent in the past—"

"How bent?"

Clough grinned nervously. "I'm not goin' to tell you that, now am I?" he asked, trying to pretend he though the Chief Inspector's question was no more than a joke.

"I'm not interested in bangin' you up for somethin' you did

when you were in Liverpool," Woodend said patiently. "All I'm tryin' to do is what your brother would probably call, 'put things in context'. So why don't you just tell me what were you involved in?"

"I used to be one of Robbie's collectors," Clough admitted.

"You want to spell that out a bit more?" Woodend suggested.

"I used to go round to the pubs an' clubs that were payin' Robbie for security, an' collect the money every week."

"That's it? No strong-arm stuff? No robberies?"

Clough shook his head. "Maybe I would have got into that eventually, but just before I married Jenny, Robbie had a quiet word with me. He said he didn't want to run the risk of his daughter's husband goin' to prison, so he'd find me a job which was legit. He also said that if he ever heard of me doin' anythin' crooked, he'd have both my legs broken."

Which, seen without the benefit of rose-coloured glasses, was pretty much what Michael Clough had said. "So I take it Robbie approved of you marryin' his daughter, then," Woodend said.

"It was his idea."

"It was *what*?"

Clough shrugged again. "His idea. I mean, I'm not sayin' I don't love her or anythin' like that, but he was the one who first suggested it."

And Woodend thought he knew *why* Robbie had suggested it. His wife despised him, and his younger daughter wanted nothing to do with him. So all he was left with was his darling Jenny, and he didn't want to lose her. What better way to make sure he still kept her affection than by marrying her to a nonentity like Terry Clough – a man who would never be serious competition for him.

"Did Robbie have any enemies?" Woodend asked.

"Not down here."

"But in Liverpool?"

Another shrug. It was almost habitual. "When you've been involved in the rackets, like Robbie was, you're bound to have crossed a good few people in your time."

"Do you know a man called Alex Conway?"

Clough frowned. "I don't think so."

"But you're not sure."

"I've never met anybody called that, but I think I may have heard the name. Robbie could have worked with somebody called Conway in the Forties."

And he could still have been working with him until a couple of days ago, Woodend thought – right up to the point when Robbie got that nail in his temple.

The Chief Inspector lit a cigarette, then realising he'd not offered one to Clough, slid the packet across the table. That was the trouble with this feller, he decided. He was so insignificant that you hardly noticed he was there – even when you were talking to him.

"Is the club openin' tonight?" Woodend asked.

"I expect so."

"But you don't know for sure? Aren't you in charge, now that Robbie's dead?"

"I'm the assistant manager, like I always was, but my mother-in-law is the boss now."

Of course she was. Doris probably wouldn't allow Terry Clough to clean the windows without supervision.

"My sergeant and I would like to join," Woodend said. "So if you wouldn't mind, we'll be needing some membership application forms."

Terry Clough tried an ingratiating smile. "You won't need a membership card to get in, Chief Inspector," he said.

"Oh, but I will," Woodend told him. "There's one thing you'd better learn about me quickly, Mr Clough. I always play things by the book."

The Red Lion was less than half a mile away from The Hideaway. It had ivy climbing up its walls, and had probably been built in the days when there was actually a Swann family living in Swann's Lake.

"Well, this is where you'll be staying," Inspector Chatterton said as he and the two detectives walked across the car park to the front door. "Like I told you before I booked it, it's only a pub."

Woodend raised his eyebrows in comic exasperation. "Only a pub?" he repeated. "Did they send you overseas durin' the War, Inspector?"

"No," Chatterton said. "I never got the chance."

"Then count yourself lucky," Woodend told him. "I went through the lot. The Western Desert. The D-Day Invasion. Crossin' the Rhine. An' apart from wantin' to see my missus again, the only thing that kept me goin' sometimes was the thought of gettin' home to my local pub."

Chatterton laughed. "Very good, sir."

Bloody fool! Woodend thought. "I'm not jokin'," he said. "I mean it. You know what they say about nookey, Inspector? They say there's no such thing as a bad jump – it's just that some are better than others. Well, it's the same with pubs. I've never seen a bad one yet."

They reached the door and were greeted by a small, round woman with a jolly red face.

"This is Mrs Thorpe, the landlady," Chatterton announced.

They shook hands. "I've made up your beds," Mrs Thorpe said. "They're nice rooms, in easy reach of the lavatory. Now I expect you're hungry after a hard day's work. What would you say to a nice plate of bacon, liver and onions?"

"I'd say, 'Grand'," Woodend told her. He grinned at Chatterton. "See what I mean, Inspector? It's times like this when I can almost believe it was worth gettin' shot at."

Seven

The Hideaway's organist leant over the microphone. "This next number's by The Crickets, an' it's called 'That'll Be The Day'," he said, with some attempt at showmanship.

"The Crickets!" Woodend said disgustedly to his sergeant as the organist played the opening bars.

Rutter grinned. "Something wrong with the name, sir?"

"When I was a lad, I used to listen to a band called Louis Armstrong's Hot Seven," Woodend replied. "Louis Armstrong was their leader, there were seven of them, an' the music they played was hot. See what I'm gettin' at, Sergeant? That name made sense, which – unless they rub their legs together on stage – this band's doesn't."

He turned to face the dance floor again. The organist looked as if he would have been much happier playing the music of an earlier era, but nevertheless his efforts had already enticed several couples onto the dance floor, the older ones doing their best to incorporate the beat into a rather uneasy foxtrot, the younger ones treating it as an invitation to jive.

"Tell me, Sergeant," Woodend said, "do you really think this so-called music's got a future?"

"Oh yes," Rutter replied enthusiastically. "Rock 'n' roll is here to stay."

The Chief Inspector sighed. "You know, lad, sometimes you make me feel very old," he said.

Woodend picked up his pint of best bitter. This was his third, which meant, he estimated accurately, that he'd probably been in the club for just about an hour. He held the beer up to the light. A grand pint – fifty times better than they served down south, and at one and tuppence, a real bargain. He liked being in

Cheshire. It wasn't as good as his native Lancashire – nothing ever would be – but it wasn't bad. He liked the club, too, and it gave him a slightly malicious satisfaction to know that his sergeant – who was only drinking halves – was nothing like as comfortable there as he was.

A man in a shabby grey suit, who had been hovering near the bar, made his way over to their table. "You'll be the two detectives from London," he said. "Chief Inspector Woodend and Sergeant Rutter, is it?"

"That's right," Woodend agreed. "And you'd be . . . ?"

"Harold Dawson. I work for the *Maltham Chronicle*. Would you mind if I joined you?"

"Be my guest," Woodend said.

Dawson slid into the chair opposite Woodend. "How's the investigation going?" he asked.

"We've been here less than a day, Mr Dawson," Woodend said. "There's not really much to report yet. So you work for the local paper. What are you? A reporter or a photographer?"

Dawson laughed and Woodend thought there was more bitterness than humour behind it. "I'm a photographer by training," he said, "but on a rag like the *Chronicle*, you're expected to turn your hand to anything. Not that there's much challenge in it. You don't have to be an Agatha Christie or a Dorothy Sayers to cover Women's Institute meetings. Just take down the full name of the old bag who was lucky enough to win the cake raffle, and you've got your scoop."

"You must be pleased about this murder, then?" Woodend said.

"Pleased?" Dawson repeated, as if the word had startled him.

"Aye. At long last you've got a story with some meat on it. A story you can probably sell to the national papers if you play your cards right."

Dawson grinned sheepishly. "You're quite right about that, Chief Inspector," he admitted. "Several of the London papers have been in contact with me." He signalled the waiter. "What can I get you and your sergeant to drink?"

"No offence, but we'd prefer to buy our own," Woodend said.

Dawson smiled, revealing a set of teeth which could have done with serious dental work. "Don't want to be accused of taking bribes – is that it?" he asked.

"Somethin' like that," Woodend agreed.

"But you've got nothing against co-operating with the press, have you, Chief Inspector?"

"Not as long as I'm dealin' with a responsible journalist who wouldn't print anythin' which might impede my investigation."

"That's me. 'Responsible' is my middle name," Dawson said.

I'll just bet it is, you slimy bugger, Woodend thought. But aloud he merely said, "I'm glad to hear it. In that case, we shouldn't have any trouble gettin' on with each other."

The waiter arrived, and Dawson ordered a pint. "I was . . . er . . . wondering if you'd give me your permission to take some photographs for the nationals," he said to Woodend.

"Of what?"

"Oh, you know – the club, the lakeside attractions, things like that."

"This isn't Russia," Woodend said. "As long as you don't trespass, you can photograph what you want."

"Ah, but there's the problem," Dawson said. "One of the things I'd like to take pictures of is Robbie Peterson's office. And that's private property."

"What possible interest could photos of Robbie Peterson's office be?" Woodend wondered.

"It's the scene of the crime, isn't it? The place where the dastardly deed was done. And most people who read the kind of newspapers I freelance for have got an insatiable appetite for blood and gore."

"I suppose I could let you have some of the official police photographs," Woodend conceded.

Dawson looked disappointed. "Official pictures don't have any atmosphere to them. I'd rather take my own, if you don't mind."

"I don't mind," Woodend said. "But there wouldn't be much

point now. Apart from one filin' cabinet, all the original furniture's been removed."

"And where's it gone to?" Dawson asked.

"You'll have to ask Inspector Chatterton about that. But wherever it is, I don't expect he'll want you fiddlin' about with it. Strictly speakin', it might still turn out to be evidence."

"Oh, I see," Dawson said. "Well, I suppose the official police photographs will be better than nothing."

He might say that, Woodend thought, but he didn't mean it. The fact was, he had absolutely no interest in the official photographs. So what was it exactly that he *did* have an interest in?

If Gerry Fairbright had been back home in Oldham, he would have been pacing the living room by now. But that was the problem. He wasn't at home. Nor was he in Port Talbot, where his wife firmly believed him to be. Instead he was stuck in this cream sodding Alpine Sprite caravan – where there was no *room* to pace – stewing in his own juice.

If only he hadn't been such a bloody fool. If only he'd learned his lesson last time. Or the time before! But he hadn't.

He must have wished Robbie Peterson dead a hundred times, he thought, but he'd done so without considering the implications of what that death might mean to him. Now that Robbie actually *was* dead, he could see quite clearly that he was in an even more difficult position than he'd been in before. True, Peterson had been a vicious greedy bastard, but at least Gerry had known the rules when dealing with him. Whereas now . . .

He looked out of the caravan window. He could see the club, all lit up, and even hear the faint strains of the electric organ. Maybe he'd go for a drink, he thought. But that really wasn't the answer. Drink might loosen his tongue – might even make him go and confess to that Chief Inspector from London. And that would never do at all.

He opened the cupboard under the tiny sink and took out his tool set. "You've got to do it," he muttered to himself. "You don't have any bloody choice."

With trembling hands, he selected a hammer, a small chisel and a screwdriver. He could do the job easily with these tools, he thought. But there was a part of him which wished that it *wasn't* easy – wished that it was bloody impossible, so that whatever happened, it wouldn't be as a result of his decision.

It would be best to break into the office at about three o'clock in the morning, when there'd be nobody around and he could do a proper job. Yes, three o'clock would be just about right. But that meant he still had a lot of time on his hands. So maybe, despite what he'd promised himself earlier, he would have a drink. After all, what harm could one pint do?

Sid Dowd lit the thick Havana cigar and inhaled luxuriantly before swinging round in his executive leather chair to face his assistant. "They say each one of these coronas is rolled individually on a dusky virgin's thigh," he said.

"Is that right, Mr Dowd?" Phil asked indifferently.

Dowd sighed. That was the trouble with this new breed of heavies, he thought – they had absolutely no sense of romance. It had been different in the old days. Certainly things had been rougher – more violent – back then, yet despite that, the people he'd worked with had had some dash about them. Now he employed fellers like Phil, who did their job well enough – *better* then well enough – but had about as much flair as undertakers' assistants.

Thoughts of undertakers reminded him of something. "They're burying Robbie Peterson on Tuesday," he said.

"So I believe," Phil responded.

"I think I'll go and pay my last respects."

"Which car will you be needing, Mr Dowd?"

Sid sighed again. That was what he meant about these youngsters. No sense of style. "I'll be wantin' the Roller, of course," he said. "An' while I'm down at Swann's Lake, I just might take the opportunity to put that Chief Inspector right on one or two things."

The atmosphere in The Hideaway was warming up in all senses of the word. Many of the women had discarded their cardigans

75

– and with them their inhibitions – and now were dancing with other women's husbands. Woodend watched as hands meant to steer partners slipped down backs and nestled, briefly, on buttocks. It was all harmless fun, he thought, though he doubted whether his sergeant, in the first flush of love, would approve. He remembered his own mild flirtation with Liz Poole during the Salton case. That had never come to anything, nor would he have wished it to, but it was strange to think that she was only a few miles away from Swann's Lake at that very moment. He wondered if she had read about the case in the newspapers, and knew he was so close to her pub. He wondered . . .

But enough of wondering. The past was the past, and he was in Swann's Lake to investigate a new murder, not to revive old memories.

"What did you make of that reporter, Bob?" he asked Rutter.

The Sergeant took a thoughtful sip from his glass of beer. "I didn't like him," he said.

"*Because* he was a reporter?"

Rutter shook his head. "No, not because of that. I got the impression that our Mr Dawson's interest in the case was more than just professional."

Which was exactly what Woodend had been thinking. "Would you care to expand on that?" he asked.

"I'd like to," his sergeant replied. "But I can't. I just get a gut feeling that he's involved in some way. Not with the murder – I'm almost sure he had no part on that – but maybe with something which *led up to* the murder. It's almost as if . . ."

But Woodend was no longer listening. Instead, his eyes were following a man of around thirty, who had just entered the club. "See him, Sergeant?" he asked. "His name's Gerry Fairbright. He owns one of the caravans, and he's here on his own because his wife had to go back to Oldham to look after her sick mother. Well, that's the story he gave me, anyway."

"But you don't believe it?"

"No, I don't. He sounded to me like he was makin' it up as he went along. An' he's not behavin' like a man on holiday.

76

He was watchin' us for a full three quarters of an hour this afternoon."

"Watching *us*?" Rutter repeated.

"That's right. Watchin' us – or maybe watchin' Robbie's *office.*"

"But there's nothing in Robbie's office that could be of any possible interest to him," Rutter pointed out.

"You know that, an' I know that," Woodend said. "But maybe Gerry Fairbright doesn't."

The steward in The Hideaway had long ago called last orders and it was hours since the final reluctant customers had drifted away to their caravans and bungalows. Now there was a blanket of silence over the whole of Swann's Lake. Now, Gerry Fairbright told himself, was the time to make his move.

He picked up the tools he had taken from the box earlier, and slipped them into his pocket. It would take him ten minutes, he thought. No more than that. He made his way through the sleeping caravan site to the fence which separated it from the club. Ten minutes – and he would finally have peace of mind.

It had been a mistake to go into the club. He'd realised that the moment he saw Woodend sitting there. But once he *had* seen him, there'd been no turning back, had there? That would have looked like turning tail and running. And that would have made the detective even more suspicious than he already was.

"It'll be all right," he whispered softly into the darkness. "Once you've done the job, Woodend won't be able to touch you."

Fairbright opened the gate – carefully, so as to avoid any noise. It was a clear night. He would have no problem seeing the lock. Everything would work out just as he'd planned.

He took two steps, and then stopped – horrified. He tried to tell himself he was imagining things, but it was no good. He was not alone in the yard. Worse! The other person – and he could not tell whether it was a man or a woman – was crouched in front of the office door, fiddling with the lock!

His heart beating so fast he thought it would burst, Fairbright turned around and made his way quickly back to his caravan.

Eight

A heavy mist swirled around The Red Lion that Monday morning. It insinuated itself through the ivy. It rolled under the tables on the forecourt. And it pressed itself against the windows of the bar parlour where Woodend and Rutter were eating their breakfasts.

Rutter nibbled at a piece of toast and wondered how his boss could manage a full cooked breakfast after eight or nine pints of bitter the night before. But speculation about his boss's iron constitution was only a temporary diversion from the matter which was really weighing on his mind. He was going to Doncaster alone, to carry out an investigation which could provide the first real breakthrough in the case. But what if he messed it up? What if, without Cloggin'-it Charlie at his elbow to guide him, he did something incredibly stupid? He had never suffered from any lack of confidence before, and was surprised that he did now. But what surprised him even more was the realisation that it was not the thought of failing to solve the case which worried him – it was a fear of letting Woodend down.

"If I was you, the first thing I'd do when I got to Doncaster would be drop in on the local cop shop, an' find out exactly what they've got on this Conway character," Woodend said, spearing a thick slice of bacon with his fork.

"And then?"

"You've got the element of surprise on your side. Pay our Mr Conway a visit."

"You're sure he *will* be surprised?" Rutter asked.

"Absolutely. As far as Conway's concerned, there's nothin' to connect him with Swann's Lake. An' he's right – nothin' except for one brown envelope which Robbie was careless enough to leave in his filin' cabinet. So even if he's as guilty as Judas Iscariot, he'll not be expectin' a bright young bobby to turn up on his doorstep an' start askin' him about Robbie Peterson's murder."

"Would you care to suggest any lines of approach, sir?"

"Well, I'd probably start by askin' him if he heard about Peterson's death," Woodend said. "An' if he said he hadn't, I'd know he was lyin' – 'cos it's been in all the papers."

"And if he says he *has* heard?"

"I'd ask him what he was doin' last Friday night."

"If he is behind the murder, but didn't do the job himself, he's probably got a watertight alibi," Rutter pointed out.

"Maybe," Woodend agreed. "But it'll still put the wind up him to know we're thinkin' that way – an' a man with the wind up him can say things he never intended to."

There was the sound of a car horn hooting outside.

"That'll be your transport," Woodend said. He grinned. "There are still some advantages to rank – if they'd been pickin' *me* up, they'd have come inside and asked if I was ready yet."

Rutter rose to his feet and was almost at the door when he stopped and turned round again. "You don't think it would be a good idea if you went to Doncaster instead of me?" he asked.

Woodend studied his sergeant for a couple of seconds, then shook his head. "The other side of the Pennines is enemy territory to a Lancastrian like me," he said. "Anyway, it's about time you got a few scratches."

"Scratches, sir?" Rutter said, puzzled.

"When you buy a new car, you're forever frettin' that you're goin' to scrape against somethin' an' damage it's lovely shiny surface," the Chief Inspector told him. "It's takes all the pleasure out of drivin'. Then you *do* have a scrape, an' you realise you don't have to keep worryin' any more."

The car horn hooted again – more impatiently this time.

Rutter smiled. "You're saying I'm like a new car, are you, sir?"

"Well, a good second-hand one, anyway," Woodend said,

grinning back. "Put it this way, Sergeant. I'm still waiting for
you to make your first big cock-up – and the suspense is bloody
near killing me."

"Thanks, sir," Rutter said.

"What for?" Woodend asked innocently, as he cut his last
remaining sausage in two.

The mist had cleared and it was promising to turn into an almost
perfect day. Woodend refused Chatterton's telephoned offer of
a lift to The Hideaway, and instead walked the half-mile from
The Red Lion to the club. It was pleasant to stroll down the quiet
country lanes, to hear tiny, unidentified animals rustling in the
hedgerows and watch the last of the swifts flying overhead.

"Creatures of habit," he said to himself, as he watched the
birds glide and swirl. "But then, aren't we all?"

He tried to imagine himself buying a club like The Hideaway
at some time in the future. Would he able to shed the persona of
'Charlie Woodend the bobby' like an old skin, and be nothing
more than 'Charlie Woodend the genial mine host'? Or would
he catch himself watching his customers – trying to work out
which of them was up to no good? And when there was a murder
in the area, would he be able to resist the temptation to go to the
same pubs as the bobbies on the case, in the hope that they might
possibly recognise him as an old Yard man and ask his advice?
No, of course he wouldn't. He'd been a policeman for far too
long to start changing now.

In that way, he and Robbie Peterson were alike, he suspected.
Robbie had come to Swann's Lake to make a new start, but it
wasn't just his family he'd brought with him – it was a whole
way of looking at things. So even though he hadn't needed the
money, when he'd seen the chance for the cigarette-smuggling
racket, he just hadn't been able resist it.

It was just after eight o'clock when he reached The Hideaway. The curtains in the Peterson house were still drawn and
the caravan site was as silent as if had been secretly evacuated
overnight.

But though nothing was stirring now, someone had been busy
only a few hours before, Woodend thought, staring down at the

lock on the office door. Very busy! Paint had been chipped away and the shiny brass lock itself had at least a dozen scratch marks on it

The Chief Inspector took his own key out of his pocket, inserted it in the keyhole and was pleasantly surprised to find that the lock still worked. As he stepped into the office, he found himself wondering who the bungling burglar had been. Gerry Fairbright's name immediately came to mind. He'd been watching the office the day before and he'd seemed very worried about something when he entered The Hideaway a few hours later. But Gerry Fairbright had a craftsman's hands. A flimsy lock like the one on the office door would have presented few difficulties for him.

Woodend sat down at the desk. Perhaps the important question was not to ask *who* had tried to break in, but *why* the attempted burglary had taken place at all. What was the burglar looking for? Surely not 50,000 cartons of cigarettes?

There was a knock on the door and when Woodend looked up he saw Inspector Chatterton standing there, with a paper bag in his hands. "I got you the hammer, sir," the Inspector said.

"The hammer? What hammer?"

"A hammer like the one which was used to kill Robbie Peterson. You said you wanted one."

"Oh, right," Woodend agreed. "Put it on the desk, will you."

Chatterton laid it neatly across the corner of the desk, frowned, then re-arranged it so it was more symmetrical.

"Have you had your lads go through Robbie Peterson's office furniture?" Woodend asked.

"Of course, sir. We had to inventory it."

"And what did you find?"

"Nothing much. Pens, pencils, blotting paper. I think Peterson had it more for show than for anything else."

Or Doris did, Woodend thought. "No secret drawers?" he asked.

"I beg your pardon, sir?"

"You know, secret drawers. Places where Peterson might have been hidin' things."

"I can't say we were really looking for anything like that," Chatterton admitted.

"Well, look now," Woodend told him. "Better yet, get somebody from the high-class furniture trade to examine it. And I want the three-piece suite taken to pieces as well."

"What are we looking for, sir?"

"Blessed if I know," Woodend said. "Anythin' worth breakin' the law over."

"I see," Chatterton said. He took a deep breath. "I was talking to the Chief Constable a few minutes ago."

"That must have been nice for you," Woodend said dourly. "Social call was it?"

"No, it was about this murder," Chatterton said, missing the point. "He was wondering how many men you'll be needing today. He's quite willing to cancel all leave and have officers reassigned from other duties."

Yes, they usually were, Woodend thought. The trouble with most Chief Constables was they liked to be seen to be doing something by the press and the public. And to them, that meant having a load of bobbies trampling all over the crime scene with their size-nine boots, being more hindrance than help.

"Like I told you yesterday, until I've got a feel for the place, I wouldn't know what to do with them," he told the Inspector. And then he remembered the burglary. "Actually, I could use one man."

Chatterton looked relieved. "Oh, good," he said. "I'll send a constable over right away. Or would you prefer a sergeant?"

"I don't want him now," Woodend replied. He stood up and looked across at the club. "I want him tonight. Round about midnight."

The white-haired man sitting opposite Rutter in the police canteen wore a sergeant's stripes and a look which managed to be both alert and world weary. His name, he'd announced when they shook hands, was Les Dash, and it was going to be his job to baby-sit the Yard man for as long as he was in Doncaster.

"I thought I knew every villain in this town personally, but you've got me stumped with this Alexander Conway," he confessed. "Nobody else I talked to had heard of him either. And there's nothin' in our records."

"He might be new to Doncaster," Rutter pointed out. "We've no idea yet how long this tobacco smuggling racket's been going on."

Dash popped an unsmuggled cigarette into his mouth and frowned. "New or not, I should know about him. This is my town, Sergeant Rutter, an' if a villain only stops on his way through to take a leak, I usually get to hear about it."

"Are you saying he's not a criminal?" Rutter asked.

"I'm sayin' that if he is, he's a very clever one." Dash lit his cigarette and stood up. "Don't you think it's about time we went to see this Mr Conway of yours and found exactly what he's up to?"

"That seems like a good idea to me," Rutter agreed.

It was the pain which woke Maria up – a stabbing at the back of her eyes, as if someone were pricking her with red-hot needles; a pounding in her head like the one she had felt when she finally came to in Belgrave Square.

Yet even through the pain, thoughts were beginning to register themselves. She was lying in her bedroom – she remembered going to bed – and it was dark so it must still be night. Yet should it be *so* dark, even at three or four o'clock in the morning? Why weren't the street lamps throwing their customary pale glow on the bedroom curtains.

She reached out her hand and groped for the switch on her bedside light. She felt it click, but still the darkness remained. A power cut? That would explain the absence of street lighting.

It was so hard to think with the constant drumming in her head. Perhaps she should follow Javier's advice and get a check-up at the nearest hospital. She wondered how long she would have to wait before the casualty department opened. She glanced down at her watch – and saw nothing!

It should be glowing in the dark, she told herself, as feelings of hysteria started to well up inside her. It should be glowing and it wasn't!

"Oh my God!" she sobbed. "I'm blind!"

Woodend stood looking out of the office window at the yard in front of the club. Scores – perhaps even hundreds – of people had crossed it in the last three quarters of an hour before Robbie Peterson met his end. Which was probably exactly why the killer had chosen that time to make his move.

He walked back to the desk and picked up the hammer which Inspector Chatterton had brought him. He closed his eyes and pictured Robbie asleep in the chair, his head resting on the desk.

The murderer comes in and hears him snoring, he thought. He doesn't know the bulb's blown, but he has no wish to turn on the light anyway. Darkness can only work to his advantage. He makes his way over to the workbench, where he knows he'll find the things he needs to commit his crime. Once he's got the hammer and nails, he returns to the desk. He places the nail on Robbie's temple – lightly, so that there's not even a slight prick to disturb the sleeping man – and wham!

It would have to have been a fairly hard blow, Woodend decided, but most men would have been capable of delivering it. And so would a lot of women. Hell, even a reasonably strong child could have killed Robbie Peterson, if he'd been really determined.

Woodend tightened his grip on the hammer, took a deep breath and swung his arm. There was no human head to get in it's way this time and the hammer's head struck the desk with a loud clang. The Chief Inspector tried to will into his mind an image of the kind of man who might have used the hammer as an instrument of death. But it wouldn't come. There was not even the most fleeting impression – the vaguest sense of what might drive that man. Well, he supposed that while handling the murder weapon was sometimes a good trick, he couldn't expect it to work every time.

He opened his eyes and looked first at the dent in the desk and then at the tool he was still holding in his hand. "You've been nothin' but a waste of taxpayers' money," he said accusingly to the hammer.

There was a dustbin by the club's rear door, and for a moment he was tempted to walk across the yard and drop the hammer into it. Then he noticed the gap in the tool rack where the murder weapon had once hung – and remembered his early days in the Army . . .

A group of raw recruits, still itching from their new haircuts, standing in an uneasy line. A small corporal, marching up and down that line, glaring belligerently at each and every one of them.

'The Army runs on discipline and order,' the corporal had screamed. 'Discipline! When I ask you to jump, you don't ask me why. You say, "How high, corporal?" Order! A place for everything and everything in it's place.' He turned his menacing gaze on a young recruit who looked scared to death. 'What does it run on, you big Northern snot-rag?'

'Discipline and order, Corporal,' Private Charlie Woodend had answered shakily.

The Chief Inspector grinned ruefully. "A place for everything, and everything in its place," he murmured.

They had drummed it into him, and even twenty years later it was still there. He walked over to the tool rack, slipped the hammer into the vacant slot and stood back to admire the result. That little corporal would have been proud of him, he thought.

Hatton Gardens was a very pleasant, tree-lined street of detached houses on the outskirts of Doncaster.

"Used to be all single family residences before the War," Sergeant Dash said, as he and Rutter walked from the car to the gate of Number Seven. " 'Course, income tax was only five an' a tanner in the pound back then. Now it's eight an' sixpence, an' nobody can afford big houses any more. Most of the street's been converted into flats."

"It's still a nice area to live in," Rutter replied.

"Oh, it is," Dash agreed. "Very respectable, the people in Hatton Gardens. I'm surprised we're lookin' for your villain here."

They opened the gate and walked up a path which was bordered with neat rows of flowers. There were two bells beside the door, each with a card next to it. The one beside the top bell was hand-written and said, 'Alex Conway'. The one below was a printed visiting card with the words 'Miss Olivia Tufton' printed on it.

"See what I mean?" Dash asked, pointing at the lower card.

"*Very* respectable."

Rutter rang Conway's bell, waited, and then rang again. When he got no answer the second time, he pressed the lower button. There was the sound of slow careful footsteps in the hallway, then the front door was opened by an old lady with blue-rinsed hair.

"Miss Tufton?" Rutter asked.

The woman looked past him at Sergeant Dash's blue uniform. "Have you come to see my television licence?" she asked, with just a hint of panic in her voice.

"No, madam," Dash said reassuringly.

"Because I'm not sure where I put it, you see. Father always used to say, 'You'll be forgetting where you left your head one of these days, my girl,' and I'm rather afraid that he was right."

"We're not really here to see you at all," Rutter said. "It's Mr Conway we'd like to talk to. Do you know when he'll be back?"

"You're wasting your time," Miss Tufton told him. "Mr Conway hasn't *got* a television. It wouldn't be worth his while paying out four pounds a year licence fee for the time he's here."

"Away a lot, is he?" Rutter asked.

"He travels a great deal for his business."

"And what business might that be?"

Miss Tufton jutted her chin forward. "I wouldn't know," she said haughtily. "Father always told me never to ask a gentleman what his occupation was. And Mr Conway *is* a gentleman, despite the fact that he sometimes drops his consonants."

"Could you describe him to us, Miss Tufton?" Rutter asked.

The old lady's eyes narrowed. "Why? He's not done anything wrong, has he? I can't believe that of him."

Rutter gave her one of his most winning smiles. "No,

he's not done anything wrong. We're just conducting routine inquiries."

"Like Superintendent Lockheart does in *No Hiding Place*?"

"Exactly."

"It was a very good story last week," Miss Tufton said with enthusiasm. "The police were looking for a man who'd been left a lot of money and . . ." She stopped, suddenly. "That's it, isn't it? Someone's left Mr Conway a lot of money?"

Rutter nodded, in a way he was sure Woodend would have been proud of. "His uncle," he said.

Miss Tufton shook her head. "Oh dear. Mr Conway's such a sensitive man. He's bound to be upset."

"His long-lost uncle," Rutter said quickly. "Lived in Australia. They've never met."

"Well, that's all right, then," Miss Tufton said, with some satisfaction.

"You were going to describe him to us," Rutter reminded her.

"He's about as tall as the sergeant," Miss Tufton said, looking at Dash.

"That would make him about five feet eleven."

"I suppose so."

"What else can you tell us about him?"

"He has blond hair and a moustache. And unlike a great many of the moustachioed men you see around these days, he trims his every day."

"How would you know that?" Rutter asked.

"Father had a moustache and *he* used to trim it first thing every morning," Miss Tufton said, slightly affronted. "I know a well-trimmed moustache when I see one."

"How old would you say Mr Conway is?"

"A young man, really. No more than fifty."

Rutter, with the arrogance of youth on his side, suppressed a smile. "Does he have any visitors?"

"There's a young lady who visits him occasionally—"

"Young?"

"Not more than in her late thirties. Very smartly dressed. But she never stops – just rings the doorbell and waits on the pavement until he goes out to her."

"Anyone else?"

Miss Tufton frowned. "There was a man, once."

"Tell me about him."

"A horrid little man. I was just coming out of my apartment as he was entering the house. He didn't look very pleased to see me."

"Did you speak?"

"*He* spoke to *me*. He said he was a friend of Mr Conway's, and would be staying the night. Then he rushed up the stairs to Mr Conway's flat without another word."

"How did you know he wasn't a burglar?" Rutter asked.

"He had Mr Conway's keys," Miss Tufton said, shaking her head slightly, as if to indicate that she considered Rutter's powers of detection to fall well below the standards set by *No Hiding Place*.

"He could have stolen them," Rutter pointed out.

Miss Tufton looked shocked. "I never thought of that," she admitted. "But anyway, he *was* a friend of Mr Conway's, because we talked about it later."

"You and Mr Conway?"

"That's right. I mentioned the way the other man had behaved towards me, and Mr Conway was most apologetic. He said he was sure his friend hadn't meant to be rude. It was just that he wasn't very well educated. I knew what he meant."

"Could you describe this friend?" Rutter asked.

"He was what Father would have called a 'runt'," Miss Tufton said. "He must have been about half a head shorter than the sergeant."

"What was he wearing?" Rutter asked.

"A suit like the ones the black-marketing spivs used to wear just after the War."

"You mean expensive, but flashy."

Miss Tufton grimaced. "I don't understand all these modern words," she said. "All I can tell you is that it was in very poor taste."

"Was he clean shaven?"

"He could have *done* with a shave, if that's what you mean?" Miss Tufton said.

"But no beard or moustache?"

"No."

"What colour was his hair?"

"Brown. And he had very shifty eyes."

Flashy suits, brown hair, shifty eyes? Rutter took a photograph of his pocket and held it out for Miss Tufton to examine. "Is that Mr Conway's friend?" he asked.

The old lady peered at it. "Yes," she said. "You can tell even from this that he's got no breeding, can't you?"

"You only saw him for a second or two," Rutter reminded her. "Could you be mistaken?"

"No," Miss Tufton said firmly. "I've got a very good memory for faces." She glanced nervously across at Sergeant Dash. "It's only things like television licences I keep misplacing."

Rutter did his best to contain his feeling of triumph. All right, so he hadn't been able to talk to Conway, but he had established a definite link between the man and Robbie Peterson, and, by implication, connected Conway to Peterson's smuggling racket.

He put the photograph back in his pocket. "When you see Mr Conway, you won't mention that we've had this little talk, will you?" he asked Miss Tufton.

"Why shouldn't I?"

"Well, you don't want to spoil his little surprise for him, do you?" Rutter asked, winking at her.

"Little surprise?"

"The legacy. From his uncle in Australia."

Enlightenment dawned. "Oh no, of course I don't," Miss Tufton said, winking back at him.

Nine

The afternoon sun shone down benevolently on both the lakeside and the people who swarmed around it. For some, it was perhaps a little too hot. In the lakeside café, grandmothers sipped at their tea and told their impatient grandchildren that *soon* they could go on another ride. Fathers, modern enough to have abandoned the use of both flat caps and trilbys, now saw the error of their ways and placed knotted handkerchiefs on their heads. Teddy boys, in their distinctive three-quarter length coats, looked distinctly uncomfortable. Even some of the older children seemed to find it too warm to run around. And the detective from London had shed his hairy sports jacket and was carrying it over his shoulder.

Woodend was standing by the roundabout, watching a succession of happy, excited faces sweep past him, only to return again a few seconds later. It didn't seem more than a few minutes ago that he'd been one of those faces himself, clutching tightly to the central pole with one hand, while waving to his father with the other. It didn't seem it – but it was. His old man had been dead and buried for years, and however much he might not like the idea, he himself was firmly into middle age. Yet there were still moments – like this one – when he could remember exactly how it felt to be one of those kids.

His thoughts turned from his own childhood to those of Robbie Peterson's daughters. Perhaps they would have been very different from each other anyway, but the experiences they'd gone through had made them chalk and cheese. On the one hand there was Jenny, the daughter who had been kept close to her dad, and who had followed her sense of duty to the extent of marrying the man Robbie had chosen for her. On the other, there was Annabel, sent away at an early age, who blamed Robbie for her own miserable life, and had done her best to make him suffer right up until the day he died. Both of them had gone to extremes, he decided, and he was glad his own daughter seemed – so far – to be much better balanced.

He turned his back on the roundabout and wandered on until he reached the ghost train. The carriage was just pulling off, leaving the Green brothers with a couple of minutes free time on their hands, and they were using this moment of leisure to give him the looks of suspicious contempt which seemed to be their trademark. Well, if that was their attitude, Woodend thought, he'd soon give them something to be suspicious *about*.

He came to a halt just in front of the train. "The Green brothers," he said, as if he were introducing them to an audience.

"What about it?" the elder one asked aggressively.

"Which is which?"

"I'm Clem," the elder brother said, "an' that's Burt, but neither of us are pleased to meet yer."

"But you know who I am, don't you?"

Clem Green sneered. "Oh, we worked that out, all right."

Woodend smiled pleasantly. "And because you're bright lads, you've probably also worked out that I think the reasons Robbie Peterson hired you had very little to do with runnin' a ghost train."

"Meanin' what?" Clem Green asked.

"Meanin' I think that sometimes, in the dead of night, when everyone else is asleep, you take little trips across the Pennines."

"If you had any proof of that, you'd have an arrest warrant in your pocket, an' half a dozen rozzers at your back."

Woodend scratched his head. "Now that is interestin'," he said.

"What is?"

"It's interestin' that you didn't ask me what I thought you were doin' on these supposed trips of yours. That's the first question *I* would have asked."

Green's sneer deepened. "Everybody knows that Robbie

91

Peterson was smugglin' stolen fags an' whisky into Yorkshire," he said.

"I didn't," Woodend replied "At least, I wasn't entirely sure about the cigarettes, and I had no idea at all about the whisky."

"But we had nothin' to do with it," Clem Green continued, "an' now that Robbie's dead, you'll never be able to prove that we did."

"Interestin' again," Woodend said mildly. "Now Robbie's dead, I can't prove you *didn't* do anythin'."

"You bobbies always twist honest folks' words," Green countered. "It's what you're good at."

The ghost train smashed noisily through the double doors and out onto the open section of the track. Burt Green went back to the booth to collect the fares from the queue which had already formed in front of it, but Clem Green, probably out of bravado, showed no inclination to move.

"Where were you two when Robbie was murdered?" Woodend asked Clem casually. "I'm sure you'll say you were both safely tucked up in your beds – but I'm willin' to bet that you can't prove it."

A look of triumph came to Green's face. "Then you lose the bet," he said. "You know The Bandbox?"

"It's one of the social clubs, isn't it?"

"That's right. It's about a quarter of a mile from The Hideaway. Well, that night the owner was a bit short-handed an' he offered me an' our Burt a quid each if we'd help out. An' that's what we did. We started servin' the tables at seven o'clock, an' we didn't stop until time was called at eleven o'clock. From what I've heard, Robbie was well dead by then."

"An' I suppose the owner of The Bandbox will confirm this?"

"Him, his barmen, an' any number of the customers we served. So you'd better go lookin' for some other poor bugger to pin this murder on."

"Any suggestions?" Woodend asked.

"You could try that Michael Clough for a start."

"And why should Mr Clough have wanted to kill Robbie?"

A look of surprise came to Green's face and then was instantly gone. "Well, if you don't know that, I'm not goin' to be the one to tell you," he said.

The well-dressed young man walked down the street at some speed, and for a while it looked as if he were planning to go straight past the front gate of the house where Annabel Peterson had her secret flat. Then, at the last moment, he checked quickly over his shoulder, slowed down and headed up the path.

Sitting behind the wheel of his battered Morris Oxford, Detective Sergeant Gower laid his binoculars on the dashboard and jotted something down in his notebook. This was the third man to have visited Annabel that afternoon, he thought, and he was starting to see a pattern – they all seemed edgy, they all wore expensive suits and they usually weren't inside the house for more than ten minutes. Two of them he had actually recognised – one was the son of a successful local businessman, the other a nephew of the mayor. None of them, he was almost sure, had a criminal record.

Gower lit a cigarette and inhaled deeply. What the bloody hell were they doing in there? he wondered. And whatever it was, did it help to explain how Annie – who he was sure was getting no money from her father – could afford to pay for this expensive flat? She couldn't be on the game, because even the chinless wonders he'd seen going in through the front door couldn't have got their ends away and been out on the street again in such a short time. So it had to something else. The problem was, *what*? He couldn't believe the mayor's nephew was dealing in stolen record players, and it was equally impossible to put forward the theory that Annie and he were planning an armed robbery together.

So what was he left with? Bugger all!

The visitor had already come out of the door and was walking rapidly down the street. It didn't make sense, any of it. Yet Gower's instinct told him there was something going on, and whatever it was, it was big.

He lit another cigarette from the first, then almost choked as he saw who was coming down the road. This young man walked with nothing of the wariness of the last three. If anything, his gait was defiant. Nor was he as well dressed as they'd been. They'd worn suits, he was wearing a corduroy jacket and grey-flannel trousers. The man did not hesitate as the others had done, either. He walked boldly up to Annabel Peterson's door, rang the bell, and was immediately admitted.

So Michael Clough not only knew about Annabel's secret flat, but had decided to pay a call on her, Gower thought. Now that was interesting.

And what was even more interesting was that it was a full hour before he came out again – and when he did, he looked as if he'd really been put through a wringer.

Woodend sat at his dented desk in what had once been Robbie Peterson's office, the telephone receiver in his right hand. "So the Green lads *were* workin' for you last Friday night?" he asked the manager of The Bandbox.

"That's right," the other man replied.

"How many waiters did you have on duty that night?"

"Four. We were so busy that I was workin' behind the bar myself."

"An' both of the Green brothers were there all the time from seven right through to eleven?"

A pause. "Yes,"

"You don't seem certain."

"Well, I couldn't say definitely they were both in the clubroom all the time. I mean, four hours is a long while to hold your water. Everybody has to go to the bog now an' again."

"And your lavatory is across the yard, like it is in The Hideaway?"

"Yes."

Woodend frowned. "How long could one of them have been out without you noticin' it?"

"It's hard to put a time on it," the manager said. "When you're workin' your arse off just to keep up with the orders, that's all that's on your mind."

"What's your best estimate?"

94

"Well, I suppose if either of them had been gone for more than ten minutes, I would definitely have noticed," the manager reluctantly conceded.

Woodend thanked the man and put the phone down. Ten minutes, he mused. The Bandbox was only a quarter of a mile away from The Hideaway. For a fit young man like Clem Green, it would have been perfectly possible to make the journey between the two clubs twice *and* kill Robbie Peterson within a ten-minute span. Motive didn't present any problem either – the Greens could easily have decided that they were tired of working for Robbie when, with one little murder, they could have the entire operation to themselves. But if one of the Greens *had* committed the crime, it was going to be a bugger to prove.

Woodend turned his mind to Michael Clough. If he was looking for a suspect, Clem Green had said, he could do worse than start with the young teacher. But why should Michael want to kill Peterson? Woodend couldn't believe that *he* was involved in any of Robbie's rackets, and the rackets, surely, were why Robbie had died.

There was a knock on the open door and Woodend looked up to see Harold Dawson, the reporter with the bad teeth, standing there. Dawson looked, if anything, seedier than he had done the previous evening, and there was an expression in his eyes which could only be described as worried.

"Somethin' I can do for you, Mr Dawson?" the Chief Inspector asked.

"No," the reporter said vaguely. "I thought I'd just drop by to see how things were going." He looked around the office. "I see what you mean about there being no point in my taking any photographs in here now. It's completely different to the way it was in Robbie Peterson's day. Except for that filing cabinet. That was Robbie's, wasn't it?"

"Aye," Woodend agreed, "it was."

"I expect it contained all Robbie's bills and things."

"That's what most people usually file away."

"Probably a few private things as well," Dawson suggested slyly. "Letters from his friends and suchlike."

"What made you say that?" Woodend wondered. "Did Robbie get many letters?"

Dawson was suddenly very guarded. "Oh, there's no point in asking me," he said. "I didn't know about his personal affairs."

"You certainly seem very interested in them now he's dead," Woodend pointed out.

"Well, I'm a reporter, aren't I?"

"As well as a close friend?"

"I knew Robbie," Dawson said, the guarded expression still in place. "But not what you might call *well*. If I saw him in the club, I might buy him a drink. But that was about as far as it went."

"But you are a regular at the club?"

"Yes, I suppose so."

"Were you in The Hideaway on the night Robbie Peterson was killed?" Woodend asked.

"Er . . . no. As a matter of fact, I wasn't."

"Then where exactly *were* you?"

"If my memory serves me well, I went for a drive," Dawson said. "I do that sometimes. It helps to clear my head."

"Did you go anywhere in particular?"

"No, I just drove around." Dawson stopped, suddenly, as if he'd been hit in the face with a shovel. "I'm not a suspect, am I?"

"Of course not," Woodend said reasonably. "You're a responsible journalist, like you told me last night. But before we can eliminate even responsible journalists from our inquiries, we have to have some account of their movements."

"To tell you the truth, I don't know where I went," Dawson said, obviously shaken. "I'm like that. Sometimes I've got so much on my mind that I can drive and drive and I have no idea where I've been."

"That must be very disconcertin' for you," Woodend said, in a tone which might have been interpreted as sympathetic by anyone who didn't really know him.

"Yes . . . well . . . if you'll excuse me, I'd better be about my business," Dawson mumbled.

"Feel free to drop by any time, sir," Woodend told him.

Sergeant Dash puffed on his cigarette and blew a perfect smoke circle. "Took me years to get that right," he said, with smug satisfaction.

"Must have done," Rutter replied, looking around the police canteen at all the uniformed officers grabbing a hurried cup of tea before they went on duty. "So what did your Super have to say to you?"

"He said he was pissed off that we appeared to have a major villain on our patch who we knew absolutely nothin' about. He went on to say, an' I'm quotin' here, 'When I was walking the beat, just before the War, not a thing slipped past me. We had an idea of how to do our job back then, but the young coppers today know less about real policin' than next door's cat does'."

Rutter smiled. "Do you think we'll ever go on about the good old days when we're his age?" he asked.

Dash grinned back. "Probably. Anyway, the upshot of it was that he wants this matter clearin' up, an' with that end in view, he's willin' to give you all the assistance you need." The grinned broadened. "Within reason, of course."

"Of course," Rutter agreed.

"So what *can* we do for you?"

"I'd like your men out doorstepping in Hatton Gardens," Rutter said. "I need a better description of Alexander Conway than Miss Tufton provided us with, and I'd be very interested in anything else the neighbours could tell us about him."

"Consider it done," Dash said.

"I'd also like to know whether Conway owns or rents the flat. If he rents it, talk to the landlord. If he owns it, have a word with the man he bought it from. And put in a request to the Yard to see if they have any idea who he is or what he's done."

"Piece of cake."

"And I want a twenty-four-hour surveillance on the house, so we'll know when Conway gets back."

Dash shook his head dolefully. "You've as much chance of gettin' the Super to agree to that as I have of joinin' the Dagenham Girl Pipers," he said.

Jenny Clough stood in the doorway of the office. She was holding a tea tray in her hands, and on the tray rested a steaming mug of tea and a plate of biscuits. Her face was pale and drawn, but she looked to Woodend like a woman who was making a real effort to get a grip on herself.

"Is it all right if I come in?" she asked, slightly hesitantly.

Woodend gave her an encouraging smile. "Anybody bearin' refreshment is always most welcome," he said, pushing aside the sheaves of notes he'd made since Harold Dawson's departure.

Jenny entered the office and placed the tray on the desk. "The biscuits are custard creams," she said, putting the plate in front of him and mug of tea to his right. "If you don't like them, I'm sure I can find you some chocolate digestives from somewhere."

"Custard creams will do me champion," Woodend assured her. "It really is very kind of you to find the time to look after me, Mrs Clough."

Jenny shrugged. "Men need a cup of char when they're workin'," she said. "Besides," she continued, almost as if she were making a confession, "I've run out of other things to do in the house." She grinned ruefully. "There comes a point when even I have to accept that the cooker's clean enough."

Woodend nodded understandingly. He'd seen this before – women attempting to cast off their grief by burying themselves in domestic chores. And sometimes it even worked. "If you ever want somebody to talk to – not as a bobby, just as another person – you can always come to me," he said.

"Thank you," Jenny said, swallowing hard. "Thank you so much."

She picked up the tray and turned to go. Then, suddenly, she froze, and the tray, which had slipped out of her hands, clattered noisily to the floor.

What the hell had happened to her? Woodend asked himself. Had she seen somebody – or something – through the window? But when he looked himself, he saw that the yard was empty. "That's the matter, lass?" he asked.

Jenny began to shake violently. "Help me!" she gasped. "Help me!"

Woodend jumped up from his desk and put his arms around her. "Tell me what you want me to do," he said.

"Get . . . get . . . me . . . out of here."

She seemed to have lost the use of her legs, and it was more a question of lifting her to the door than helping her to it, but once she was outside her body started to relax and her breathing became more regular.

Still holding onto her, Woodend checked the yard again. If Jenny Clough *had* seen anyone through the window, there was no sign of him now. "What happened in there, Mrs Clough?" he asked.

"Nothin' . . . nothin' happened," Jenny said. "It was just *bein'* there. I thought I could handle it, but I couldn't. It brought Dad right back to me, and it was all so . . . so painful."

"Is it all right if I let you go now? Do you think you can stand on your own?"

Jenny nodded. "Yes, I'll be fine. I'm sorry, Chief Inspector, you must think me a complete fool."

"Not at all," Woodend assured her. "Your reaction is perfectly understandable under the circumstances. Probably something to do with shock."

But if it was shock, then it was *delayed* shock, he thought – because both when he'd interviewed her the day before, and when she'd brought him the beans on toast, being in the office hadn't seemed to bother her at all.

Wally the steward was polishing pint glasses behind the bar and a few couples who didn't have kids to put to bed were already occupying the tables near the stage, but other than that Woodend and Rutter had The Hideaway to themselves.

"I tried to push Sergeant Dash to keep a round-the-clock watch on Conway's flat, but he said the best he could do was to have the bobbies on regular beat keep an eye on it," Rutter explained. "It's not that he doesn't want to help, but they're very short-handed up in Doncaster."

"They're very short-handed everywhere," Woodend said

sourly. "Nobody ever wants to pay for a decent police force until they need it themselves." He took a sip of his pint. "So have you got any theories about this Alex Conway feller?"

"Miss Tufton told me he always keeps his hair and moustache neat and tidy," Rutter said. "According to her, he must trim his moustache every day."

"So?"

"So maybe he's an ex-military man."

"We're all ex-military men," Woodend said. "The only difference is some of us were in the War an' had nasty men firin' real bullets at us, an' some of us, like a certain sergeant I know, spent two years doin' their national service an' never got further than sunny Aldershot."

Rutter grinned. "It wasn't that easy being a conscript. We had to make our own beds, you know."

"That's my point," Woodend told him. "Whatever kind of soldier you were, you were subjected to the same sort of bull. The same sort of spit an' polish." He thought of how the gap in the tool rack had annoyed him earlier in the day. "A place for everythin', and everythin' in its place."

"Maybe," Rutter admitted. "But for most of us, especially the ones who were only in for two years, it starts to wear off in time." He looked down at his feet. "When I first left the Army, I used to buff my shoes until I could see my face in them. Now, if I've got a reasonable shine, I'm happy to leave it at that."

"So you're sayin' for the habit to be so ingrained, this Conway feller must have served for quite a long time?" Woodend asked thoughtfully.

"That would be my guess."

"An' what else do we know about him?"

"That he's away from Doncaster a great deal, and that Robbie Peterson has a key to his flat."

"Not really enough to put a rope round his neck, is it?" Woodend asked.

"Nothing like enough," Rutter agreed.

The phone rang on the bar, and Wally picked it up. "It's for you, Chief Inspector," he said. "Your wife."

Woodend made a comical face. "First time in years she considered me worth checking up on," he said.

He rose to his feet and made his way to the bar. Rutter lit a cigarette, and though he was not consciously listening to the conversation, he couldn't help hearing Woodend's half of it.

"Hello, luv," the Chief Inspector said. "What's brought this sudden bout of concern on? . . . What? . . . Oh, my God! No—"

Rutter turned round, alarmed. Woodend's strong features had crumpled, and he was gripping the telephone so hard his knuckles had turned white.

"Yes . . ." Woodend was saying. "Yes, I'll tell him."

Tell *him*, Rutter repeated to himself. He was the only person in Cheshire who Joan Woodend knew, apart from her husband. "What's happened?" he asked. "Has anything . . . has somebody—"

"Two whiskies, quick!" Woodend said to Wally. "And you'd better make them doubles."

The barman stuck the glasses under the optics, then handed them to Woodend. The Chief Inspector carried them back to the table. "Joan got a phone call from Maria this afternoon," he said. "She was ringin' from the eye hospital."

"The eye hospital!" Rutter repeated. "But Maria doesn't even wear reading glasses."

Woodend put his hand on his sergeant's shoulder. "I'm afraid it's a bit more serious than short-sightedness," he said. "You're goin' to have to catch the first available train back to London."

Ten

Woodend made his way up the country lane which led towards the Church of St Mary in Swann's Lake. It had been raining quite heavily earlier that morning, but by half-past ten the clouds had completely disappeared, the hedgerows had lost their glossy sheen, and even the small puddles which had formed at the edge of the road were almost dried out.

The church loomed up ahead. It had been built early in the nineteenth century, the Chief Inspector guessed, before they had got the concept of the Gothic Revival quite right. Now it stuck out like a blot on the landscape – a small church trying to pretend it was a cathedral, a structure which attempted to soar and only succeeded in being a dwarf standing on tiptoes.

There was time for one more cigarette before he reached the churchyard, Woodend thought. He lit a Capstan Full Strength and wondered how his sergeant was getting on. Had he already seen Maria? And if not, what had they told him about her? He wished he could be there with the lad. But he had a job to do and it was time he got on with it. Grinding the half-smoked cigarette under the heel of his right shoe, he strode on towards the church.

A group of mourners had already gathered by the time Woodend arrived. There was the widow – scarcely grieving, but at least appropriately clad in a black dress which covered her attractive legs right down to the middle of the calves. There was Robbie's eldest daughter, Jenny. She was clutching tightly to her husband's arm for support, and from the pained and sympathetic expression on Terry Clough's face, it was obvious that even if Robbie had talked him into marrying Jenny, he truly loved her now. Michael Clough was there, too, wearing

102

his brown corduroy jacket with a black armband and looking, as John Donne had once said, as if the bell also tolled for him. Of Annabel Peterson, there was no sign – but that was probably to be expected.

Woodend let his glance fall on the other mourners. The Green brothers had turned up, looking as shifty and mistrustful as they habitually did, and there were several other faces unknown to Woodend. But there was no tall, blond man with a carefully clipped moustache. Alexander Conway, whatever his connection with the murder, had clearly decided to stay away.

Heads were turning towards the gate, and when Woodend allowed his to follow them, he saw that a shiny black Rolls Royce Silver Dawn had just pulled up in front of the church.

"Well, look what the cat's dragged in," Doris said to her daughter. "I'd never have thought he'd have put in an appearance. Not in a million years."

The man getting out of the back of the Rolls was wearing an expensive black mourning suit, which contrasted most attractively with his mane of silvery hair. He was somewhere between fifty-five and sixty, Woodend guessed, but he had the body of a much younger man, with powerful broad shoulders and a barrel chest.

Seemingly unaware that all eyes were on him, the man in the mourning suit made his way straight to the widow, bent down, and kissed her on the cheek. "My deepest condolences, Doris," he said.

"It was good of you to come, Sid," the widow replied.

Woodend's plain Lancashire Methodist background had ensured he'd not been inside many Anglican churches, but even from his limited experience this one seemed much more ornate than the average. Certainly, it was not somewhere he would have felt comfortable worshipping in. He wasn't comfortable with the vicar, either. The Reverend Wilfred Cunliffe Jones, now standing at the lectern, was a florid man with an aquiline nose and a superior tilt to his chin – the sort of fashionable priest who went down well in some of the more prosperous areas of London, but would have been laughed out of the East End.

The vicar cleared his throat, and gazed down on his congregation with a look which may have contained compassion, but seemed awfully close to disdain. "I did not know Mr Robert Peterson long," he said in a plummy voice. "Indeed, he was a comparative newcomer to this area. But by all accounts he was very happy here and made some good friends in the time he spent amongst us. I'm sure those friends will miss him deeply."

Is that it? Woodend wondered.

Was the funeral oration going to be no longer than the message on the back of one of those comic picture postcards people sent when they were staying at the seaside? Apparently it was. The vicar nodded his head solemnly and stepped down.

The doctor was a short man, and his small, tired steps along the never-ending hospital corridors seemed infuriatingly slow to the man who had been pacing the waiting room for what had felt like an eternity.

"Try not to get her too excited, and if she appears to be getting tired, tell her you'd better go," the doctor said.

"Why won't you tell me exactly what the situation is before I see her?" Rutter asked. "It would help to assess how I should deal with her."

"Believe me, I'd like to give you the information," the doctor replied, "but there are rules governing these matters. She can tell you what she likes, but we're only allowed to reveal her medical status to close relatives."

"I'm going to marry her," Rutter pointed out. "You don't get much closer than that."

"Hmm," the doctor said.

Rutter stopped walking, took the doctor by the shoulder and swung him round so they were facing each other. "And what's that 'hmm' supposed to mean?" he demanded angrily.

"I'm sorry," the doctor replied. "I'm exhausted. If I hadn't been without sleep for the last forty-eight hours, I probably wouldn't have said that."

"But you *did* say it," Rutter insisted. "And now I want to know what you meant by it."

"I'm sure that you're a fine young man and that you love my patient very much, but—"

"But what?"

The doctor sighed. "I've seen scores of young men in your situation," he said. "They know they're in love, and they're sure they can cope with whatever fate throws at them. And then they think about it. I mean *really* think about it. They ask themselves what their lives will be like in five years' time. In ten years' time. In *twenty* years. And in the end, they decide that love is simply not enough to sustain them through such a difficult existence."

"Take me to my fiancée," Rutter said, through gritted teeth. "Take me to her now."

The doctor sighed again, as if such shows of determination were nothing new to him. "As you wish," he said.

The burial was over, and the mourners began to drift away from the grave. The vicar bestowed a few platitudes on the widow, told her that his door was always open should she need comfort, then turned and walked rapidly towards the vicarage, where he would just have time for a small sherry before lunch. He did not get far. Standing between two lines of graves – and effectively blocking his path – was the big man in the hairy sports jacket he'd noticed in church earlier.

"I'm Chief Inspector Woodend," the big man said. "Could you spare me a couple of minutes, Mr Jones?"

"Cunliffe Jones," the vicar corrected him.

"Could you spare me a couple of minutes Mr *Cunliffe Jones*?"

The vicar glanced down at his watch. "I have got rather a busy day ahead of me," he said irritably.

Woodend nodded. "Of course you have," he agreed. "What with buryin' the dead and visitin' the sick, you must be run off your feet. Tell you what, I'll come round to the vicarage tonight. Would nine o'clock suit you?"

It wouldn't suit him at all, the Reverend Cunliffe Jones thought. And it wouldn't suit the guests at his wine and cheese party, either. "You said you only wanted two minutes?" he asked.

"Well, not more than ten, anyway," Woodend said cheerfully.

The vicar gave in to the inevitable. "What would you like to ask me?"

Woodend rested his right hand on the nearest gravestone. "You didn't like Robbie Peterson much, did you?" he said.

The vicar looked vaguely offended – but only vaguely. "Mr Peterson was one of my parishioners, and as such—" he began.

"I'm investigatin' a murder," Woodend told him. "I go a lot by impressions, an' most of the time I'm spot on. An' I get the definite impression that you didn't like Robbie Peterson much. Are you goin' to say I'm wrong this time?"

The vicar hesitated for a second. "Perhaps it would kinder to say that I was not used to his city ways," he conceded. "After all, as you will have seen for yourself, we are largely a rural parish here."

"Did he often come to church?"

"He attended quite regularly when he first arrived in the village. It would be misleading to say he has worshipped with us recently."

"Have you any idea what made him stop?"

Again, the vicar hesitated. "When he'd been here for a few months, he came to see me at the vicarage."

Woodend could well imagine it. He could see Robbie, perfectly at home and in control in any of the tougher areas of Liverpool, looking totally lost as he knocked on the vicar's door. He could picture Cunliffe Jones, too – smug and superior. "I expect you offered him a sherry, did you?" he asked.

"If memory serves, I did."

Woodend grinned. "Bet it wasn't your good stuff, though. You'd never waste any of that on somebody like Robbie. I'd guess you fobbed him off with some Australian plonk."

"If I remember rightly, it was a perfectly acceptable Cyprus sherry," the vicar said huffily.

Woodend assumed a look of mock-contrition. "Sorry to have

interrupted you," he said. "You were tellin' me Robbie came to the vicarage. What did he want to see you about?"

"He'd noticed our church roof appeal fund hadn't been as successful as we hoped. He offered to make a substantial contribution."

"Which, of course, you readily accepted."

The vicar frowned. "At first I did. Just as, at first, I accepted his offer to cater for the Sunday school picnic."

"But then?"

"Then it became plain to me that Mr Peterson was not being purely philanthropic."

"Strings attached, were there?"

"Indeed."

"He wanted you to co-opt him onto the parish council, did he?" Woodend asked.

Cunliffe Jones's mouth dropped open in surprise. "However did you know that?"

"What else could you have had to offer that he'd want?" Woodend replied. "Anyway, I imagine you told him the answer was no."

"I put it to the sitting members," the vicar said defensively.

Woodend grinned again. "Backed with your own strong recommendation that they agree to let him into their exclusive little club?"

"I'm not sure I care for your tone, Chief Inspector," the vicar said. "Try to understand our position. We have retired army officers on the parish council. There are headmasters, solicitors and justices of the peace. They reflect the community they live in."

"An' Robbie Peterson wouldn't have, would he?"

The vicar looked at his watch again. "Mr Peterson wasn't really one of us. I think, despite what I said in my funeral oration, that he would have been happier back in Liverpool. With people of his own kind. And now, if you'll·excuse me . . ."

As the vicar turned and walked away, Woodend became aware of a slow, methodical clapping sound. He turned and saw that the noise was coming from the broad, silver-haired man who'd arrived in the Rolls Royce, and now was standing a few feet to his left.

"Well, you really showed that pompous bastard up for what he was, didn't you?" the man asked. He stepped forward and held out his hand. "Sid Dowd."

"Charlie Woodend," the Chief Inspector replied, taking the proffered hand. "I've heard a lot about you, Mr Dowd."

Dowd grinned. "All good, I hope."

"You'd be surprised if I said yes, wouldn't you?" Woodend asked.

"Surprised? I'd be bloody astounded," Dowd admitted. "Look, I've got a bit of time to spare before I go back to Liverpool. Don't you think you an' me should have a little talk?"

"It might be a very good idea," Woodend agreed. "I'll see you in Robbie's office in ten minutes."

"I don't like offices that aren't my own," Dowd said, grinning again. "They intimidate me."

"I don't think there's much that intimidates you, Mr Dowd," Woodend told him. "But if you'd prefer it, there's a pub up the road called The Red Lion. We could meet there"

"That'd do nicely," Dowd said.

The room was painted in a gentle pastel blue, the carpet was a shade darker. There was a window facing the hospital grounds, and through it the patient could see a fine clump of elm trees. It was a pleasant room – a soothing room – and it was completely wasted on its present occupant, because *she* couldn't see *anything*.

Rutter stroked Maria's hand. "They've told me so little," he said. "Only that you've had an accident and it's affected your sight. What happened?"

"A policeman at the demonstration hit me over the head with his truncheon," Maria said simply. "The doctors think *that's* what caused the loss of vision."

She sounded so weak, Rutter thought. She sounded as if she had sobbed herself into a state of complete exhaustion. And she probably had. "I think you're being very brave," he said.

"It . . . it was terrifying at first," Maria told him. "When I realised I couldn't see, I was in the bedroom, and the phone was in the living room. I knew I had to get to it, but it was so hard."

"I understand," Rutter said, stroking her hand again.

Maria shook her head. "No, you don't. You can't until it's happened to you. I thought I knew my flat like the back of my hand, but I was very, very wrong. When you can't see, everything's different. I . . . I kept banging into my furniture. It felt almost as if it was lying in wait to ambush me."

"What happens now?" Rutter asked.

"They're going to operate on her tomorrow," Joan Woodend said from her chair in the corner of the room. "They think there's a very good chance it will be successful."

"How good?"

"Sixty per cent. Maybe even as much as seventy."

Which meant there was at least a thirty per cent chance of failure. The doctor's words came back to Rutter. *'They know they're in love, and they're sure they can cope with the situation. And then they think about it. I mean really think about it. They ask themselves what their lives will be like in five years' time. In ten years' time. In twenty years.'*

"You're going to be all right," he said. "But even if you weren't, it still wouldn't make any difference."

Maria looked up at him, even though she could see nothing through her bandaged eyes. He thought about how beautiful she looked – and how vulnerable. "Of course it would make a difference," she said softly.

"Not to us," Rutter argued passionately. "I want to be with you whatever happens."

He meant every word of it, he thought. He truly did. But even as he'd been speaking, there'd been a tiny corner of his brain which had asked him if he was lying – even to himself.

Maria squeezed his hand tightly. "I didn't want you to come, you know," she said. "Joan never told me she was ringing you, or I'd have asked her not to. But I'm glad you came. You've given me new strength. And now I want you to go back to Cheshire."

"And leave you alone?" Rutter protested. "I could never think of doing that!"

The pressure of Maria's hand increased. "You would go insane sitting around and doing nothing," she said. "It will be much better for you to be kept busy – and I know that Mr Woodend will see to that."

How could she think of him, and *his* feelings, at a time like this? he marvelled. How could any woman be strong? So loving? "I want to stay," he said.

"And *I'd* rather you went back to your case," she told him firmly. "I don't want to have to worry about you, as well as worrying about myself. Please do this one thing for me. Is it *so* much to ask?"

"No," Rutter said gently. "No, it isn't."

But he already knew that forcing himself to get on a train back to Cheshire would be the hardest thing he'd ever had to do in his life.

The uniformed constable stood in the hospital corridor, fiddling with his jacket buttons and wishing that his Super had sent someone else out on this particular job. He heard the click of the door handle, then the door itself opened to reveal a young man who looked like he'd just been through hell.

"Detective Sergeant Rutter?" the constable asked.

The other man nodded. "That's right. What can I do for you?"

The constable shifted his weight awkwardly from one foot to the other. "My guv'ner sent me down. He'd like to see you."

"Your guv'ner?" Rutter repeated. "And who might he be?"

"Superintendent Jackson, Sarge."

The name rang no bells with Rutter. "You wouldn't have any idea *why* he wants to see me, would you?" he asked.

The constable looked down at his boots. "I think it might be about what happened at the Spanish embassy on Sunday," he admitted. "You see, Superintendent Jackson was the man in charge."

"Then we'd better not keep him waiting, had we?" Rutter said, fighting for breath as he felt an iron band suddenly start to tighten across his chest.

Eleven

The lounge of The Red Lion was full of horse brasses and plush seating, but almost entirely empty of customers. Woodend bought a pint of bitter for himself and a double whisky for Sid Dowd, then took them over to the table where the Liverpudlian was waiting. "Doris seemed very appreciative of the fact you'd turned up for the funeral," he said as he sat down.

"Doris is a two-faced cow who'll suck up to anybody with money," Dowd said, without obvious heat. "Now if I was still Young Sid – the lad who used to deliver groceries on his push-bike when she was a little girl – it would have been an entirely different story. She'd have told me to piss off before I even got through the churchyard gate."

"You've know her a long time, then?"

"Too long."

"If she's as bad as you're makin' out, what did Robbie Peterson ever see in her?" Woodend asked.

"She was a good-lookin' girl," Dowd replied. "But that's not really the point. It's what *she* saw in *him* that mattered."

"An' what did she see?"

"She saw a young man who was goin' places in the rackets." Dowd shook his head. "Poor Robbie. Once she'd got her hooks into him, he had no chance. It was years before he even started to suspect that she'd married him for what she could get out of him. Still, once he *had* realised it, he didn't let history repeat itself."

"How d'you mean? Repeat itself?"

"With Jenny," Dowd said. "When she was no more than a kid, she had this lad sniffin' after her. A good-lookin' boy,

112

he was, but it was Robbie's dosh, not Jenny herself, that he was after."

"An' what happened?"

"Robbie warned him off."

"Worked him over, you mean?"

Dowd shook his head. "There was no need for violence. A stern warnin' an' a hundred quid in his pocket, an' the lad was soon gone. Mind you, if he hadn't taken the hint, then Robbie really would have got nasty."

"He didn't do such a good job of protectin' his other daughter, did he?" Woodend asked.

Dowd frowned. "Annie was a lovely little kid," he said, "as soft an' sweet as you could ever wish for. But she changed completely when Robbie sent her to that fancy boardin' school."

"In what ways?"

"All sorts of ways. She started shop-liftin', but stupidly – as if she *wanted* to get caught. She was never charged, of course – Robbie saw to that – but if she hadn't had a dad with influence, she'd probably have ended up in a remand home."

"Maybe she would have considered that preferable to her posh boarding school," Woodend said thoughtfully. "What else did she do?"

"She liked throwin' bricks through windows an' smashin' up cars – especially if they were her dad's windows or her dad's cars. It was like she hated the whole world in general, but Robbie in particular." Dowd's eyes suddenly widened. "You don't think Annabel could have killed Robbie, do you?"

"I'm more interested in findin' out whether *you* think she could have done it," Woodend said.

Superintendent Jackson was around forty-five years old, with a square head and belligerent eyes which, for the moment, he was trying to infuse with sympathy. "I was very sorry to hear about what happened to your fiancée, Sergeant," he said to Rutter, who was sitting opposite him. "A tragic accident."

Accident? Rutter thought. Accident! "There'll be an inquiry, of course," he said.

"Indeed there will," Jackson assured him. "My men came under very heavy attack from stones and bottles. I've no intention of letting the perpetrators get away with it."

Rutter gripped the arms of his chair. "I meant an inquiry into what happened to Maria. I want to see the policeman who assaulted her up on serious charges."

"We don't even know it was a bobby," Jackson said. "Perhaps she was hit by one of the bricks or bottles. Maybe she fell down and got kicked in the head by one of her own people. I'm afraid those are the chances you take when you go on that kind of violent demonstration."

"I've talked to her," Rutter said, holding his rage in – but only just. "She's quite clear in her mind about what happened. She was attacked by one of the officers outside the embassy."

"Assuming that's true," Jackson said. "Assuming that, as a foreigner with left-wing views, she's not just saying it to discredit the British police."

"What!" Rutter exploded.

"Let me finish," Jackson said firmly. "Assuming – as I think likely – that she's not merely confused by the blow to the head. Where does that leave us?"

"With a policeman who's a disgrace to his uniform," Rutter said through gritted teeth.

"For all we know, she might have been threatening the officer concerned," Jackson continued. "Or *appearing* to threaten him. And let us say, for the sake of argument, that this officer made a poor decision and lashed out. Not meaning to hurt her, you understand, but only to drive her back. Are you prepared to ruin that young officer's career for one momentary mistake? How will that help your fiancée?"

"*Young* officer?" Rutter repeated. "I never said anything about him being young."

"*Most* of the officers on duty that day were young," Jackson said.

It was a good attempt at covering his gaffe, but not quite good enough. "You know who did it, don't you?" Rutter demanded. "You bloody know. And you're going to do all you can to protect him."

Jackson's face hardened into its normal unyielding expression. "Given how upset you must be, I'll ignore your tone on this one occasion," he said. "In answer to your question, no, Sergeant, I *don't* know. As I've already said, it's far from clear that any of my officers was involved in the incident at all." He spread his hands out in a gesture of reasonableness. "You're a bright young bobby, Sergeant Rutter. You have a great future ahead of you in the police. Don't jeopardise that by taking any ill-considered actions in the heat of the moment."

Rutter stood up. "Do you really think you can threaten me?" he asked. "Do you seriously believe that my job means so much to me that I'll take what happened to Maria lying down?"

"Listen to me, Sergeant Rutter—" Jackson said, with a warning edge to his voice.

"No, you listen," Rutter interrupted. "Sod the job! And sod you as well, *sir!*"

"Isn't it about time we got around to the real purpose of this meetin'?" Woodend asked, taking a sip of the pint that Sid Dowd had just bought him.

"You're probably right," Dowd agreed. "The fact is, I'm a little bit worried that this investigation of yours might start movin' along the wrong lines."

"Now why should you think there's any danger of that?"

"You know that one of my bright young men was at the club the night Robbie was killed, don't you?" Dowd asked.

"I had heard."

"An' you know that I've got what you might call a chequered past?"

"I know you're a Class A villain, Mr Dowd, if that's what you mean," Woodend said.

The other man laughed. "So it'd be very easy for you to put two an' two together an' come up with five."

"When I was at school, I was always slow at sums," Woodend said. "I think you're goin' to have to explain it a bit clearer."

"All right," Dowd conceded. "A Class A villain wants to buy a share of Robbie's club, Robbie won't sell, and before you can say Jack Robinson, the poor bugger's dead. Naturally, the villain comes out near the top of your list of suspects. But he doesn't belong there."

"I'm still listening," Woodend said.

Dowd glanced around the pub. "Can I assume we're talkin' strictly off the record, here?" he asked.

"As long as you're not admittin' to any knowledge of the crime," Woodend agreed.

"I'm not," Dowd assured him.

"So go ahead."

"I'm not claimin' to be as pure as the driven snow," Dowd said. "A couple of the things I've got a hand in are a bit dicey, but in the last few years most of my businesses have gone legit, so that now I've barely got a bent penny in me pocket."

"What's this got to do with Robbie Peterson?"

"I fancied havin' a share of his club. Why wouldn't I? It was a good business opportunity. But he said he didn't want to sell, and that was it."

"Stop playin' games, Mr Dowd," Woodend said. "If that had been it, you'd wouldn't have sent one of your lads up to The Hideaway last Friday night."

Dowd grinned like a guilty schoolboy who'd been caught out in a lie. "All right," he said, "I don't give up easily, an' I don't take kindly to bein' turned down. But I'd never have used strong-arm tactics to get The Hideaway. Why run the risk when there are so many other ways I could have got the same result?"

"Are there?"

"Of course there are. Money's the real muscle in this day an' age, an' I've got plenty of it. All I'd have to have done to bring Robbie to heel was to sell booze at cost price to some of the other clubs – on the understandin' that they passed the savings on to their customers. I'd have had The Hideaway empty in a week."

"Maybe," Woodend admitted. "If it had worked out like that. But what if the other clubs didn't want to play along?"

"Then I'd have come up with some other scheme," Dowd said, without a second's hesitation.

"Like what?

Dowd thought about it. "I'd have turned up at The Hideaway with a couple of charabancs every Friday and Saturday night," he said, "an' as the customers were goin' in, I'd have offered them a free trip to Blackpool, and all they could drink when they got there. A month or two of that and Robbie would have been out of business."

"It would have cost," Woodend pointed out.

"Like I said, I can afford it. You think I'm in business now 'cos I need the dosh? Hell, I could have retired years ago if I'd wanted to."

"And Robbie?"

"He wasn't poor when he left Liverpool, but he invested all he had in Swann's Lake. He needed the cash that was comin' in from his businesses."

It all made sense, Woodend thought, yet he was still suspicious of the man from Liverpool. "Why are you tellin' me all this?" he asked.

Dowd shrugged. "Like I said, it's in my interest not to have you barkin' up the wrong tree."

"An' there's really nothin' more to it than that?"

Dowd looked a little embarrassed. "All right," he admitted. "There *is* more to it. Robbie worked for me for years. He was a good kid – a loyal kid – an' I don't like the thought of whoever topped him gettin' away with it."

"You're offerin' me your help?" Woodend asked incredulously.

"Much as it goes against the grain, yes, I am," Dowd told him. "I'm not sure if there's anythin' I can actually do, but—"

"I am," Woodend interrupted. "Did you know about Robbie's rackets?"

"I heard he'd gone straight," Dowd said.

"You heard wrong. He was in it up to his neck – smugglin' stolen fags across the Pennines."

Dowd made a tutting sound. "I've never liked that kind of racket myself," he said. "The trouble with it is, since you're operatin' outside your own patch, you need to take on partners."

117

"Exactly," Woodend agreed.

"An' you think it might have been one of his partners who killed him?"

"It's a possibility."

Dowd nodded his head sagely. "Yes, I like that better than the idea that young Annie might have done it," he said. "So what exactly do you want me to do?"

"I want to know who Robbie was workin' with, and where they were the night he died. An' I think you're the man who could find out for me."

Dowd took a pensive sip of his scotch. "I'm not turnin' coppers' nark," he said.

"I'm not askin' you to," Woodend told him.

"Aren't you? Suppose I gave you a list of names tomorrow mornin'. By nightfall, everybody on it'd be in gaol."

"That won't happen," Woodend said firmly. "I'll only use your list to track down the murderer. It's not my job to do the local bobbies' work for them."

"What guarantee have I got of that?" Dowd asked dubiously.

"You've got my word."

Dowd sneered. "The word of a bobby?"

"No," Woodend said, his voice turning ice cold. "The word of a man who'll take you outside and try to beat the crap out of you if you ever say anything like that again."

"Try?" Dowd repeated. "I must have ten years on you."

"And a lifetime's experience of fighting dirty," Woodend pointed out. "So I think there's a fair chance I'd be the one who ended up on my back. But I'm still willing to give it a bash."

Dowd smiled. "You know what they told me in Liverpool?" he asked.

"Who's *they*?"

The smile broadened. "Best not to go into details. It's enough to say that 'they' told me you can't be bought. An' after ten minutes of sitting with you, I think they're right."

"Which means that you'll help me?"

Dowd nodded. "You'll get your list," he said. "Maybe not by tomorrow, but you'll get it."

Twelve

The woman standing next to The Hideaway's organ was middle-aged, just a little overweight – and clearly regretting her decision to climb up onto the stage.

"I'm . . . I'm goin' to sing a song which was a big hit for Connie Francis," she said, peering myopically into the bright lights. "It's called 'Who's Sorry Now?' and I hope you'll all join in on the chorus."

The organist struck up the opening chords and the woman came in just a couple of beats too late. Woodend shifted his attention from the stage to the rest of the club. A syndicate from the caravan site was clustered around the one-armed bandit, one of them holding the plastic bag containing their sixpences, another feeding the coins into the slot, a third pulling the handle. In one corner, a group of old men in cloth caps were playing dominoes. The singer's friends, more out of loyalty than interest, were giving her their full attention as she gamely struggled her way through the song. It was, in other words, a typical night in the place which styled itself 'Swann Lake's Premier Social Club'.

"Chief Inspector," someone called from the bar.

Woodend looked round. Wally the bar steward was holding the phone in one hand and gesturing with the other. A call for him. He hoped it wasn't Bob Rutter phoning with bad news.

The Chief Inspector walked over to the bar and took the phone from Wally. "Is that you, Charlie?" asked the voice at the other end of the line.

Woodend covered his left ear which his free hand. "It's me," he admitted. "Who am I speakin' to?"

"Andy Jackson."

119

Woodend grimaced. There were officers in the Met he liked and officers he didn't. Superintendent Jackson fell firmly into the latter category. "What can I do for you, Andy?" he asked.

"I had a talk with your boy Sergeant Rutter today," Jackson said.

"Oh aye," Woodend replied neutrally.

"I didn't like his attitude at all. Just before he left my office – without first getting my permission, mind you – he told me I could sod off."

Woodend allowed himself a small smile at the thought of how Jackson must have reacted to that, then his face was serious again. "That doesn't sound like Bob Rutter," he said. "What had you done to provoke him?"

"Provoke him!" Jackson repeated. "I'm his superior! It doesn't matter what I said to him. It's how he spoke to *me* that counts."

"Is this something to with that lass of his?"

"Well, yes," Jackson admitted grudgingly. "He more or less accused me of deliberately protecting whoever was responsible for injuring her."

And I wouldn't put that past you, Woodend thought. Not for a second. "The lad was probably distraught," he said.

"I don't care about that," Jackson told him. "He's been guilty of extreme insubordination, and I feel under an obligation to put in a report."

With visible relief, the singer had finally finished her number and was climbing down the steps to a smattering of applause. Who's sorry now? Woodend thought. And who's goin' to be sorry in the future?

"Did you hear what I said?" Jackson asked. "I'm going to put in a report on him."

Woodend took a deep breath. "I'd much rather you didn't do that, Andy, at least for the moment," he said. "I don't want the lad suspended. I need him for the case I'm working on up here."

"But damn it, Charlie, if I let him get away with it—"

"Give me a few days," Woodend said. "We'll talk it over when I get back to London."

"There are prescribed procedures in these cases."

"It'd be a pity for us to fall out over this, *sir*," Woodend said, with a new edge in his voice. "I don't think that would do either us any good. Best to leave it till we can talk."

There was a hesitation on the other end of the line, then Jackson said, "When do you expect to be back at the Yard?"

"In a few days. A week at the latest."

"I won't file my report until I've talked to you," Jackson promised. "But I'm warning you now that whatever you say isn't going make any difference."

"Thank you, sir," Woodend said, replacing the phone on its cradle.

"From the expression on your face, I'm guessin' that wasn't exactly a friend of yours you were just talkin' to," Wally said.

"His name's Jackson," Woodend replied. "An' if the bastard ever calls again, I'm not here. Got that?"

Wally nodded. "Understood."

It was that time of night when nothing stirred; the time when shift workers were beginning to look forward to going home, but day workers still had a few hours more sleep left to them; the time between the last sleeper train leaving for London, and the first mail train arriving with the national newspapers. It was, in other words, the insomniac's waking nightmare, a lonely, aching time, midway between the bubble which appeared on the screen as the television closed down at ten-forty-five and the first crackle as the radio came to life with the programme for farmers at six o'clock.

Constable Len Taylor stepped well away from his observation post at the window of The Hideaway, flicked on his torch and read his watch face. Half-past two. That meant he had been sitting there, watching the office door, for nearly three hours. He'd seen American coppers doing this kind of work on programmes like *The Naked City* and *77 Sunset Strip*, and somehow when Bailey and Spencer had been involved, it had all seemed rather glamorous. Now he knew the truth. It was dull. It was mind-numbingly boring.

"No smokin' while you're at that window, lad," the Chief Inspector from London had told him. "And if you feel like goin' to the bog, pee into a bottle or a bucket or somethin'. Because the last thing I want is for you to miss anythin' while you're answerin' a call of nature."

As if there was anything to miss! Taylor thought. All there was out there was an empty yard, and an office door which nobody seemed to have the slightest interest in.

It was just as this bitter thought was going through his head that he saw the man standing hesitantly at the gate which led to the caravan site. Taylor whistled softly to himself. This might turn out to be like *The Naked City* after all, except – he hoped – there wouldn't be any shooting.

The man at the gate seemed to have reached a decision and now made his way across the yard. But instead of stopping by the office, he walked straight past it. Taylor felt a stab of disappointment. The feller wasn't planning to break in – he just felt like a breath of fresh air.

The dark figure returned to Taylor's line of vision and this time he did stop in front of the office door. With his back to the window, it was impossible for the constable to say exactly what he was doing, but Taylor was willing to bet that he was trying to force the lock. The constable tensed, but did not move.

'Don't be hasty, lad,' that Chief Inspector had said earlier. 'Give him enough rope to hang himself. I don't want him collared until he's right inside.'

The door swung open, the man entered the office and Taylor rose from his chair and headed for the exit. Once outside, the constable sprinted across the cinder yard, because there was no point in trying to be quiet now – it was speed which mattered.

The man inside the office heard the running feet and panicked. His tools clattered to the floor and he rushed back to the door. But he was too late! Before he even had time to reached the yard again, his terrified face was squarely in the beam of Constable Taylor's torch.

Like many of the buildings in Maltham, the police headquarters was mock Tudor.

"It's because of all the subsidence caused by the minin' around here," the Duty Sergeant explained helpfully. "See, none of these buildin's have any foundations, so that if the ground starts to sink, you can just jack them up an' put in half a dozen layers of bricks under them. Course, that means you have to climb up a few steps to get in through the door, but it's a damn sight better than climbin' *down* a few steps once you're inside."

Woodend yawned. "That's very interestin'," he said, rubbing his eyes. "In fact, if it wasn't half-past three in the mornin' I'm sure I'd find it bloody fascinatin'. Can I see the prisoner now?"

The Sergeant looked crestfallen. "I'm sorry, sir, I didn't mean to be borin'."

"You weren't, lad," Woodend said. "It's just that it's been a long day, an' I'd rather like to see the prisoner."

"Of course, sir," the Sergeant said. "If you'll follow me, he's waitin' for you in the interview room."

Gerry Fairbright didn't look as if he was waiting for anything, except perhaps the imminent end of the world.

"You're in big trouble, son," Woodend said as he sat down the chair opposite him.

"Don't you think I know that?" Fairbright replied miserably.

"But from what they tell me, you've refused to see a lawyer," Woodend mused. "Why is that?"

"A lawyer wouldn't do me any good."

Woodend shrugged. "Well, if you change your mind—"

"I won't."

The Chief Inspector took out his packet of Capstan Full Strength and offered one to the other man. "You made a better job of breaking into the office this time than you did the last," he said.

"I never tried to break in the first time."

"Somebody did."

"I know," Fairbright admitted. "I saw him."

"And who was it?"

"I couldn't tell you. He was just a dark shape. But the

123

moment I saw him, I got out of there as quickly as I could."

Woodend took a deep drag on his cigarette. "What did you think was so important in that office that you'd run the risks you did?" he asked.

"I'm not sayin' any more," Fairbright told him.

"We've already got you on a burglary charge," Woodend told him. "Do you want to make it murder, as well?"

Fairbright's jaw dropped. "You surely don't think I killed Robbie Peterson, do you?" he gasped.

"Do you have an alibi for the time of the murder?"

"Yes . . . no."

"Which is it, son?"

"I went for a walk."

"Where?"

"Down by the lake."

Down by the lake! At exactly the same time as Terry and Michael Clough claimed to have been there!

"Did you see anybody while you were takin' this walk of yours?" Woodend asked.

"No."

"You're certain about that? You didn't hear two fellers arguin' with each other?"

"I told you, there was nobody down there but me."

So either he was lying, or the Clough brothers were – and at that moment the Chief Inspector had no idea which it was.

"Have you ever been in trouble with the police before, Mr Fairbright?" he asked.

Fairbright's jaw quivered, as if he were on the point of bursting into tears. "No, I haven't," he said.

"Not even when you were a youth? Drunk an' disorderly? That kind of thing?"

"My dad would have killed me if I'd done anythin' wrong," Fairbright said bitterly. "He were right strict. I never even had a proper girlfriend before I went into the Army. You know why?"

"Why?"

"Because all the lasses used to laugh at me when I told them

I had to be home by ten o'clock. That's what my dad made me
– a bloody joke."

"He won't be too chuffed when he hears you've been
arrested, then, will he?" Woodend asked. "An' he will hear.
In fact, I think I just might give him a ring in the mornin' an'
ask him to come down here an' have a word with you."

Gerry Fairbright laughed. "You're a bit late for that. He's
been dead for over two years."

Woodend sighed. Luck just wasn't running his way on this
case. "Nasty places, police holdin' cells," he said, trying a new
tack. "Oh, they don't look too bad at first, but when you've
been in one of them for a few hours, you start to feel the walls
closin' in on you. You don't want to go through that, do you,
lad? Especially when you know, deep down, that the truth's
bound to come out sooner or later?"

"You're wastin' your time," Fairbright said. "I've told you
I'm sayin' no more, an' I meant it."

Woodend stubbed his cigarette exasperatedly in the ashtray.
"It's your choice, lad," he said, "but I think you're makin' a
bloody big mistake."

Thirteen

E ven before he opened his eyes, Woodend realised that he had woken up grumpy, and the sound of drizzle pitter-pattering against his bedroom window did nothing to improve his mood. He checked his watch and saw that it was nearly noon. For a moment, he considered feeling guilty about making such a late start. But why the hell should he? He'd been up half the night trying to talk some sense into Gerry Fairbright, so wasn't he entitled to have a lie-in? Besides, what would he have done with his time if he'd got up earlier?

As he got dressed, he found himself remembering his child-hood, back in Lancashire, and, in particular, the soapbox cart he and his mates had built. It had been a rickety old thing, crudely hammered together – and running on four pram wheels of slightly differing sizes – but his gang been incredibly proud of it. But it had also been a great bone of contention. Every time they took it out, they would row furiously about who got the first ride. Jack, who had gone last the time before, would argue he should be given priority this time. Albert, who'd provided the clothes line which was an integral part of the steering mechanism, would claim this gave him precedence. Each member of the gang, it seemed, had natural justice on his side.

The Chief Inspector pictured himself, his turn finally having arrived, sitting in it at the top of the hill near the Co-op shop. Little Charlie Woodend, wearing short grey trousers, a grey flannel shirt and the sleeveless jumper his Granny Woodend had knitted for him. Little Charlie Woodend, bursting with excitement, knowing that once he got going, he'd fly down the steep slope like buggery. But before that could happen,

126

he needed a push – and the teasing sods behind him seemed to think it was the best joke in the world to keep him waiting.

This murder case was like that, he recognised. He needed some kind of push. It could be anything. The Doncaster police might uncover some telling information on Alex Conway. Gerry Fairbright might get fed up of being confined in a police cell, and finally be willing to come clean about why he broke into Robbie Peterson's office. Someone in Swann's Lake – Harold Dawson and the Green brothers immediately came to mind – might do or say something which would give him the new lead he needed. But until one of those things happened, he was left sitting at the top of the hill, bursting with frustration.

"You're gettin' fanciful, Charlie," he said aloud. "If you don't watch yourself, you'll be writin' poetry next."

It was early afternoon when the police Wolsey pulled up in front of The Hideaway, and Rutter got out.

Woodend, who was shuffling his notes around in the vain hope they might suddenly tell a coherent story, followed his sergeant's progress across the yard. By Christ, Bob looked rough, he thought. More than rough – the poor devil looked completely crushed.

Rutter entered the office and flopped down in the visitors' chair opposite his boss. "I need to talk to somebody," he said.

"I'm sure you do, lad," Woodend said sympathetically. "An' I'm right willin' to listen."

It was like inviting the flood gates to open. Rutter told of Maria's terror when she'd first discovered she'd gone blind – how even the furniture in her own flat had seemed hostile. He talked of the need for an operation and its chances of success. "She insisted I come back here," he said, with tears in his eyes. "Can you imagine that? As scared as she was, she could still find time to think about what was best for me."

"Aye, she's a grand lass," Woodend said, sincerely. "One of the best."

Rutter took a deep breath. "So what's happened while I've been away?" he asked, trying to sound his usual crisp, efficient self.

127

"You're sure you want to stay on the case, lad?" Woodend asked.

Rutter nodded. "Yes, I want to stay on it – at least, for as long as I can."

"An' what exactly does that mean?"

"While I was in London, I had a run-in with a bastard called Superintendent Jackson. It was about—"

"I know what it was about," Woodend interrupted him. "He rang me up last night."

"So you know he's probably already set the wheels in motion to have me suspended pending an official inquiry."

"You just leave Jackson to me," Woodend said. "There'll be no official inquiry. I may not be able to sweep it under the carpet completely, but you should get away with no more than a slap on the wrist, and that won't really hurt your prospects."

"My prospects don't matter, because as soon as we get back to the Yard, I'm going to hand in my resignation," Rutter said.

"I wouldn't do that if I was you, lad," Woodend advised.

"I don't have any choice," Rutter retorted. "How can I continue to be a policeman when I've no faith in the Force any more?"

"An' what would you do once you were on Civvie Street?" the Chief Inspector asked. "Become a bank clerk? I can't see you sittin' behind a desk, Bob."

"Maybe I'll go to Australia," Rutter said. "The assisted passage is only ten pounds, and even an honest detective sergeant can afford that. And when I get there, perhaps I'll join the Australian police, because it's just possible that *they* might have a little integrity."

Woodend shook his head. "You can't go condemnin' the whole barrel that makes up British policin' just because you think one apple's bad," he said.

"Do you *think* Jackson's bad?" Rutter demanded.

"At the very least, he's badly bruised," Woodend admitted.

"And the animal who attacked Maria? That's two bad apples so far, and we haven't even started."

Woodend sighed. There was no reasoning with the lad at that moment. "You may well be right," he told Rutter, "but there's nothin' we can do about it until we get back to London. So do you want to hear about the developments in the case or what?"

"Yes," Rutter said. "Give me all the details."

Holding his trousers up with one hand, and conscious of his shoes slip-slopping with every step he took, Gerry Fairbright paced his small cell. When the Custody Sergeant had taken away his braces and his shoe laces, he'd felt insulted. Did the Sergeant really think he was the kind of man to do away with himself? he'd demanded. But now, after twelve hours in captivity, he saw the sense behind the regulation, because there had been moments – mad, mad moments – when death had seemed the easiest way out.

He heard the key click in the lock and the heavy door swung open. The Custody Sergeant entered the cell, carrying a metal tray. "I've brought your tea, lad," he said, not unkindly.

"Has . . . has anythin' happened?" Fairbright asked.

"Happened?" the Sergeant repeated.

"Have they come any closer to catchin' Robbie Peterson's murderer?"

The Sergeant laid the tray on top of the fold-down table. "Ee, I wouldn't know anythin' about that, lad," he said. "I've got enough on my hands just lookin' after you lot."

The Sergeant turned back towards the door, and Fairbright felt an urge to ask him to stay – to sit down, so they could have a good natter about Bolton Wanderers' chance of winning the FA Cup again. But he knew it would do no good. For all the Sergeant's friendliness, he was a gaoler, and Gerry was the prisoner.

The door clanked hard behind the Sergeant, and Fairbright was alone once more. He lifted the lid which had covered his tray. Greasy sausages and lumpy mashed potatoes. Institutional stodge, the like of which he hadn't seen since National Service. And not even a knife to eat it with, because criminals like him were expected to manage with a spoon.

He sat down and lethargically began eating. His father was to blame for all this, he thought. If the old man hadn't kept such a tight rein on him when he was living at home, he'd have been an entirely different person now – a person who'd have seen no reason to make the kind of mistakes he'd made.

"I hope you're satisfied, you miserable old bugger," he said to the dead man. "I hope you're really pleased with yourself."

Was it possible that Woodend had been right in what he'd said the previous evening? Fairbright wondered. Wouldn't it be better to confess now, and get it all over with? No! There was still a slim chance he would get away with it, and as long as he had that hope to cling on to, he was determined to keep his mouth firmly shut.

From his corner table in The Hideaway, Woodend watched Harold Dawson knock back yet another double whisky at the bar. "That bugger wants to come an' talk to us," he said to Rutter. "Only he's not quite sure if it's such a good idea."

"I still don't see how he fits into the picture," Rutter said.

"Neither do I," Woodend agreed. "But forget him for minute. I'm tired of sittin' on my arse, doin' nothin'. It's time to put the cat among the pigeons."

It sounded just like vintage Woodend, and Rutter could hardly resist smiling. "And how do you propose to do that, sir?" he asked.

"By breakin' the habits of a lifetime an' goin' to Yorkshire voluntarily," Woodend said. "If Alex Conway won't come to us, maybe it's about time we went lookin' for him. I've had a word with the Doncaster police, an' by tomorrow mornin' they should have got a search warrant sworn out on Conway's flat."

"What about Michael Clough, sir? Clem Green did seem to suggest he might be worth taking a closer look at."

"He's on my list, Sergeant, especially since, bearin' in mind what Gerry Fairbright said, it's possible he wasn't down at the lake at all when Robbie was killed. But as a suspect, he ranks a long way behind Alex Conway." He glanced across at the bar. "Ay up, I told you yon bugger would make his move sooner or later."

Rutter looked in the same direction as his boss. Harold

Dawson was approaching their table and there was definitely a slight stagger to his step.

Dawson came to a shaky halt directly opposite the Chief Inspector. "I hear you've arrested Gerry Fairbright," he said.

"I'm surprised you know him, sir," Woodend replied. "I wouldn't have thought the paths of a gentleman of the press and a fitter from Oldham would have crossed very often."

"I met him in here a couple of times," Dawson said. "We got talking, like you do."

"That would explain it then," Woodend replied, making no effort to sound as if he believed the reporter for a minute.

Dawson swayed a little. "Thing is, does it have anything to do with the murder?"

"He's been charged with breakin' into private property," Woodend said evenly.

"And has he explained *why* he did it?"

"Yes sir," Woodend lied. "He said he was lookin' for somethin'."

Dawson gulped. "Did he say what?"

"That's as far as I'm prepared to go at the moment," Woodend told him.

Dawson shook his head, as if he were trying to clear his fuzzy thought process. "Well, if you'll excuse me," he said, slurring his words, "I'd better get off home."

"You do that. An' drive carefully," Woodend advised him.

But Dawson didn't head for the door. Instead he went back to the bar and ordered himself another double whisky.

"What did you make of that, Bob?" Woodend asked.

"He's very worried indeed about what Fairbright might have said," Rutter suggested.

"Aye, he is, isn't he?" Woodend agreed. "An' I'll tell you somethin' else for nothin'. If we want to find out who made the first, botched attempt to break into Peterson's office, we'll not have to look much further than Mr Harold-bloody-Dawson."

Fourteen

"Well, I must say it was easier getting into Yorkshire today than it was the last time," Rutter said as the police Wolsey approached the sign which welcomed it to Doncaster. "Passport control hardly looked at us, and there was absolutely no trouble at the customs' post."

"Sarcastic young bugger," Woodend growled – but he was pleased that his sergeant seemed to be in good enough spirits to be able to make a joke.

The Wolsey turned into Hatton Gardens, and Woodend saw two men standing on the footpath outside Number 7. One of them was a white-haired sergeant. The other, the police locksmith, was wearing a khaki storeman's coat and carried a tool box in his hand.

"So that's your Sergeant Dash, is it?" Woodend asked Rutter. "Looks like a good lad – for a Yorkshireman."

The Chief Inspector and the uniformed Sergeant shook hands. "Have you found out anythin' that's goin' to be useful to me, Sergeant?" Woodend said.

"Yes an' no, sir," Dash answered. "We know that at least one Alexander Conway of the right age exists. Somerset House has confirmed he was born in Huyton, Liverpool, in June 1910. But that's as far as the trail goes. He's not registered with the National Health, the Inland Revenue hasn't got any record of him, and he doesn't have a file in Scotland Yard. The Liverpool police haven't come up with anythin' either, but they're are still workin' on it."

Woodend frowned. "Hmm," he said. "Have you tried the War Office?"

"Yes, sir. They've never heard of him either."

Woodend handed the cigarettes around. "How about your investigations here in Doncaster?" he asked.

"We talked to the feller Conway bought the flat from. They never met. It was all done through Conway's solicitors, and they're claimin' client confidentiality."

"They would," Woodend said gruffly. "An' did you get any results from the door-to-door?"

"Quite a few of the neighbours confirm Miss Tufton's description of him – about five eleven, blond hair etcetera – but they've really not much more to add. They may have nodded to him in the street, but we couldn't find anybody who'd actually had a conversation with him."

He was a slippery customer all right, Woodend thought, but given the game he was in, that was hardly surprising. "Have you got the paperwork with you?" he asked Sergeant Dash.

Dash patted his pocket. "Right here, sir."

"Then let's get started."

The four men walked up the path to the front door. Rutter rang Conway's bell first, but as on the last visit there was no response.

"Have to be the old biddy who lets us in then," Woodend said.

Miss Tufton was overwhelmed to find *four* men standing on the doorstep. She was quite pleased to see the nice young detective again, though she was less enthusiastic about the reappearance of the uniformed sergeant who seemed to be obsessed with television licences. And she simply didn't know what to make of the man in the hairy sports coat and the other one carrying a toolbox.

"Have you seen Mr Conway since the last time I was here?" the nice young detective asked her.

"No, I haven't" Miss Tufton confessed. "And I'm getting quite worried about him."

"Why is that?"

"Well, you got me thinking," Miss Tufton explained. "I don't actually count the number of days he's gone, but after your visit I did try to remember the last time he was here, and I have this feeling he's been away for much longer than normal."

133

"He sounds like he's big enough to take care of himself," Woodend said.

Miss Tufton gave the man in the hairy sports coat a look of mild dislike. "Mr Conway is a very gentle man," she said.

"I'm sure he is," Woodend agreed.

"Far too gentle for the wicked world which seems to have grown up since the War," Miss Tufton added.

"I'm . . . er . . . afraid we are going to have to have a look around his flat," Rutter said. "We'll try not to make too much noise."

"Oh dear," Miss Tufton said. "Have you got a search warrant?"

Woodend shot Rutter a questioning look, as if to ask how the old girl knew about anything as technical as a search warrant. "Miss Tufton's a big fan of *No Hiding Place*," the Sergeant explained.

"Yes, we do have a warrant," the Chief Inspector said. "Would you like to see it?"

"Good heavens, no," Miss Tufton replied. "But I'd quite like it if you'd wave it in front of my face, like they do on television."

"Anything to oblige, madam," Woodend said, thinking to himself that if he was running some kind of criminal activity, he couldn't think of a better person to live above than an innocent, confused old dear like Miss Tufton.

It took the police locksmith a good five minutes to pick the lock on the door to Alex Conway's flat. "Beautiful workmanship," he said when he'd finished. "Almost a pity to mess about with it."

The main door opened straight into the lounge. It was a square room, with a leather three-piece suite dominating the centre of it. A radiogram stood against one wall, and even a cursory glance was enough to tell Woodend that Conway had quite a collection of records. Facing the radiogram was a bookcase, and it seemed that in addition to being a music lover, Conway was a voracious reader. The Chief Inspector looked around and took in the rest of the details. The carpet had a muted floral pattern, and the curtains were plain, and corn gold. It was a pleasant room – a restful room with a definite feminine touch – and Woodend, who had been half-hoping to find several thousand cartons of stolen cigarettes stacked up against the wall, felt vaguely disappointed.

"Where shall we start, sir?" Rutter asked.

"You an' me'll take the record collection," Woodend said. "Sergeant Dash, check to see if any of them books is stuffed full of used fivers."

Woodend and Rutter knelt down beside the radiogram. The Chief Inspector flicked through the records. They were all classical. He went through them again, more slowly this time, noting the titles. "What do you make of this, Sergeant Rutter?" he asked.

"Not a great deal," Rutter admitted. "What *should* I have made of it?"

"How about the way they're filed?"

"They're not alphabetical," Rutter said, "so judging by the wear and tear on the sleeves at the left hand, and the shininess of the ones on the right, I'd say they were filed according to when he bought them."

"You're gettin' there," Woodend said, "but you've missed the main point, which is *the order* he chose to buy them in."

"You've lost me again, sir," Rutter confessed.

"Look at the records he bought first. Strauss and Rossini. Now go to the other end. Bruckner and Sibelius."

"I still don't get it."

Woodend sighed. "Rock 'n' roll is here to stay," he said, with mild contempt. "I don't know much about classical music – jazz is more my sort of thing – but I do know enough to realise that Strauss is what they call light classical, an' Sibelius is much heavier stuff. *Now* do you get it?"

"He's been educating himself," Rutter said. "Starting with easy pieces, then moving on to the more difficult ones."

"Go to the top of the class." Woodend stood up. "I don't think there'll be anything hidden in the record sleeves," he said. "But you'd better check anyway. I'll go an' see how Sergeant Dash is gettin' on with Conway's book collection."

Dash was holding a large book by the spine, and shaking it to see if anything fell out. When nothing did, he replaced on the shelf, picked up the next one, glanced briefly at the title, then gave that a good shaking, too.

"Found anythin' interestin'?" Woodend asked.

"There's nothing hidden between the pages of the books, if that's what you mean, sir" the Sergeant replied. "But the books themselves might be of interest."

"Oh? In what way?"

"Go through most people's bookcases an' you'd be bound to find Zane Grey, Ellery Queen an' Dennis Wheatley," Dash said. "But there's none of that here. They're all what I suppose you might call 'quality' books."

"Quality books?"

"Yes, sir. History, literature, stuff like that. He seems especially enthusiastic about paintin'. There are a lot of books about Italian artists."

"Canaletto, Titian, fellers like that?" Woodend asked.

"Yes, sir," Dash said, with a hint of surprise in his voice. "Know about art, do you?"

"Oh, I like a good picture," Woodend said. "Thing is, Sergeant, apart from tellin' us that Conway's more cultured than your average villain, I don't see where this is leadin' us."

"About a dozen of the paintin' books are from one of the sub-branches of the Doncaster library, if that's any help," Dash said.

"About a dozen?" Woodend repeated. "How many books are you normally allowed to take out of your library, Sergeant?"

"Three or four I think," Dash said. "But most of these books haven't been taken out in the normal way." He opened one and showed it to Woodend. "See, it's still got its little card inside. That should have been filed back at the library when Conway withdrew the book."

"Now that *is* interesting," Woodend reflected.

Alexander Conway's kitchen was well equipped with pots and pans, but there was no evidence of food, in either the fridge or the cupboards.

"Seems our Mr Conway isn't much of a one for throwin' dinner parties," Woodend said.

There were two bedrooms. The wardrobe in the smaller of the two was empty and the bed was stripped down to the bare mattress.

"Still, it must be handy when he has a visitors – like his mate Robbie Peterson, from Cheshire," the Chief Inspector commented.

The larger bedroom was very tidy, but obviously lived in. Woodend opened the wardrobe and saw that it was full of suits. "He won't have bought any of these down at the fifty-shillin' tailors," he said to his sergeant.

"No," Rutter agreed, running the cloth of one of the jackets through his fingers. "These are expensive. Tasteful, too. The sort of clothes a chief inspector might be seen wear—" He stopped, suddenly. "I'm sorry, sir, I didn't mean to suggest—"

"I know exactly what you meant," Woodend assured him. "An' you're quite right. It's the sort of clobber you'd wear if you were tryin' to impress somebody. Now let's put all this stuff on the bed, so we can see exactly what we've got."

They spread all the clothes out over the counterpane. In addition to the suits there were over a dozen shirts, three ties, underwear, socks, two pairs of casual trousers and a couple of pullovers. Rutter checked through every garment which had pockets and came up empty-handed.

"There's two things that bother me about this lot," Woodend said thoughtfully.

"And what are they, sir?"

"First of all, wouldn't you say that wardrobe was almost full to burstin' when we first opened it?"

"Yes, I would," Rutter agreed.

"An' that Conway would be really pushed to fit much more inside?"

"I suppose so."

"So where does he keep the clothes he takes with him when he's off travellin'?"

"Maybe he usually stores them in the wardrobe in the guest room," Rutter speculated.

"Maybe he does," Woodend agreed. "But wouldn't that suggest, since he chooses to separate them like that, that they're not the same *kind* of clothes."

"How would they be different?"

Woodend shrugged. "I'm not sure. Like you said, what he keeps in this room is all top-quality stuff. Perhaps he dresses down when he's away from Doncaster."

"Most people take their best clothes with them when they go away," Rutter pointed out.

"You're right," the Chief Inspector said. "It's all a bit of a mystery, isn't it?"

"You said there was something else bothering you," Rutter reminded him.

"Oh aye," Woodend said. "This bloke Conway's got a lot more clothes than I have – he could go a fortnight without doin' any washin' if he wanted to – but there's one thing he hasn't got multiples of."

"His shoes!" Rutter said.

"Exactly. Where are his spare pairs of shoes?"

Maria was aware of time passing since the doctor had put something over her mouth and told her to take short, deep breaths, but whether that was an hour earlier, or a day – or even a year – she had no way of knowing. What she *did* know was that she was lying flat on her back.

She reached out and ran both hands along the edges of the bed. Her palms brushed against the cold metal and her fingers touched the ends of the familiar bolts which held the frame together.

For a second, she was shocked at how quickly she learned to use touch as a substitute for seeing. And then that thought was swept aside by the realisation that if she wasn't under anaesthetic any more, the operation must be over.

She listened carefully, and thought she heard someone else breathing. "Is anybody there?" she asked.

"I'm here," said a familiar voice.

Joan Woodend! Of course she's here, Maria thought. She's hardly left my side since this nightmare began. "Have the doctors told you anything?" she asked.

"They said there were no complications," Joan replied. "Everything went just about as smoothly as it possibly could have done."

But was it a success? Maria wondered in anguish. Will I able to see again? "When do the bandages come off?" she asked.

"On Sunday."

How long it seemed until Sunday. How much darkness lay ahead before then. And there was always the possibility – the *strong* possibility – that once the bandages were removed, the darkness would remain.

Maria contemplated a bleak future. To be blind! To be constantly aware that there were obstacles lurking out there in the darkness, waiting to bang against her shins or trip her up. To be helpless in the face of tasks which caused absolutely no problem for normal people. She thought of the life she'd been half-planning with Bob. What would happen to that now? How could she have the children she'd so looked forward to, when she wouldn't be able to look after them?

"I'm sure it will be all right," Joan Woodend said comfortingly.

But how *could she* be sure, if even the surgeons didn't know?

Sitting at a table in the pub closest to Number 7, Hatton Gardens, Woodend took a generous slurp of his pint and then smacked his lips contentedly. "There are some good things about Yorkshire after all, Bob," he said. "Mind you, if you ever quote me on that, I'll deny I ever said it."

"Thank you, sir," Rutter said.

Woodend put his glass down. "What exactly is it you're thankin' me for, Sergeant?"

"Most bosses I've worked with would already have asked me three or four times how I was bearing up under the strain. You haven't mentioned Maria since we left Swann's Lake."

Woodend looked distinctly uncomfortable. "Aye, well, I

figured that when you want to talk about it, you will," he said.

"So what do you make of Alex Conway?" Rutter asked, indicating that time had not yet arrived.

"He's not your average villain, is he?" Woodend replied. "He might not exactly be as well educated as a grammar school boy like you – but he certainly wants to better himself."

"Maybe he's not a villain at all," Rutter suggested, picking up the double Scotch which he'd chosen in preference to his usual half of bitter.

"I'd agree with you on that, but for one thing – his flat," Woodend said. "It's like he'd never been there."

"Never been there?" Rutter repeated. "He's got his records, his books, his clothes—"

"Listen, lad, if you were ever to break into my house, you'd come away knowin' a lot about me," Woodend interrupted. "I don't mean you'd know I liked Dixieland jazz or the Italian school of paintin' – though you'd have a fair idea about that. No, what I'm sayin' is, you'd know when I was born, when I was married, where I bank whatever's left of my miserable salary, how much my life is insured for – all kinds of details."

"Documentation," Rutter said, grasping the point.

"That's right. Bloody hell, I think I've still got my old army pay book. But this feller Conway has bugger all in the line of papers, which suggests to me that he's been anticipatin' the day when a couple of nosy bobbies like us would get a search warrant and turn his flat over. An' to think things through like that, you've simply got to be a villain."

"You could be on to something there," Rutter admitted.

"Add to that what your Miss Tufton said about him bein' away for rather longer than usual, and you've got the finger of suspicion in the death of Robbie Peterson pointin' straight at Mr Alex Conway."

"You think they had an argument and Conway decided Peterson had to go?" Rutter asked.

"Not necessarily. Maybe Conway goes down to the club on Friday night just to talk. Then he finds Peterson asleep at his desk. 'Hang on,' he says to himself, 'with Robbie out of the way, I could be in charge of the whole racket.' It doesn't take more than a few seconds to pick up the hammer and nail, and bam! Peterson's dead. Now all Conway has to do is lie low while the murder investigation's goin' on, an' then he's back in business – this time on his own."

Rutter looked distinctly dubious. "You think that Conway has gone into hiding?"

"That's what it looks like to me."

"But why should he have done that? You said yourself that the only thing which connected him with Robbie Peterson – as far as we know – is an envelope. And what reason would he have had for thinking we'd get our hands on it? Does he even remember it? I know I'd probably have forgotten it, if I'd been in his place."

Woodend gave his sergeant a look which could almost have been mistaken for dislike. "I hate it when you shoot down my theories with logic," he said. "I bloody hate it. But if you're right, how do you explain the fact that Alex Conway has been away from his flat for so long?"

"We don't know he has," Rutter argued. "Miss Tufton *thinks* he might have been gone for an unusually long time, but even she admits that she's very vague about such matters."

"You're right again," Woodend admitted reluctantly. "But I still think Alex Conway is our man."

"So what are you going to do about it?" Rutter asked.

"I'm goin' to find him, of course."

Rutter drained his whisky and signalled to the waiter that he'd like another one. "It's all very well to say you're going to find him," he told his boss. "But where, exactly, do you plan to start looking?"

"Well," Woodend said, "I could do worse than begin with the public library."

Fifteen

Woodend's local library in Kilburn was similar to ones he remembered as a child, a grey, intimidating place presided over by a grey, intimidating woman who seemed to take it as a personal insult whenever anyone wished to check out a book. The library Alexander Conway made frequent use of, on the other hand, was a completely different story. It was light and airy. Selected books were displayed enticingly, instead of being confined to the shelves. There were paintings – mainly from the Italian school – on the walls, and pot plants which the Chief Inspector was willing to bet had not been provided by Doncaster Council. Someone had worked very hard to make this a pleasant place to be.

A plump young woman with a jolly red face and long, undisciplined brown hair was sitting behind the main desk reading a true romance magazine. When Woodend coughed she looked up, smiled and said, "Can I help you, sir?"

"I'm looking for the librarian," Woodend told her. "The *chief* librarian, I mean."

"Then you'll be wanting Miss Noonan," the girl said, still smiling. "I'm afraid she's out on her coffee break. I'm Miss Jones, the assistant librarian. Is there anything *I* can do for you?"

"Very possibly," Woodend said. "I'm a policeman." He produced his warrant card and held it out for her to see.

The girl's eyes widened and her smile disappeared. "*A chief inspector,*" she said. "Has somebody done something wrong?"

"If somebody somewhere hadn't done something wrong, I'd be out of a job," Woodend said, grinning reassuringly. "But it probably isn't anybody you know."

Miss Jones relaxed slightly. "What do you want to ask me?" she said.

"I'm interested in one of your customers—"

"Patrons. Miss Noonan doesn't like the people who come into the library being called customers. She says we're running an institution for enlightenment – not a shop."

"Patrons, then," Woodend agreed. "The one I'm interested in is probably a regular. He's about my height, somewhere around fifty, has blond hair and a moustache, which he always keeps well trimmed—"

"Oh, that'd be Mr Conway," the assistant librarian said.

"You're not telling me that he's—"

"I'm sure he's as pure as the driven snow," Woodend lied. "But I'd still like to find out a little more about him. Would that be all right?"

The girl nodded doubtfully. "I suppose so."

"How long has Mr Conway been coming here?" Woodend asked, starting with an easy one.

"Well, he's certainly been a regular patron for as long as I've been working here."

"And that would be . . . ?"

"Three years now. Of course, he's not regular in the sense that he comes in every week. We can go a whole month without seeing him."

"He's a keen reader, isn't he?"

"*Very* keen. Sometimes we have to order the books from the central library especially for him. But Miss Noonan doesn't mind doing that. She says that's all part of the service."

"What kind of person is he?"

"Oh, he's very nice. Very soft-spoken. And a little shy," Miss Jones lowered her eyes, "at least, he is with me."

"But not with Miss Noonan?"

Miss Jones looked as if she wished she could cheerfully have bitten off her own tongue. "And he's a very smart dresser," she said, side-stepping the question. "Always has a nice suit on."

"What about his shoes?"

Miss Jones gazed at him in wonder. "You've never met Mr

Sally Spencer

Conway, have you?" she asked. "You wouldn't be asking all these questions if you had."

"You're right," Woodend admitted. "I've never met him."

"So how do you know about his shoes?"

I don't, Woodend thought. All I do know is that they were the only articles of clothing missing from his flat. But aloud, he said, "Why don't you tell about the shoes, Miss Jones?"

"Well, they're very smart, too. Black leather. And he always keeps them beautifully polished. But—"

"But he only has one pair?" Woodend interrupted.

Miss Jones's awe of the Chief Inspector was growing with every second which passed. "Some of the clothes he wears would go much better with a pair of *brown* shoes."

"You think he's only got the one pair, don't you?" Woodend asked.

"It's the only explanation."

Woodend grinned again. "On the quiet, you're a bit of a detective yourself, aren't you?"

Miss Jones giggled conspiratorially. "I wonder what he does when they need repairing?" she asked. "Does he go around in his carpet slippers all day?"

"Now that really would look strange," Woodend agreed. "But let's go back to what we were talking about earlier, shall we? You said that he was shy with *you*, but he wasn't—"

Behind him, Woodend heard the door swing open. The effect on Miss Jones was immediate. With one hand she opened her desk drawer, and with the other hastily stuffed her true romance magazine into it. Then, smoothing down her hair, she assumed an expression the Chief Inspector supposed she thought was appropriate for an assistant librarian.

"Is everything all right, Miss Jones?" asked a woman with a brisk, businesslike voice. "Can you handle this gentleman's problem, or do you want me to take over?"

Woodend turned round to face the owner of the voice. She was about middle height, wore severe steel spectacles and had her hair in a tight bun – none of which really disguised the fact

144

that with her oval face, almost rosebud lips and wide green eyes, she was a rather attractive woman.

"I said, can you handle this gentleman's problem, Miss Jones?" the formidable Miss Noonan repeated.

"I . . . er . . . he's a . . . um—" Miss Jones mumbled.

"I'm a policeman," Woodend said, rescuing the struggling library assistant. "Chief Inspector Woodend."

He handed her his warrant card. Miss Noonan studied it carefully and then turned it over, almost as if she expected to see a label from Joe's Joke Emporium on the other side.

"I see," she said, finally handing the card back. "And what possible business can a Chief Inspector all the way from Scotland Yard have in a small branch library such as ours?"

"If you don't mind, I'd like to ask you a few questions," Woodend said.

"Me?" Miss Noonan said.

"You," Woodend confirmed.

"What kind of questions?"

Woodend glanced meaningfully at Miss Jones, who was pretending to readjust the wheels on her date stamp. "I think it might be better if we talked in private," he said.

"Perhaps you're right," Miss Noonan agreed. "We'll use my office. It's this way."

It was not so much an office she led him to as a stock cupboard, but there was just enough room for the two of them to sit down without any indecorous rubbing of knees.

Now that she was sitting still, Woodend had a chance to look at her more closely. His initial impression of her face was confirmed. She was very attractive, despite her attempts to hide it. Her linen suit was severely cut – almost on masculine lines – but it didn't quite conceal the fact that she had a good figure underneath. She was in her late thirties or early forties, Woodend decided – and she wore her age extremely well.

"I'm inquiring about one of your customers . . . er . . . patrons," the Chief Inspector said. "A Mr Alexander Conway."

The librarian made a slight adjustment to her spectacles. It did not look like a natural gesture and was designed – Woodend guessed – to give her time to think. "May I ask what all this about?" Miss Noonan said finally.

"I'm afraid not," Woodend told her regretfully. "Police inquiries are always confidential, as you'll appreciate. Believe me, it's as much to protect the innocent as it is to detect the guilty."

"And *I'm* afraid that without knowing more, I couldn't possibly consider discussing one of the library's patrons," Miss Noonan said.

Woodend sighed. "You're an intelligent woman, Miss Noonan," he said. "You should know that it's not in your own interests to start making things difficult for the police."

Miss Noonan stood up, her face filled with outrage. "Are you threatening me?" she demanded. "In my own library?"

In your own little kingdom, more like, Woodend thought. "No, I'm not threatening you, Miss Noonan," he said. "But you must understand that just as you have rules about how you run the library, so we have rules about how we conduct our investigations."

The woman sat down again. "Ask your questions," she said. "But I can give you no guarantee that I'll answer them."

It wasn't his argument about breaking rules which had made her change her mind, Woodend thought. Nor was she intimidated by him. Her about-face had been brought on by the fact that there was at least a small part of her which wanted this conversation as much as he did. He wondered why that should be.

"How long has Mr Conway been coming here?" he asked.

"Just over five years."

"Regularly?"

A pause. "I would say he's fairly regular, yes."

"So he comes in, say, a couple of times a week?" Woodend asked, still not able to guess whether or not she was going to lie to him.

"When he's here, he does."

"Would you mind explainin' that?"

"He's often away for quite long periods of time. Being a successful businessman, he naturally has to do a considerable amount of travelling around the country – or so I understand."

The last four words – the afterthought – were delivered with some style, but just a little too late. Woodend remembered that Miss Tufton had told Bob Rutter about the woman who rang Alex Conway's doorbell, then waited on the pavement – and he knew he was definitely on to something.

When Billy Morrison was first starting out in the rackets just after the end of the War, he'd boasted that one day he would be the Sid Dowd of Leeds. And up until that very afternoon, he'd really believed he'd achieved his dream. After all, he had the same outward trappings as Sid had – the nice clothes, the flash cars, the big house with an indoor swimming pool. He owned theatre clubs like Sid did. Other criminals came to him – just as they did to Sid – to ask his permission to pull jobs on his patch. So how was he any different to the Liverpudlian?

The difference had been made screamingly obvious by the arrival of the two young men in smart blue suits – young men so hard they made his own minders look like lollipop ladies. And now, sitting in his expensive office – which was probably every bit as good as Sid's – Morrison realised that he wasn't Dowd at all, but strictly small fry.

Morrison looked nervously across his expensive teak coffee table at the two heavies, who had introduced themselves simply as Phil and Jack. Considering they were on his territory, they looked far too relaxed, he thought. Far too confident. Jesus, they scared him!

"Have a cigar, boys," he offered, reaching across for the silver box that usually impressed people.

Phil and Jack shook their heads politely, but said nothing.

Morrison reached for a cigar himself and lit it. It wasn't until he had taken a puff that he realised he had forgotten to snip off the end first. He reached for his gold cutter and tried to make it look as if this roundabout route was the way he always lit his cigars.

"You . . . er . . . mentioned that good old Sid wanted to do a bit of business," he said shakily.

"No, we didn't," Phil corrected him. "We said that Mr Dowd wanted some information from you."

"Information," Morrison repeated. "Well, I'll be glad to do whatever I can to help you. Any friends of Sid's are friends of mine."

"We're Mr Dowd's employees, not his friends," said Phil, with just a hint of rebuke in his voice, "but we take your point. What we'd like is information about the contraband whisky and cigarette racket."

"Which contraband whisky and cigarette racket?"

Phil leant forward slightly, somehow managing to make the gesture seem both casual and menacing. "The racket Robbie Peterson was running out of Swann's Lake," he said.

Morrison felt a cold chill in the pit of his stomach. He'd been worried when he read about the murder that the police might connect Robbie with him. But this was worse. Much worse. For all he knew, it was Sid Dowd who had done for Robbie – which meant that he himself could be next on the list.

"I . . . I don't know anything about that," he said.

A thin, humourless smile came to Phil's lips. "Mr Dowd doesn't want to take over anybody else's business," he said. "All he needs is the names of all the people involved."

"Why should he want that?" Swanson asked. "He's not turned coppers' nark, has he?" He realised his mistake the second he'd spoken, and held up his hands defensively. "Just a joke, boys."

"But not a very good one," Phil said severely.

"Seriously, why should he want the names? I don't go stickin' my nose into his business, now do I?"

"I'm sure he has his reasons," Phil replied, "and he said I was to be sure to tell you that if you ever want a favour in return, you've only to ask."

They were throwing him a bone, Morrison thought, but he supposed that was better than nothing. At least this way he might emerge with a shred of his self-respect intact. "Robbie's people, a couple of lads called Green, have been bringin' the goods across the Pennines," he said. "My lads meet them somewhere on the road. From there on in, it's been up to me."

"If the eventual destination is Leeds," Phil pointed out.

"That's right."

"What if they were supposed to go somewhere else? Say to Sheffield or Rotherham?"

"Rotherham's Maltese Freddie's patch. Most of Sheffield belongs to Albert Strong."

"So they would have made their own arrangements?"

"I expect so."

"One more question," Phil said. "Did you have Robbie Peterson knocked off, Mr Morrison?"

"No, I bloody didn't!" Morrison exploded.

Phil nodded. "Just checking," he said.

"So when Mr Conway's not travellin', he makes a great deal of use of this library, does he?" Woodend asked.

"Yes, indeed. He's very interested in the arts. As I am myself."

"Especially paintin'?"

"I think you could say that painting is his favourite branch, yes."

"The Italian school."

"Yes," Miss Noonan said enthusiastically. "There's so much breadth and feeling to it, isn't there?"

"What I don't understand is why, if he wanted such specialist books, Mr Conway didn't go to the central library," Woodend said.

"This is much closer to his fl—" Miss Noonan said, before she could stop herself.

"Oh, you know where he lives, do you?"

Miss Noonan laughed. "Of course I do. His address is written on his library cards."

"So it is," Woodend agreed. "Still, you'd have thought that if he couldn't wait to get his hands on a particular book, he would have used a bigger branch."

"Perhaps the reason he chose to keep on coming to this branch after his first few visits was because of me," Miss Noonan admitted.

"Aye," Woodend said. "I thought that might be it."

"You see," Miss Noonan continued hastily, "though we share the same interests, I have rather more experience, and I have, in my humble way, been able to guide him in his reading a little."

Miss Noonan smiled – and her face became suddenly radiant. But it was not a smile for the man sitting opposite her, and Woodend wondered if she knew what Conway's business was – or whether she'd ever met his partner, Robbie Peterson, whose idea of a good picture was probably something sent through the post in a plain paper wrapper.

"What concerns me at the moment," the Chief Inspector said, "is that Mr Conway appears to have several books from this library which have not been properly stamped out."

Miss Noonan was outraged. "You've been to his flat. You had absolutely no right—"

She realised what she was saying, and stopped abruptly.

"Yes, we did search his flat," Woodend said mildly, "but if anyone has cause to complain about that, it's Mr Conway himself, wouldn't you say, not the someone from the local branch library?"

"Surely a Chief Inspector from New Scotland Yard is not interested in a few library books," Miss Noonan said, trying a fresh line of attack.

"They are pertinent to our inquiries, and all policemen have a responsibility to investigate any crime they encounter – however petty it may seem. Did Mr Conway steal the books?"

Outrage again. "Certainly not!"

"Then how did he get them?"

"He . . . I . . . As I think I explained earlier, Mr Conway is interested in making a fairly extensive study of art. Three or four books are simply not enough for that. I know him to be a responsible gentleman of serious intent, and so I sometimes lend him more books than he is strictly entitled to."

"And is this a service you extend to other readers?"

Miss Noonan put her hands up to her face. "No . . . I . . . that is . . ."

She took her hands away, and Woodend could see the tears streaming from her eyes.

"Chief Inspector," she said, "what, for the love of God, has happened to my darling Alex?"

Then she buried her head in her hands, and sobbed in earnest.

Woodend watched the second hand of the institutional clock behind Miss Noonan's head complete a full circle. If this had been Jenny Clough who'd burst into tears, he thought, he'd have put his arms around her and uttered soothingly meaningless words. But Miss Noonan was a very different sort of person, and he was sure that any contact would only have angered her.

The second hand had passed twelve again before Miss Noonan looked up. Her eyes were red, but the resolution had returned to her face. "I must apologise, Chief Inspector," she said. "I rarely give in to public displays of emotion."

"I'm sure you don't," Woodend said sympathetically. "Shall we start again? Right from the beginning?"

Miss Noonan nodded. "Alex first came here, as I told you, about five years ago. What you must accept, if you're ever going to understand him at all, is that though he is a very successful businessman, he's had a very limited education. But his thirst for knowledge – for an understanding of the finer things of life – puts me, with my grammar school background, completely to shame."

"Understood," Woodend said.

"On his initial visit, he didn't know where to start. He was almost like a child, who realises he wants something, but doesn't know exactly what."

"An' you recognised that, and decided to help him?"

Miss Noonan gave him a small, grateful smile. "Exactly. For the first year or so, we had a purely professional relationship – me on one side of the counter and him on the other. But then, as we both seemed to love the same things, it was only natural that we should start going to exhibitions and concerts together. Then we began seeing each other on more purely social occasions, and finally—"

"You became his lady-friend," said Woodend, tactfully.

"I became his mistress," Miss Noonan answered defiantly.

"I know society frowns on such things – I know it could cost my job – but I don't care. The pleasure Alex has brought me, *in every sense of the word*, has been more than worth whatever suffering I have to go through as a result of it."

"I'm not here to judge you," Woodend said. "You don't happen to have a photograph of Mr Conway you could show me, do you?"

Miss Noonan shook her head. "No, I don't."

"Isn't that rather a strange thing to have to admit, given the nature your relationship?"

"You'd never say that if you knew Alex," Miss Noonan replied. "He's a very shy man. Whenever we go out, he seems to be nervous that people might be looking at us. And he absolutely refuses to have his photograph taken."

In case it falls into the wrong hands, Woodend thought. In case some bright bobby somewhere happens to recognise him from it. "I have just a few more questions and then I'll leave you in peace," he said. "If you often don't see Mr Conway for long periods of time—"

"That's not his fault," Miss Noonan said fiercely. "He has his business commitments."

"I understand that. But if he does spend so much time away, why does his absence distress you so much this time?"

"He hasn't rung me since last week."

"That doesn't seem very long."

"It is for him. Besides, there are arrangements to be made."

"Arrangements?"

"We're supposed to be going away on holiday on Saturday. It will be the first time we've ever been away together."

"And where are you planning to go?"

"Venice."

Of course! Woodend thought. With their mutual interest in Italian painting, where else would they be going? "Do you happen to know if Mr Conway has his passport yet?" he asked.

"Yes, that's one thing we don't have to worry about," Miss Noonan said. "It arrived a couple of weeks ago."

"Are you sure of that?"

"Of course I am. He showed it to me. He was so excited about it. He saw it as the final proof that the dream we'd been planning for so long was actually going to come about. And, of course, it was the all more exciting for him because he's never been abroad before."

"Not even during the War?"

Miss Noonan shook her head. "He didn't serve in the armed forces. He volunteered, of course – Alex would never try to shirk his duty – but he was turned down. He had flat feet, you see. Maybe that's why he wears—" She stopped, as if she had suddenly realised she'd said too much.

"Wears what?" Woodend asked.

"I . . . I don't know what I'm saying. You've got me confused."

"You were goin' to tell me about his shoes, weren't you?"

Miss Noonan looked him straight in the eye. "I would like you to give me your word, Chief Inspector, that you do not suspect Alex of having done anything criminal."

"You know I can't do that," Woodend said.

The librarian stood up. "In that case, I don't think we have anything else to say to each other."

She wanted to stop talking before she inadvertently gave anything else away, Woodend thought. And for the moment, what she wanted was all that mattered – because he hadn't even the smallest shred of evidence to use as an excuse for pulling her in for questioning. Miss Noonan already had the door open and was gesturing that he should leave. There seemed no alternative but to do just that.

Woodend rose to his feet. "If you change your mind and decide you have anythin' more to tell me . . ."

"I won't," Miss Noonan said. Her lower lip quivered. "But if you do find Alex," she implored, "you will let me know, won't you? Please!"

The pub was called The King's Arms, which was rather a fancy name for a place with long cracks in the leather settle and patches of mildew on the wall. But as Woodend had pointed out when he and Rutter entered the snug bar, it didn't really matter what the place looked like, as long as the ale was good.

"The most significant thing I learned from Miss Noonan is that Conway was plannin' to go away for his holidays on Saturday," Woodend said.

"Because that means he wasn't planning to kill Robbie Peterson?" Rutter asked.

"Exactly. Either it was like I said earlier – he found Robbie asleep an' it was too good a chance to miss – or he didn't kill Peterson at all, but knew who did, an' realised he was next in line."

"So if he's not in hiding because he's a murderer, he's there because he's frightened of *being* murdered?"

"Spot on," Woodend agreed. "An' whichever it is, it's in our interest to find him as soon as possible."

"The only problem is, we've no idea where he is," Rutter pointed out.

"You're right," Woodend agreed. "But we've got a couple of real beltin' leads."

"And what are they?"

"The passport and the shoes! The passport office must have the application form Conway sent in, and that will give us more details about him. And then, of course, there'll be a photograph. He was too wily to let Miss Noonan have one, but he'll have had no choice if he wanted a passport. So we'll soon know exactly what he looks like."

"What about the shoes?" Rutter asked.

"That's a bit more of a long shot," Woodend admitted. "But the way I've got it figured out, if he wears the same pair most of the time he's in Doncaster, they must need solin' and heelin' fairly often. So maybe they're sittin' in some cobbler's shop right now – just waitin' to be picked up. All we have to do is find out which shop, an' then ask the Doncaster police to keep an eye on it."

"I'll get Sergeant Dash on the job right away," Rutter said.

"I don't think we'll use the local bobbies on this job," Woodend told him. "Can't trust them not to make a cock-up of it."

"You said yourself that Dash had the look of a bloody good bobby," Rutter said.

"For a *Yorkshireman*," Woodend countered. "No, that's not fair. He is a good bobby within his limitations. But I'd still rather keep this lead to ourselves."

"So the two us are going to check every single cobbler's in the Doncaster area?" Rutter asked incredulously.

"Not us, lad. You."

"But it could take days!" Rutter protested.

"Not if you put your back into it," Woodend said cheerfully.

"This isn't just a way of keeping me busy, is it? You've not given me this job so I'll have no time to worry about Maria?"

"Of course I haven't, lad," Woodend lied.

Sixteen

E ven as a kid, Woodend had been able to smell impending trouble, and now, as the police Wolsey made its way along the lakeside road, it filled his nostrils like the smell of burning paper.

"Stick your clog down, lad," he said to his driver. "There's somethin' I don't want to miss."

As the driver accelerated, Woodend scratched his head and wondered why, when the solution to this case probably lay in Doncaster or Liverpool, he should be getting such an uneasy feeling so close to The Hideaway.

The answer was clear the moment the Wolsey pulled into the yard. Jenny Clough, a pinny over her skirt and cardigan, was standing in front of the club talking to her sister, who was wearing another of her revealing dresses. But they were not *just* talking. Their bodies were stiff and their necks were arched forward. They looked, the Chief Inspector thought, exactly like two unfriendly cats who were sizing each other up.

What the bloody hell could have brought this confrontation on? he asked himself. True, there was often ill feeling in families after funerals, but money was usually at the bottom of that, and he was pretty sure that Doris would have seen to it that everything went to her. Besides, Jenny Clough didn't strike him as the kind of woman who would be much concerned about material things.

The driver parked the car by the garage and Woodend got out. Whatever the two women had been talking about, Annie had obviously had enough, because she'd turned her back on Jenny and started walking away. But *Jenny* hadn't finished with *Annie* yet. Showing a passion Woodend wouldn't have thought her capable of, she flung herself onto the back of her retreating sister, and dragged her down to the ground.

The fight was so fast and so vicious that it was almost a blur. The two women rolled over and over, with first one on top and then the other. Jenny clawed at Annabel's face as if she wanted to gouge out her eyes. Annabel bit deep into Jenny's shoulder. It only took Woodend a few seconds to cover the distance between the car and the fight, but by the time he got there, both women were already bleeding and gasping for breath.

Annie was on top. Woodend grabbed her under the armpits and hauled her away from her sister. Jenny scrambled quickly to her feet and would have launched a fresh attack had not Terry Clough appeared on the scene and got a hold on his wife. For a few moments, both women continued to struggle, and then, seeing it was pointless, they relaxed.

"If we let you go, you're not going to start fightin' again, are you?" Woodend asked, using his best constable-dealing-with-a-domestic-disturbance voice.

"I won't," Annie said sulkily. "I didn't start it in the first place."

"What about you, Jenny?"

Jenny shook her head. "That bitch isn't worth it."

Woodend released his grip, and, after a second's hesitation, Clough did the same.

"Now what was that all about?" Terry asked his wife, his voice more puzzled than angry.

Jenny looked him straight in the face, then swung round and pointed angrily at Annie. "Ask her!" she screamed. "Ask that connivin' cow!"

"Well?" Terry said.

Annie looked as if she were going to give him the answer he was searching for, then changed her mind. "If she won't tell you, I don't see why I should," she said. "But I shouldn't have to, anyway. If you weren't such an incredibly thick bastard, Terry, you'd be able to work it out for yourself."

And suddenly, it seemed as if Terry Clough had. A smile of the purest happiness came to his face – a smile which quickly changed to a look of concern when he heard the muted sob which escaped from Jenny's throat.

"It's all right, Jenny," he said softly. "From now on, *everythin's* goin' to be all right."

He put his arm around his wife's shoulder and led her back towards the house. She made no protest – all the resistance seemed to have been knocked out of her. Annie Peterson, biting her bottom lip, watched them until they reached the door. Then she turned and hurried away from the club.

Woodend looked down at the scratches on his hand – inflicted by either Jenny or Annabel, he wasn't sure which. The scratches would sting like buggery when he put antiseptic on them, he thought – but that had been a small price to pay for witnessing something which had cleared up at least two mysteries.

Bob Rutter looked out of the Doncaster boarding-house window, down onto the street below. He had already been through the telephone directory to establish just how many shoe-repair shops there were in the Doncaster area, and he would have a busy morning ahead of him. But what was he to do until then? How was he to fill in the long hours in which there was nothing to do but worry about Maria?

He studied his room. Bed. Wardrobe. Small table and chair. The basics. He closed his eyes, so that he could see as little as Maria had that fateful morning, then made his way slowly across the room to the bed. He thought he had calculated it perfectly, yet it still came as a surprise when his shin barked against the edge of the frame. God, it was horrible, he thought. It was frightening. Without sight, you were helpless as a baby. It was enough to make a person go mad.

He forced himself to repeat the operation, walking to the door this time. The experience did not get any better with practice. He opened his eyes again. What he really needed, he decided, was a drink. More than one drink.

Annie Peterson sat bathing her wounds with Dettol in front of her dressing-table mirror. She looked a real mess, she told herself. She was sorry about the fight with Jenny, but not about its cause. Her needs were as great as Jenny's. Greater! Jenny hadn't endured the humiliation of a posh boarding school. Jenny wasn't trapped between two worlds, belonging to neither.

"I've got the right to reach out and grab happiness with both hands," she told her scratched reflection in the mirror. But even as she said it, she knew she was not convincing herself. Hadn't her sister the same right to happiness as she had – and who was to judge which of them had suffered more from being Robbie Peterson's daughter?

She forced the issue to the back of her mind, and thought instead about her plans for the evening. She had to go out again. She and Michael had agreed on that. She didn't want to go – aching after her fight with Jenny, she longed for nothing more than a hot bath – but there really was no choice. She had an appointment she didn't dare not keep. But then that was it! Just this one last meeting, then she would put it all behind her. For ever.

She walked over to her wardrobe and took out a short red dress with a plunging neckline which she had nicknamed 'Slag 3' to distinguish it from all the other 'slag' dresses she owned. Yes, that would do nicely. The perfect dress for this final encounter. And when it was over, she would burn the bloody dress – along with all the others.

Going to the pub had not been a good idea, Rutter decided. Men like Cloggin'-it Charlie Woodend could knock back pint after pint of the old neck oil without it having any visible effect apart from giving them a rosy glow, yet for him the more he drank the more he seemed to see the gloomy side of life.

He thought about his career, which had once looked so promising. He was the youngest detective sergeant in the Yard. Why shouldn't he also eventually be the youngest ever Commissioner in the Met? Now it would never happen – not because he'd been rude to a superintendent, Charlie Woodend would handle that – but because he simply didn't want to be a policeman any more.

He remembered what the doctor had said about Maria – about how many young men found that faced with the prospect of a lifetime of living with a blind person, love was simply not enough. Well, it would be for him. It *had* to be for him – or he was not the man he'd always taken himself to be.

He seemed to have lost control of his elbow and it slid along the bar, colliding with a pint glass and spilling its contents all over the bar.

"Hey you, that was my drink!" an angry voice said.

Rutter turned to face the man who made the complaint. He was big and had the look of a natural street fighter about him. "Your drink, wash it?" he asked, realising he was slurring his words. "Well, show bloody what?"

"You can buy me another one," the big man said threateningly. "An' a whisky to go with it."

"And you," Rutter said, doing his best to focus on the other man, "can go and get stuffed."

The big man leant forward. "We don't want any trouble in here," he said, almost in a whisper, "but if you'd like to step outside, we'll soon find out whether you're goin' to buy me another drink or not."

Even at his best he would have no chance in a fight with this bloke, Rutter thought. And after the amount of whisky he had drunk, he was feeling far from at his best. "Yesh," he heard himself say. "Let's go outside and sort it out there."

The big man headed towards the door and Rutter followed him. He was going to get the beating of his life, the Sergeant thought – and wondered why that should make him feel better.

Annabel Peterson got off the train at Manchester Central Station, walked straight to the taxi rank, and gave the driver in the front cab an address.

"You don't want to go there, luv," he said. "That's right down by the docks, that is."

"I know where it is," Annabel told him.

"It's a real rough area," the cabbie warned her.

Annabel sighed. "Look, I'm on the game, and I'm meeting my bloody pimp down there," she said loudly. *"All right!"*

160

The taxi driver raised his hands. "Whatever you say, luv," he assured her. "You're the one who's payin' the fare."

Annabel climbed into the back of the cab. She did not glance over her shoulder, but if she had done, she would have seen Detective Sergeant Gower getting into the taxi just behind hers.

"You want me do *what?*" Gower's cabbie asked, when the Detective Sergeant gave him his instructions.

"Follow the taxi in front," Gower replied. "But try not to let him *know* you're doin' it."

"Are you off your chump, or what?" the cabbie asked.

"No, I'm not off my chump. I'm a copper, workin' on a case."

"Where's your warrant card, then?"

Handed in to the Super when the bastard suspended me, Gower reminded himself. "There's no time for bleedin' warrant cards," he growled menacingly. "But let me tell you somethin' for nothin', Sunshine. I've got friends in the Manchester police, an' if you don't get this thing into gear right now, I'll tell them to make your life a bloody misery."

"Follow that cab!" the driver said sullenly. "As if we was in bloody America or somethin'." But he pulled off from the kerb anyway.

This excursion to Manchester might lead to nothing, Gower thought, as he watched the taxi just ahead of them. Annabel Peterson might be doing no more than visiting an old school friend. But the feeling in his gut told him that tonight was definitely *the* night – that he'd finally get his reward for all the weeks of patiently watching the flat which Annie could not possibly afford.

The two taxis travelled through the city centre, then left the impressive civic building and big stores behind. Soon they were making their way along narrower, meaner streets, streets full of terraced houses squatting against the skyline like malignant goblins.

"Well, she certainly won't be meetin' any of her posh friends in *this* area," Gower said happily to himself.

Annabel's taxi driver stuck out his indicator and pulled up in front of a rough-looking dockside pub called The Grapes.

"You want me to stop as well?" Gower's driver asked.

"No I don't, you bloody fool," the Sergeant hissed. "Drive round the corner an' park."

The cabbie did as he'd been told. Gower gave him a ten shilling note and, without waiting for his change, walked quickly back to The Grapes. There was no sign of Annabel Peterson on the street – but that was only to be expected.

The Sergeant approached the pub cautiously and had to stand on tip-toe to look over the frosted glass that ran halfway up the window. The Grapes was a scruffy, run-down place, typical of the area. The bar was crowded with dockers and merchant seamen, all dedicated to drinking down ten or twelve pints before last orders were called. He could see Annie at the bar, sitting with her back to him. Apart from two obvious prostitutes, she was the only woman in the pub.

Had she merely dressed the part, or was she really on the game? Gower wondered. But if she'd been selling her body, surely she'd have stuck to her poncy boyfriends back in Maltham, instead of coming all this way to give one of these rough fellers a cheap knee-trembler in a back alley. No, she had to be up to something else, and given where she'd come looking for it, he had a pretty good idea what that *something* was.

He didn't dare go into The Grapes – they could smell the police a mile off in that sort of place. So he would have to rely on arresting Annabel once the exchange had been made. True, this was not his manor, but he thought he could justify making the arrest himself by saying that he hadn't had time to contact the local police. Anyway, thinking through the consequences of his actions had never been his strong point. As far as he was concerned, all that would be sorted out later.

He moved away from the pub and leant against a lamp-post on the street corner. The light wasn't working – probably vandals had broken the bulb so many times that the city council had got tired of replacing it – so Gower was virtually invisible, except from close to. On the other hand, he had a clear view of the pub. Anyone entering or leaving was illuminated by its bright lights.

He saw a coloured seaman in a woollen cap walk down the

street and enter The Grapes. Black bastards, they should never be allowed into the country in the first place, he told himself. And evidently the landlord shared his opinion, because the seaman was only inside for thirty seconds before he emerged again. But he didn't go away! Instead, he cut up the alley at the side of the pub.

About half a minute later, Annie Peterson came out, and also disappeared up the alley. Gower strode quickly after her, pulling his torch out of his pocket as he went. His beam caught them in the act – the black seaman taking the money off Annabel, her taking the package off him.

"Police!" Gower shouted. "Don't move!"

They both began running, and so did the Detective Sergeant. The black man streaked ahead, but Annie Peterson, hampered by her high heels and tight skirt, soon came to a resigned halt. Gower charged on anyway, ploughing into Annie and knocking her off her feet. He helped her, none too gently, into a standing position again.

"You, my princess, are bleedin' well nicked," he said with malicious glee.

The night-time duty sergeant at the Manchester River Police headquarters, his eyes red with tiredness, looked up from his paperwork at the man in the hairy sports jacket. "Can I help you?" he asked.

Woodend produced his warrant card and held it out for the Sergeant to see. "I got a call from one of your lads. He told me you're holding a girl called Annabel Peterson," he said.

The Sergeant nodded. "That's right, sir." He stepped from behind his desk. "She's waitin' for you in Interview Room Three. Straight down that corridor and third door on your right."

Woodend walked down the empty corridor, listening to the echo of his own heels. What a cock-up Annie Peterson had made of her life, he thought. What an absolute bloody mess.

He counted off the doors, reached the third one, knocked and entered. Like so many of the interview rooms he'd spent countless hours in, it was a depressing place, small and cramped, with chocolate-brown paint to waist height and institutional cream from there to the ceiling. The wooden table which took up most of the space looked incredibly rickety, and the two straight-backed chairs on each side of it had definitely seen better days.

A bovine-looking WPC, with a bored expression on her face, sat on one of the chairs, Annie Peterson on the other. Annie had a cigarette in her mouth and was using an Individual Fruit Pie aluminium plate as her ashtray. From the number of crushed cigarette ends it contained, she had obviously been chain-smoking. She was wearing one of the tartish dresses that were the uniform of her battle against the rest of the world, Woodend noted, but though her thick make-up was smudged, she had not been crying.

"Thank you, Constable," Woodend said. "I'll take over now. Just wait outside the door."

The WPC rose to her feet and squeezed past the Chief Inspector. When she had closed the door, Woodend eased himself into the seat opposite Annie. She looked quiet and subdued. The fire – the aggression – seemed to have left her. She gave him a friendly smile, but one tinged with sadness.

"One last pick-up," she said. "That's what it was going to be. One last pick-up. I didn't want to do it, but they told me they needed time to recruit someone to take my place. I said that was their problem, and they said it would be a pity if such a pretty face as mine ended up covered in razor scars. They meant it."

"I'm sure they did," Woodend agreed. "But what I don't understand is why, in God's name, you ever allowed yourself to get involved with people like that in the first place."

Annabel Peterson shrugged. "It gave me freedom, I suppose. I didn't have to depend on Robbie anymore; I didn't have to depend on *anyone*."

Woodend shook his head in disbelief. "That's not it," he said. "Or at least, not all of it. You're a bright girl, Annie. You could have made yourself independent of Robbie in hundreds of different ways. So there has to be somethin' else, doesn't there? Another reason you chose to go the way you did?"

Annabel Clough looked him straight in the eyes. "Do you really want to know? she asked.

"Yes, I do."

"Why?"

"Because I think that somewhere below that hard-bitten exterior, there's somebody I could like," Woodend said. "All I want you to do is help me find her. Are you willin' to do that?"

Annabel nodded. "I used to think the men I went out with accepted me for myself," she said tiredly. "I was wrong. I was out with one of them at an exclusive country club one night and I went to the toilet. When I got back to the table, my date was talking to one of his friends. They didn't see me, and I accidentally overheard what they were saying. Shall I tell you exactly what that was, Chief Inspector?"

"If you want to."

"The friend said he'd heard I was a great girl, and the man I was with said, 'Yes. She'll let you do anything you want to her. And the best part is, she doesn't even charge for it. Not that I'd mind paying if she asked.' Do you know how that made me feel?"

"I can imagine," Woodend said.

Annie shook her head vehemently. "No, you can't. Nobody can, unless it's happened to them. I felt so worthless. I saw that whether I took money or not, I was still nothing more than a common prostitute to him. To all of them! I rushed back to the toilet and was sick in the basin. I don't know how long I was there, heaving my guts up, but all the time I was thinking, I want to die. I just want to die. And I swear to God that if I'd had a packet of razorblades on me, I'd have slit my wrists then and there."

"Go on," Woodend said sympathetically.

"But I didn't have any razorblades, and by the time I was cleaning myself up, I'd thought of something better to do than kill myself. My 'boyfriends' had been using me, but now I was going to start using them. Instead of *me* being their plaything, I'd introduce them to a new one. I'd help them to destroy themselves, just as they'd been working so hard at destroying me."

165

Sally Spencer

"But *heroin*, Annie!" Woodend exclaimed. "My God, there can't be more than a few hundred heroin users in the whole of the British Isles."

Annie smiled with what looked like genuine amusement. "That was part of its appeal to them," she said. "They always like to feel they belong to an elite."

"Did you kill your father?" Woodend said.

"I've often thought about it."

"That wasn't what I asked."

"No," Annie said. "I didn't kill Robbie. How could I? When all's said and done, he was my dad."

There was the sound of a scuffle coming from the other end of the corridor, but Woodend felt no inclination to hurry towards it. Whatever was going on, it was the Manchester Police's business, not his. And then he saw what was causing the disturbance. Two uniformed constables were struggling to restrain a frenzied young man. And that young man was Michael Clough.

The sight of Woodend had an instant calming effect on Clough. He stopped trying to break free, and became, once again, the calm, detached person Woodend had come to know.

"Tell them I have to see Annabel, Chief Inspector," he said.

"I can't," Woodend replied. "There are rules, Mr Clough. Until she's charged – and she *will* be charged, you know – the only person she can see is her solicitor. After that, she'll be allowed visitors, but only from her immediate family. Of course, it shouldn't be long before you can count yourself as one of them, should it?"

"What do you mean?" Clough asked.

"Well, you are plannin' to marry her, aren't you?"

For once, Michael Clough looked as if he'd been caught off-guard. "How . . . how did you know?" he asked.

"Jesus, lad, for anybody who's got eyes to see, it's bloody obvious," Woodend told him.

166

Seventeen

Woodend had not been expecting the black Rolls Royce Silver Dawn to pull up in front of The Hideaway, but neither was he particularly surprised when it did. Men like Sid Dowd didn't bother making appointments – if they wanted a meeting, even one with senior police officers, then that meeting usually happened.

The driver's door opened, and a hard-looking young man in a smart blue suit got out. His eyes quickly swept the area around the club, looking for any source of trouble. Very professional, Woodend thought. Sid Dowd was wise to employ someone like Phil to watch his back. But just how far would Phil go in the service of his boss? Would he, if Dowd asked him to, drive a nail into an enemy's skull? Yes, Woodend decided, he would. Probably without a second's thought!

Satisfied that the yard was safe, Phil opened the back door of the Rolls, and Dowd, as immaculately dressed as he'd been at the funeral, stepped out with all the grace and assurance of a visiting royal.

Woodend suppressed a yawn. His visit to Manchester the night before had meant he'd only managed to grab a few hours' sleep, and he was feeling the effect. He wasn't as young as he used to be, he told himself. It was about time he let that keen young sergeant of his do most of the running about. Except that, unless Woodend could come up with a very good argument against his resigning, Rutter wouldn't be around to do the running much longer.

The sound of Sid Dowd tapping lightly on the open door snapped Woodend out of his contemplation. "Come in and take a seat, Mr Dowd," the Chief Inspector said.

Dowd sat, placed his expensive leather briefcase on his lap and snapped it open. "My lads have been workin' very hard on your behalf," he said.

"I appreciate their efforts."

Dowd extracted a manila file from the briefcase. "Before we begin, can we just make sure we both understand the ground rules," he said. "I don't care what you do in Swann's Lake, but you're not to use the information I give you to arrest anybody anywhere else. Unless, of course, he's the one who topped Robbie."

"Agreed."

Dowd spread the file out on top of the briefcase. "Robbie supplied several firms in Yorkshire," he said. "Probably his best customer was Billy Morrison, in Leeds. Robbie used to send him a shipment at least once a month."

"Let's hear the rest of the list," Woodend said.

It took Dowd a few minutes to reel of all the names and places. The gangster was right, Woodend thought, his lads *had* been working hard. By they still hadn't come up with the name *he* wanted.

"You haven't mentioned Doncaster," he said, when Dowd had finally finished reading.

"I haven't mentioned Halifax, either," Dowd replied. "That's because Robbie didn't do business in either of them places."

Was he lying? Woodend wondered. Was it possible that both Dowd *and* Conway had been involved in Robbie's death, and that the Liverpudlian's offer of help had been nothing more than part of an elaborate smokescreen?

"You haven't mentioned Alexander Conway, either," the Chief Inspector said.

Dowd looked genuinely surprised. "Clumpy Conway? He's nothing to do with any of this. Why, he must have been dead for nigh on twenty years now."

Woodend shook his head. "No, he hasn't."

"I saw his body myself."

"An' if I check with the Liverpool police, they'll confirm it?"

Dowd grinned. "Not exactly. You see, we didn't want the

bobbies stickin' their noses in where they weren't wanted, so we didn't give him what you might call a proper funeral."

If Dowd was telling the truth – or at least what he *thought* was the truth – that would go a long way towards explaining why Sergeant Dash had so far come up with so little on Conway. On the other hand, if he was lying . . .

"He's dead," Sid Dowd said. "You've got my word on it."

I believe him, Woodend thought. As far as he's concerned, Alex Conway really *is* dead. "You want to tell me how it happened?" he asked.

For the first time since he'd entered the office, Dowd looked wary. "Still off the record?" he said.

"Still off the record," Woodend agreed.

"It's 1940 I'm talkin' about," Dowd said. "A lot of lads had been called up by the Army, which left most businesses a bit short-handed. Well, that was all right for the farmers an' the factory managers, because they soon had women trained up to fill the gap. But I couldn't really use women in most of my businesses, could I?"

Despite himself, Woodend couldn't hold back a smile. "I see your dilemma," he said.

"Anyway," Dowd continued, "along came this new bunch of lads who figured my operation was ripe for the pickings. It was never really on – I still had more muscle on my side than they could muster – but they were a nuisance for a while. You know how it goes. They beat up some of my lads, and I had a few of theirs worked over. In the end, I think they must have decided to go for broke—"

"Where does Conway fit into all this?" Woodend interrupted.

"I was just comin' to that. See, it was Clumpy they decided to make a real example of. I was usin' him as a fence at the time. Well, if truth be told, he wasn't much use for anythin' else. Anyway, this new firm raided the place he was operatin' for me, put a shotgun to his head and pulled the trigger. Nasty way to go, but that was the point of it, you see – they wanted to show me they really meant business. It didn't take them long to realise their mistake. I couldn't have 'em knockin' off my

169

fellers – even useless little sods like Clumpy. I hit back, and a week later they'd all left Liverpool with their tails between their legs." He grinned again. "Them as still *had* their tails, that is. The ones who did for Clumpy, I handled personally."

"Shotgun wounds," Woodend said reflectively.

He'd once handled an investigation involving a shotgun. The victim in that case had taken it full in the face, too, and he was so messed up even his own mother wouldn't have recognised him. Conway was not the idiot Dowd imagined him to be, the Chief Inspector thought. Far from it, he was a calculating man who had faked his own death in Liverpool, only to emerge again in Doncaster, eighteen years later.

"I expect his head was a bit of mess, then, was it?" Woodend said.

"Worst case I've ever seen," Dowd replied, matter-of-factly. "His brains, what few he had, were spattered all over the walls."

"Then how did you know it was Conway's body you saw?" Woodend asked, pouncing.

Dowd shrugged, as if he'd never really given the matter any thought. "Well, there were his clothes – he was never much a dresser – an' his general physique," he said finally.

Woodend nodded. "His clothes an' his general physique? An' that's all."

Dowd laughed. "You're sayin' he did a switch, aren't you?" he asked. "That it was some other poor sod who got killed?"

"It's a possibility, isn't it?"

The Liverpudlian shook his head. "There weren't two like him," he said. "I'd have recognised him even if that shotgun had cut him in two an' only left the bottom half."

Weren't two like him? Recognisable from his bottom half alone? And the nickname? Woodend saw his most promising line of inquiry melting away before his eyes. "Spell it out for me?" he said roughly. "How could you be so sure the dead man was Clumpy Conway?"

"I was sure because of his club foot," Dowd replied.

Woodend sat at his desk with his head in his hands, listening to the purr of Sid Dowd's Rolls Royce as it passed the window. What a bloody disaster of a morning it had been, he told himself. He desperately needed to talk to Alex Conway, but he was no nearer finding him now than he'd been at the start of the investigation – because the man he was looking for wasn't really Conway at all. He had merely borrowed the name from a dead man he'd probably known back in Liverpool.

The Chief Inspector stood up. He really needed Bob Rutter to bounce his ideas off, he thought, but Rutter was away pounding the streets of Doncaster.

"Who will have known Conway apart from Robbie Peterson?" he asked Rutter's empty chair.

The Green brothers! They delivered the stolen goods to *all* of Robbie's partners. They would be able to tell him where to find Conway. But what was the probability they would co-operate with the police? Not a chance in hell!

"Unless . . ." Woodend said, pacing the floor, ". . . unless I had some lever I could use to put pressure on them."

He needed to tie them in with Robbie Peterson's rackets. But how could he do that now Robbie was dead?

The cigarettes! he thought. The bloody stolen fags!

He lit a Capstan Full Strength as his mind raced along this new track. What Robbie Peterson had been, in fact, was a wholesaler, and – criminal or not – he would have to keep his goods in stock until there was a demand, just like all other wholesalers. So even though he was dead, his warehouse must still be around. And once he'd found the warehouse, he might find some way to connect it to the Green brothers – which was just the lever he'd need.

"So where were you hiding the stuff, Robbie?" he asked the empty office. "Where would *I* hide it if I was you?"

The Chief Inspector found Doris Peterson sitting at her kitchen table. There was a bowl of water in front of her, and she was shelling peas into it. Woodend did his best to hide his surprise.

"Didn't expect to see a gangster's moll doin' anythin' as domestic as this, did you?" Doris asked, seeing right through his masked expression. "Brassy blonde turned housewife. It makes you think."

"Yes, it does," Woodend admitted.

"I've had the good times while they were there for the takin' – bathin' in champagne an' all that sort of thing," Doris told him, "but I've never neglected my family. I wasn't brought up that way." She paused from her shelling and gazed thoughtfully into the water. "I miss him, you know," she continued. "Robbie. I never thought I would. But I do. I got used to havin' him around, an' now he's not here any more, it's like there's a big gap in my life."

Woodend nodded sympathetically. "I think it might help us to find his murderer if we knew more about his rackets," he said.

Doris's face hardened. "I've told you the last time you asked, I know nothin' about them."

"I'm sure you don't," Woodend agreed. "But you knew *Robbie*, and you know Swann's Lake."

"How will that help?" Doris asked suspiciously.

"If he'd been dealin' in stolen cigarettes, would he have kept them close to him, or would he have been happy to warehouse them in, say, Manchester?"

Doris popped another pod, and tipped the peas into the water. "Robbie wasn't big on trustin' most other people. If he been storin' nicked fags, he'd have wanted them close enough for him to be able to go an' check on them every day. Maybe even two or three times a day."

"You've got some holiday bungalows around the lake, haven't you?" Woodend asked.

"There's nothin' there," Doris said firmly.

"How can you be so sure?"

"I checked," Doris said. "I told you I didn't know if Robbie was involved in anythin' criminal, but if he was, I wanted it to die with him. So I checked. There's nothin' in any of the bungalows that shouldn't be there."

"Do you mind if the local bobbies have a look for themselves? Not that I don't trust you. It's just that it'll give Inspector Chatterton's lads somethin' to do."

"They can look if they like," Doris said indifferently. "But like I told you, they won't find nothin'. Even if there *had* been somethin', I'd have chucked it in the bloody lake."

Woodend returned to Robbie Peterson's office with Doris's words ringing in his ears. Robbie wouldn't want to be too far away from the stolen goods, she'd said, but he hadn't been keeping them in any of the bungalows. He wouldn't have kept them around the club or the house, either – not unless he got a thrill out of running incredible risks.

"So where else would he hide crates of booze and thousands of cartons of cigarettes?" Woodend asked Rutter's empty chair.

And once he'd put the question into words, the answer was obvious.

Detective Sergeant Rutter found that the bruising to his ribs caused him to walk more stiffly that he would normally have done, but other than that, he had come away from the battering outside the pub with far less damage than he'd expected. It had been stupid to provoke the fight, he thought, yet it had served as a release – an escape from the emotional pain he had been feeling since he'd heard the terrible news about Maria. And perhaps, in a way, he was trying to share her pain. Or maybe that was too fanciful.

He forced thoughts of his fiancée from his mind. He had a job to do – a job which he had always considered important, but now, as he entered his last few days as a policeman, took on even greater significance. He had already visited five cobblers' shops in Doncaster without even a whiff of success, but, as was the usual case in this kind of work, he was driven on by the thought that it was always possible the very next one would give him exactly what he needed.

He paused in front of the shop. Johnson's High Class Boot and Shoe Repairers was spelt out in a half-circle of gold letters on the front window. It was an old-fashioned establishment which had seen better days. People today preferred to drop off their shoes at the local branch of Timpson's, Rutter thought. Besides, the sort of shoes they were making now didn't really merit the craftsmanship that Mr Johnson was probably capable of.

He opened the door and heard a brass bell tinkle above his head. The sound brought a man scurrying from the back of the shop. He was aged and shrunken, with a bald head and half-moon glasses perched precariously on his nose. But his hands looked strong, and Rutter noticed the ridges of hard skin on his thumbs.

"I'm looking for a man who might have brought a particular pair of shoes in here to be repaired fairly often," Rutter said, showing the cobbler his warrant card. "He's about five feet eleven tall. And he has blonde hair and a blonde moustache – both of them neatly trimmed."

"Foreign accent?" the cobbler asked.

"Foreign? You mean, like French or something?"

The old man shook his head. "Nay, lad. Like yours. Not Yorkshire. Well, not quite as foreign as yours. From Liverpool, or somewhere like that."

Rutter felt his pulse start to race. The Alex Conway whose birth certificate Sergeant Dash had come up with had been born in Liverpool – which would explain how he came to know Robbie Peterson. "He might well be a Liverpudlian," he told Mr Johnson.

"Well, there's a turn up for th' books," the old man said, giving a dry, rasping chuckle.

"Have I said something funny?" Rutter asked, bemused.

"If he's the man I think he is, then you're dead wrong on the height," the cobbler explained. "But sithee, that's hardly surprisin'."

"What do you mean by that?" Rutter said, but the old man had already turned and was making his way, crab-like, back into the bowels of the shop.

The cobbler returned a couple of minutes later, holding a pair of black shoes in his hands. They looked well-cared for, Rutter noted, although there were signs, on one instep, of the leather cracking.

"Beautiful things," the old man said, laying the shoes on the

174

counter for Rutter to examine. "Look at the great workmanship. That stitching alone's a work of art."

"So they're not factory made?"

The old man tut-tutted. "Definitely not. They was made by a craftsman who loved his trade. There aren't so many of us left now."

Rutter picked up one of the shoes. "Did you happen to notice what he was wearing when he brought these in?"

"Of course I noticed," the old man said. "It's my job to notice."

"And what *was* he wearing?" Rutter asked, doing his best to hide his exasperation.

"Various things. No definite style or colour. Sometimes black, sometimes brown, now an' again suede. He even come in once wearing a pair of them daft things with pointed toes."

"Were they custom made as well?"

The old man shook his head. "They were decent quality – at least what passes as decent quality these days – but they weren't in th' same class as the one's you're lookin' at."

There was something wrong with these shoes, Rutter thought. Something about the insides, just above the heel.

"It's never bothered me, bein' small," the old cobbler said.

"I beg your pardon?"

"Bein' small. It's never bothered me. But it must bother him, or he'd never have spent so much money on a pair of elevator shoes."

It was too early in the day for there to be much business at the fairground, and the Green brothers were both sitting sullenly on the painted wooden fence which led up to the pay box. They had been watching Woodend, DI Chatterton and the two uniformed constables ever since the four men first came into sight, but now, as the policemen stopped in front of the ghost train, they gave no sign of even knowing that they were there.

Woodend stepped forward. "I'd like a guided tour," he said to the elder brother, "and I'd like *you* to take me on it."

Clem Green sneered. "Got a search warrant you can show me?" he asked.

175

Woodend beamed at him. "I don't need one, Sunshine," he said. "The Ghost Train is owned by Mrs Doris Peterson – and she's given us her permission to look around all we want."

Led by the reluctant Clem Green, Woodend and Chatteron walked carefully down the track, past papier maché skulls and crudely carved wooden skeletons. The rafters were not the crumbling oak beams of which haunted houses are made, but blunt, unadorned steel girders. Deprived of its lighting effects, and the illusion created by the speed of the journey, the tunnel looked makeshift and seedy. The track twisted and turned, and, almost before they knew it, Green was pushing open the double doors that led to the exit.

"Satisfied?" he asked Woodend, once they were on the outside again.

"You'd be surprised if I said yes, wouldn't you?" the Chief Inspector asked. "Where's the engine?"

Green pointed to the buttons and levers next to the pay box. "That's it."

Woodend leant over until his face was almost touching Green's. "Maybe most of the bobbies you know are thick enough to swallow that, but I'm certainly not," he said. "That's the control panel, lad. Where's the bloody thing that drives this lot?"

For a split second, Clem Green looked as if he might make a run for it, but the two constables were watching him closely, and it was obvious to him he wouldn't get more than a few yards. Slowly, fatalistically, he turned round and led Woodend back into the tunnel.

It was not surprising that they had missed the door to the engine room the first time through. It was hidden by the figure of a decapitated monk, the severed head residing under one arm and grinning ghastlily from the power of a sixty-watt light bulb.

Green took hold of the catch and pulled, and both monk and door swung outwards, to reveal a fair-sized room.

Green stepped back. "It's in there. You want to take a closer look?"

"I most certainly do," Woodend said. "But if you don't mind, I rather think I'd like to follow you."

Green stepped inside, with Woodend at his heel. The engine was big, but it took up less than half the area inside the room. Not that the rest was empty. There was a camp bed, with filthy sheets and blankets on it – used no doubt when one of the Green brothers had to stay on guard duty – but most of the space, floor to ceiling, was crammed with cartons of cigarettes.

Woodend turned to look at Clem Green. "Heavy smoker, are you, son?" he asked genially.

Eighteen

Clem Green had not spoken a word since the discovery of the thousands of cartons of cigarettes, and now, back in Robbie Peterson's office, with the two constables guarding the door, he still showed no inclination to open up.

"I think you might be able to help us find Robbie Peterson's murderer," Woodend said.

Green stared at a point on the wall two feet above the Chief Inspector's head, but said nothing.

"Don't you want his killer brought to justice?" Woodend asked.

"It's no skin off my nose one way or the other," Green muttered.

No, it probably wasn't, Woodend thought. People like Clem Green had no idea of what society was or how it operated. To him, the law was not something designed to create order – it was an inconvenience which should be side-stepped as often as possible. "Tell me everything you know about Alex Conway," he said.

Green's eyes remained firmly fixed on the wall. "Never heard of him."

"He may be goin' under another name. He's good at doing that. But he's the man you did business with in Doncaster."

"Didn't do business with no man in Doncaster. Didn't do business with no man anywhere."

"It's too late to play the innocent," Woodend told him. "We found you with a room full of stolen fags, for God's sake."

"Don't know nothin' about them," Green said.

Woodend sighed. The trouble with dealing with petty criminals like Clem Green was that they were often too stupid to appreciate their own position. In the face of the evidence, most men would be trying to negotiate the best deal they could for themselves. All Green was offering was sullen defiance.

"Look, there isn't any way in the world you're goin' to walk away with this charge," the Chief Inspector said. "You'll be goin' back to prison whatever else happens. The question is, how much porridge will you do? Now, if we arrest Alex Conway, we'll charge him not only with the murder of Robbie Peterson, but also with bein' the big wheel behind the smugglin' racket. If we can't find him, well, we'll probably say it was entirely your operation. And that could have a significant effect on your sentence. So come on, Clem, tell me how I can collar him."

"I've never heard of no Alan—"

"Alex."

". . . no Alex Conway. An' somebody must have put them fags in the engine room since the last time I looked in there."

Woodend shook his head despairingly. "I'd really advise you to think it over very carefully, lad. An' soon. Because if we find Conway on our own, we won't need your help any more. An' if *you* haven't helped us, there's really no reason why *we* should help *you*." He turned towards the constables standing in the doorway. "Take him down to Maltham Central," he said. "Maybe a few hours in the cells'll drum some sense into him."

The Green brothers had been gone for only five minutes when Inspector Chatterton arrived with Harold Dawson. The journalist/photographer looked his normal seedy self, but now there was an added element – he was twitchy, too. The overall impression he gave, Woodend thought, was of one of those dirty old men who waited to talk to little boys outside public lavatories.

"It was good of you to come, Mr Dawson," the Chief Inspector said.

"Good of me?" the reporter repeated. "I wasn't given much choice, was I?"

Woodend turned his attention to Chatterton. "I do hope you've not been intimidatin' Mr Dawson, Inspector," he said, pulling a wry face. "I'm very keen on maintainin' good relations with the press."

For once Chatterton seemed to get the joke, and grinned. "All I did was suggest that if he didn't want to come here, we could have our little talk down at the station, sir. He didn't seem too keen on that idea, so here we are."

"Take a seat, Mr Dawson," Woodend said, pointing to the chair on the other side of the desk.

"I'd prefer to stand," the journalist replied.

"Oh, for goodness sake, take the weight off your feet," Woodend said exasperatedly. "It's making me tired just looking at you."

Unwillingly, Dawson sat.

"Strictly speakin', this matter is none of my affair, but Mr Chatterton has been kind enough to allow me a few minutes with you," Woodend said.

"What matter?" Dawson asked belligerently. "I haven't a clue what you're talking about."

Woodend reached into the drawer and produced several bulky brown envelopes. He place them on the desk and divided them into two piles, a large one and a small one.

"Pornographic photographs," he said, indicating the larger pile. "Nasty, filthy muck, but very well done. The work of a professional, I would say. A professional who works locally. And how do I know that he works locally? Because Mr Chatterton here recognises the woman who's the star of most of the pictures. Isn't that right, Inspector?"

"Down at the station, we call her Ten-bob Mary," Chatterton confirmed. "Been on the game in Maltham for years."

Woodend pulled one of the photographs out of an envelope and held it up for Dawson to see. "She must have rubber bones to be able to do that," he said.

"What's all this got to do with me?" Dawson asked.

"Oh, that's easy to answer," Woodend said. "You're the photographer, and Robbie Peterson, that well-known art lover, was the distributor."

"I never—"

"Shut up!" Woodend said loudly. "I haven't finished yet. This lot," he indicated the smaller pile of envelopes, "is even more interestin'."

He removed a photograph and laid it in front of Dawson. It was not particularly hot in the office, but he noticed that tiny droplets of sweat were forming on the photographer's brow.

"Now the quality's not as good as the ones in the other batch," Woodend said, "but considerin' the conditions you were workin' under, it's still not bad."

Dawson's eyes were fixed firmly on the wall, just as Clem Green's had been earlier.

"Why don't you look at the picture, Mr Dawson?" Woodend suggested.

"I don't want to," Dawson muttered.

"Look at it!" Woodend snapped, in a voice that startled even Inspector Chatterton.

Dawson reluctantly picked up the glossy photograph.

"What can you tell me about it?" Woodend asked.

"It's a picture of a copse of trees."

"Accordin' to Mrs Clough, it's called Sutton's Copse," Woodend said. "It's just beyond the caravan site, an' it's a favourite spot for courtin' couples. Now you're the expert, Mr Dawson. Perhaps you could help me out here. What time of day would you say this picture was taken at?"

"From the shading, I'd guess it was taken in early evening," Dawson said reluctantly.

"Time of year?"

"Is this necessary?" Dawson protested.

"Time of year?" Woodend repeated.

"The trees are in full leaf, so it's probably late spring or early summer."

"Can you see anythin' else apart from the trees in the picture?"

"Two figures. It's impossible to say whether they're men or women, but they seem to be bending down."

Woodend handed several more photographs across to Dawson. As the series progressed, the photographer got closer and closer to his subjects. For the final one, he couldn't have been more than a few feet away. It was a side-on view. It was not a good composition

– there were too many blurred trees – but the centre of the picture was well in focus.

The figures were on the ground now, one on top of the other. The lower one was a woman, her skirt billowing around her waist. The upper was a man; his trousers were round his ankles, his naked backside was stuck up in the air, pale and mottled. His face was turned towards the camera and there was a look of horror on it, registering the fact that he had spotted the photographer.

"Read the back," Woodend ordered.

"Alice Priddy, Tom Tideswell. June 18th," Dawson said mechanically.

"There are six sets of photographs," Woodend told him. "Six poor sods who have probably been payin' through the nose for their bit of fun. It must have been quite easy, really. They came up here, had a few drinks in The Hideaway, and started to feel amorous. With the combination of alcohol and passion, they weren't likely to be very careful. And once they were on the job, it would probably have taken a peal of bells in their ears to disturb them. Even if they did notice in the end – as this Tideswell feller seems to have done – well, it didn't really matter, because you had that well-known hard-case, Robbie Peterson, along with you for protection."

"It wasn't Ro—" Dawson began, before he realised what he was saying.

"What was that, Mr Dawson?"

"Robbie Peterson might have been involved in this, but I can assure you that I wasn't."

"I assume you started out just with the smut, and then Robbie came up with the idea of blackmail," Woodend said, ignoring Dawson's protest. "How much did he give you as your share? Half?"

"You can't prove any of this," Dawson said defiantly, mopping his brow with his handkerchief. "You wouldn't be badgering me like this if you could."

Woodend did not look in the least dismayed. "Maybe you're right," he said. "Only you know for sure whether that's true or not."

"What do you mean?" Dawson asked, as some of his new-found courage started to desert him.

"You don't seem to me to be the kind of man to leave yourself without insurance – especially when you were dealin' with a feller like Robbie Peterson. So I'm bettin' that after you developed your mucky pictures, you gave most of them to Robbie, but kept some of the prints back for yourself. That's why I asked Inspector Chatterton to get a search warrant sworn out – and why he's havin' your house gone over at this very moment. You may have destroyed the pictures after Robbie was killed, of course, but I'm bankin' on you bein' too greedy."

Dawson licked his dry lips as the bolt hit home. "I . . . is there anything I can do to make things easier for myself?" he asked, after he'd had time to consider his position.

"Maybe," Woodend conceded. "We'd certainly show our appreciation if you could tell us where we might find Mr Alexander Conway."

"Who?" Dawson asked.

"Alexander Conway. I thought you might have heard the name durin' your business dealin's with Robbie."

"I never had any dealings with Robbie."

"It's a bit late to start pleadin' the innocent now, don't you think?" Woodend said, suddenly angry.

Dawson held up his hands in a placatory gesture. "I'm not denying I took the photographs," he said, "and I knew what they were used for. But Robbie never mentioned them to me. He was too smart for that. Didn't want the trail leading back to him if anything went wrong."

"So who *did* you deal with?"

"That son-in-law of his. That Terry. He was the one who paid me. And he was the one who minded me when I went out takin' photographs of all those couples on the nest."

Terry Clough had sworn he had had nothing to do with Robbie's rackets, but now Woodend found himself wondering why he had ever accepted such a ludicrous statement at face value. Clough had worked for Robbie in Liverpool. Clough had married Jenny because Robbie had asked him to. Was it really very likely that if Peterson had wanted him to help run the rackets around Swann's Lake, Clough would have had the strength of character to resist?

"There is one more thing, Mr Dawson," Woodend said. "And you might as well be honest, because whatever your answer, nothing bad's going to happen to you as a result of it. It was you who tried – but failed – to break into this office the other night, wasn't it?"

"I never was much good with my hands," Dawson said.

"I take it you were hopin' to get the photographs back."

"That's right," Dawson admitted. "I thought this was where Robbie would keep them. That's why I kept trying to find excuses to be left in the office alone. Were they here?"

"No," Woodend said.

"So where *did* you find them?"

"In the engine room of the ghost train. Along with about fifty thousand fags and a few crates of whisky."

Dawson shook his head in reluctant admiration. "He was cunning bastard, that Robbie, wasn't he?" he said.

"If he was *that* cunnin', how come he's dead?" Woodend asked dryly.

The time he'd spent in the Maltham holding cells had done Gerry Fairbright no good at all. He hadn't shaved, and as a result had grown dark stubble on his chin and upper lip. It didn't suit him. The rest of his face was no more appealing. His eyes were hollow and his jaw quivered spasmodically. When Woodend invited him to sit down, he virtually collapsed into the metal chair.

"What amazes me, Mr Fairbright," the Chief Inspector said, "is that for the last two days you've been content to sit and wait things out in a police station cell."

"Content!" Fairbright retorted. "I've hated every bloody minute of it."

"An' yet you did nothin' about it. You didn't ask for a solicitor, you didn't request bail. You didn't even call your wife."

For a second, Woodend thought that Fairbright was going to cry. "I'm supposed to be on a special plant refittin' job in Port Talbot this week," he said. "That's where my wife thinks I am anyway, and I don't want her to know no different. Though Christ knows what I'm goin' to say when she asks me for my pay packet."

Woodend held up some of the photographs he'd found in the ghost train engine room. "These might be what you were lookin' for when you broke into the office," he said. "Who's the lady?"

"Her name's Elsie," Fairbright said. "She's married, like me."

"How do you get on with your wife?" Woodend asked.

"I love her," Fairbright replied, as though he considered it a particularly stupid question.

"So what the hell were you doin' playin' away from home?"

Fairbright shrugged. "The way I saw it, I was only makin' up for lost time – sowin' the wild oats I never got to sow when I was a lad."

"You're a bloody fool," Woodend said. "You know that, don't you?" He slid the photographs across the desk. "Here you are. They're yours. A little souvenir."

Fairbright picked up the photographs with trembling hands. Relief flooded his face, rapidly followed by fear.

"Does my missus have to know about these?" he asked.

Woodend smiled. "No," he said. "She doesn't. Nobody does. There's nothin' illegal about having a bit on the side, although in your case I would have thought the anxiety outweighed the pleasure. How much was it costin' you to keep Robbie Peterson quiet?"

"Two quid a week," Fairbright said. "That was enough of a strain, but then Terry Clough came up to me on Saturday night an' told me Robbie had decided to raise it to three and . . ." He stopped suddenly, the horrified expression on his face showing that he'd realised how what he'd just said gave him an even stronger motive for killing Peterson. "I didn't . . . I wouldn't . . . I couldn't . . ." he gasped.

"If you'd killed Robbie Peterson, you'd also have searched for your photographs," Woodend said kindly. "And there was no evidence of anythin' in the office being disturbed. Besides, you wouldn't just have had to kill Robbie, you'd have had to get rid of Terry as well."

"That's . . . that's true," Fairbright said gratefully. "And I didn't, did I? I mean, I'm not sayin' I killed Robbie but I *didn't* kill Terry. I'm sayin'—"

"I know what you're sayin', Mr Fairbright," Woodend interrupted. "Were you really down by the lake at the time Peterson was killed?"

"No," Fairbright admitted.

"So where were you?"

"Hangin' around the club, waitin' for a chance to break into this office."

"So why did you lie?"

"I finally plucked up the nerve to come an' have a look about ten minutes before Robbie was found," Fairbright muttered. "The office was in darkness an' the door was slightly open. I stepped inside an' then . . . an' then I lost my nerve. Robbie must already have been dead by then, but I thought if I told you I'd been here, you'd think it was me what killed him."

Woodend tried to picture Fairbright murdering Robbie Peterson. Creeping into the darkened office where Robbie was asleep at the desk. Taking a nail from the box and picking up the hammer. Placing the nail against Peterson's temple and striking it so hard that it penetrated the brain. No, he just couldn't see it. The murder had not been committed by an ordinary person. A killing of such a nature required either a man with ice in his veins or one driven on by complete desperation – and it was impossible to see Gerry Fairbright in either of those roles.

"All right, you can go now, Mr Fairbright," he said.

"Go?" Fairbright repeated. "Go where?"

"Wherever you want to. But I'd recommend you head straight home to Oldham."

"I . . . I don't have to go back to Maltham police station?"

"No," Woodend said. "I've persuaded Inspector Chatterton that in view of the strain you were under, it would be wisest to let you off this time."

"But I've already been charged."

"Charge sheets get lost sometimes. It's regrettable, but it happens."

Fairbright looked around the office as if he suspected this was all a trick, and any second half a dozen bobbies, truncheons in their hands, would come bursting out of the filing cabinet. "I can *really* go?" he asked. ıf

"Yes," Woodend said. "But I was you, Mr Fairbright, I'd think twice before I opened my fly buttons the next time."

"I will," Fairbright said. "I promise I will."

He stood up and rushed out of the door. Woodend watched him making his way back to his caravan – uncertainly, as if he still suspected a trick. "Good luck, Mr Fairbright," the Chief Inspector said softly. "Because when you get back home to your missus and haven't got that fat wage packet from Port Talbot with you, you're certainly going to need it."

Jenny Clough had crossed the yard five times since Fairbright had made his hurried exit from the office, Woodend counted. Each time, she'd walked as far as the gate to the caravan site, stood there for a while – gazing at the office window – and then returned to the house. She looked like a lost child, the Chief Inspector thought, and in a way, he supposed, that was exactly what she was.

On her sixth trip across the yard, Jenny hesitated for a second, then strode over to the office and knocked on the open door.

"Come in, lass," Woodend said.

"I'd . . . I'd rather you came out," Jenny told him. "I . . . I still can't face being in the office."

"Is something the matter?" Woodend asked, then cursed himself for being so insensitive. "I mean – well, you know what I mean."

"You remember what you said about us having a talk like two ordinary people?" Jenny asked.

"I remember."

"I'd really like to have that talk right now, if you can spare the time."

" 'Course I can, lass."

Woodend stood up, and walked around the desk to the door. Jenny was not looking good, he thought. Her face – her whole bearing – seemed to have altered since her fight with her sister. There had been lines of grief for Robbie before then, but now

187

there was hollowness in her cheeks, a pinchedness about her nose, a despair in her eyes.

"Would you like a cup of tea?" Jenny asked. "It's already made."

"That would be grand," Woodend agreed.

He followed Jenny into the living room, which, like the office, seemed to have been furnished on the principle that if it cost a lot, it must be in good taste.

"Take a seat," Jenny said.

"Thanks, lass," Woodend said, heading towards the leather rocker which had its back to the window.

"No! Not there!" Jenny said, with a hint of panic in her voice.

Woodend switched directions and lowered himself into one of the armchairs. "You're goin' to have to let it go in the end, lass," he said gently, as he watched Jenny pour out the tea.

"Let *what* go?" Jenny asked.

Woodend sighed. "You're goin' to have to get used to the fact that your dad's gone. You can't stay out of the office for ever, an' you can't get into a 'tiswas every time somebody sits in his favourite chair."

Jenny passed him his tea. Her hand was trembling and the cup rattled in the saucer. "Do you have a family, Chief Inspector?" she asked, unexpectedly.

"A wife and a daughter," Woodend said. "My daughter's called Annie, just like your sister. Well, not really, just like her. I mean, it's not short for Annabel or anythin' like that."

"Do you love your wife, Mr Woodend?"

"I beg your pardon?" Woodend said, not sure he'd heard her correctly.

"I asked you if you loved your wife."

There'd been no mistake. She had actually voiced the question. He wondered what had motivated her, and guessed that it was not so much to learn something about him as to understand something about herself *through* him.

"You don't have to answer me if you don't want to," Jenny said.

"I don't mind," Woodend told her. "Do I love Joan? Yes, I

do. Maybe I don't feel the burnin' passion I felt when we first got married, but yet in some ways I think I love her *now* more than I've ever done. Over the years, she's become part of me."

"And have you ever been unfaithful to her?"

It was an impertinent question, by any standards, but again Woodend had the distinct impression that there was a purpose behind it. "I've been tempted to stray a couple of times," he said honestly, thinking about Liz Poole, "but I've never succumbed."

"Tell me about your father," Jenny said, suddenly changing direction.

"What do you want to know about him?"

Jenny shrugged, as if she didn't know the answer herself. "Anythin'."

"He's dead now," Woodend said. "He worked in the mills up in Lancashire. He was a tackler – it was his job to fix the looms when they went wrong." He could read in her face that was not what she wanted from him. He tried harder. "You could always depend on my dad. He wasn't like some fathers who say they'll take you out fishin' and never do. If he'd promised we were going down to the river on Sunday, we went – even if it was pourin' down with rain."

"Did people like him?"

"Oh, I suppose he was popular enough. He had his mates down at the pub and the cronies he raced his whippets with. There was a decent turn-out at his funeral. But he didn't what you might call – stick out. If he thought he was in the right, he could be as determined as buggery, but most of the time he just drifted through life without leavin' much impression."

"But you loved him, didn't you?"

Woodend chuckled. "Oh aye. He was me dad, and when I was little, I thought he was the best feller in the world." He was hit by an unexpected revelation. "I still do think that, as a matter of fact," he said.

A tear fell from Jenny's eye, making a dark stain on her white blouse. Woodend noticed that even her breasts seemed to have lost their firmness and thrust. It was as if she was contracting into herself.

"I mustn't keep you from your work," she said. "You can find your own way out, can't you?"

Then she stood up and ran into the kitchen.

The police car pulled into The Hideaway's yard just as Woodend was leaving the house, and a uniformed constable with a brown paper envelope in his hand got out of it. "Inspector Chatterton's sends this with his compliments, sir," he said, handing the envelope over.

"Any idea what's in it?" Woodend asked.

"Mr Chatterton said it's from the passport office in Liverpool. Apparently you put in a request for somebody's application."

Alexander Conway's passport application! Finally there was a chance of tracking the bloody man down. First there would be a picture of him, which – even though passport photographs were notoriously distorting – was worth a thousand words of written description. Secondly, and perhaps even more importantly, someone – a professional person who had known Conway for years – would have to have signed the photograph to certify that it was a good likeness. And there was a very good chance that that person, whoever he was, would be able to lead them to wherever Conway was hiding.

Woodend took the envelope into the office, slit it open and pulled out the form. The photograph was clipped to the corner of the application. Conway appeared to be much as witnesses had described him – except that no one had mentioned the heavy spectacles he was wearing.

The Chief Inspector ran his eyes down the form. Conway had given the flat in Doncaster as his home address, and under occupation had written 'company director'. That was only to be expected – but the name of the guarantor took Woodend completely by surprise.

"Bloody hell!" he said aloud, hardly able to believe his eyes.

The man who had vouched for Conway claimed to have known the man for ten years. His occupation was listed as 'teacher', and it wouldn't be at all difficult to contact him, because he lived very close to Swann's Lake. His name was Michael Clough.

Nineteen

Just from the way Rutter walked across the yard, holding the brown paper bag in front of him like a trophy of war, Woodend could tell that his sergeant had met with success in Doncaster. And if any more proof were needed, there was the fact that the Sergeant did little more than nod to his boss before upending the bag and tipping the shoes onto the desk.

"Elevator heels," he announced. "We've been looking for a man of around five feet eleven, when we should have been after someone who was at least three or four inches shorter."

Woodend shook his head despairingly. How many false leads would there be on this bloody case? he wondered. "Sit down, lad," he said. "Sit down, an' we'll see if we can make any sense of this."

Rutter straddle the chair opposite him. "All the way back in the car I've been asking myself why he should wear elevator heels, and the only answer I could come up with was vanity."

"Did you ask the cobbler if he was wearin' elevator heels when he took these shoes in to be repaired?" Woodend asked.

"Yes, I did. And he wasn't."

"Then it's not vanity," Woodend said. "If it had been, all his shoes would have built-in lifts."

"They're an expensive item to buy," Rutter pointed out.

"Everythin' in the flat was expensive," Woodend countered. "Whatever else Alex Conway is, he's not short of a bob or two."

"So what's your theory?" Rutter asked.

"I'm not sure how this will work, so bear with me," Woodend said. "He wants to look taller when he's in Doncaster, but anywhere else he couldn't give a toss. An' since he isn't in Doncaster that often, he only needs one pair of shoes."

191

Sally Spencer

"But if being short doesn't bother him in other places, why should it have bothered him in Doncaster?"

Woodend picked up the passport photograph and showed it to his sergeant. "What's the one recurrin' theme runnin' through all the descriptions we've had of him?" he asked.

"Blond hair and pale moustache?" Rutter hazarded.

"Spot on," Woodend agreed. "But you're missin' out one important thing in that description."

Rutter frowned. "I'm afraid I'm not following you, sir."

"Why did you think he might have been a military man?"

The light of understanding dawned in Rutter's eyes. "Because they were always so well trimmed!"

"Or perhaps they don't need trimmin' at all."

"A wig and a false moustache!" Rutter exclaimed. "But surely, if that were true, the librarian – Miss Noonan – would have told you about it.

"Not after she started to suspect we might want to lock him away," the Chief Inspector said. He took a Capstan Full Strength from the packet on his desk and lit up. "So let's assume the hair and moustache are fake. Seen from that angle, the shoes are no more than part of his disguise. But it isn't a disguise he wears all the time, or there'd have been more pairs of shoes. So the question is, why does he only feel the need of a disguise in Doncaster?"

"Maybe there's someone there he doesn't want to recognise him," Rutter said.

"Like who?"

Rutter shrugged. "Some other gangster who he's done the dirty on in the past?"

"Then he's taking a hell of a chance being in Doncaster *at all*. Besides, he's probably from Liverpool – he wouldn't have known the other Alex Conway if he wasn't – and if he's got enemies, *that's* where they'll be."

"Maybe it's to disguise himself from *himself*," Rutter said suddenly.

"How do you mean?"

"I suppose it was what Maria did which gave me the idea . . ." Rutter began. Then he stopped, and put his hands up to his

192

head. "Oh God, my mind's been so much on the case that I haven't thought about her since I entered that shoe shop. Just what kind of heartless bastard does that make me?"

"You're not doin' any good worryin' about her," Woodend said. "An' it's not what *she'd* want you do."

"I know."

"So why don't you tell me your idea?"

Rutter took a deep breath. "A few weeks back, she got very depressed," he said. "There were lots of reasons for it – she was worried about her father's health, she didn't like her new supervisor, the situation was getting very bad in Spain. I was really concerned about her. Then, one day, out of the blue, she turned up all bright and chirpy."

"What's the point?" Woodend asked.

"It wasn't that all her problems had magically disappeared overnight, just that she had decided to adopt a new, more positive attitude to them. She *looked* different too. Physically, I mean. I thought at first that it was just that she was more animated. But it wasn't. She'd had her hair done. A completely new style. New attitude – new look."

His sergeant might just be onto something, Woodend thought. After all, didn't his own wife always buy a new frock when she felt she was getting into a rut? And wasn't that new frock always a contrast to everything else in her wardrobe?

And then there was Annie Peterson – pretty, mixed-up Annie – who always wore revealing dresses and heavy make-up, as if to convince herself that she fitted into the new life she'd chosen for herself.

A new person – a new start. Woodend's mind was going into overdrive. "Get me somethin' out of the filing cabinet," he said to his sergeant.

"Something?" Rutter repeated quizzically. "Nothing specific?"

"A receipt," Woodend said impatiently. "A manifest. A letter. Anythin' will do."

Maria had been dozing, but now she was awake again. She could hear the birds chirping happily in the hospital grounds, and feel the breeze which blew in through the open window, carrying with it the subtle fragrance of flowers. She wished she could see the birds and the flowers, but her world, as it had since Monday morning, contained nothing but darkness.

"Are you there, Joan?" she asked.

"Yes, I'm here," came a soft voice from somewhere to her right.

"It hasn't worked," Maria said as calmly as she could muster.

"What hasn't worked?"

"The operation. I know it. I can feel it. When they take the bandages off my eyes on Sunday, it won't make any difference at all."

"There's no point in speculatin'," Joan Woodend told her. "Why worry yourself unnecessarily. You'll be far better off if you just wait and see."

The second the words were out of her mouth, she realised her mistake. Wait and *see*. Oh God, what a thing to say!

But Maria didn't seem to notice – or if she did, pretended not to. "I think Bob was planning to ask me to marry him," she said.

"So do I," Joan said candidly.

"Do you think he'll still ask if the operation's a failure?"

There was a pause which seemed to Maria to last for a thousand years, then Joan said, "Yes, I do."

"So do I," Maria said, a tear slowly coursing down her cheek. "I know it wouldn't be fair to accept. I really do. Why should he be saddled with a blind woman for the rest of his life?" She clutched her bed sheet tightly with both hands. "But sometimes I get . . . so scared . . . of being alone that I worry I might say yes."

Clem Green, looking no less shifty after his arrest than he had before it, was already sitting at the interview table in Maltham police station when Woodend arrived. The Chief Inspector pulled out the chair opposite him and sat down.

"Mr Chatterton called to tell me you wanted to speak to me," he said.

"That's right," Green agreed. "I've been thinkin' over what

you said this mornin'. I don't see why me an' our Burt should take the whole rap for this. I want to make a deal."

Woodend shook his head. "You're too late, lad. The deal was that if you could tell us somethin' which might lead us to Alex Conway, I'd ask the local bobbies to go easy on you. Well, we know where Conway is now, so we don't need you any more. You should have taken your chance while you had it. Now, since they can't send your boss to jail – on account of him being dead – they're likely to try an' get the maximum sentences they can for you an' your brother."

Green threw back his heard and roared with laughter.

"I wouldn't have thought I'd said anythin' particularly funny," Woodend said

"Funny?" Clem Green spluttered. "It's bloody side-splittin'. With my *boss* dead, you said! You really have got it all wrong about Robbie Peterson, ain't you?"

Terry Clough shuffled into Peterson's office, looked suspiciously over his shoulder at the two uniformed officers who were standing by the door, then slid into the chair Woodend was gesturing towards. "What's this all about?" he asked.

Woodend held out the brown envelope which had first put him on the trail of Alex Conway. "Do you know what was in this envelope originally?" he asked.

Clough's eyes flickered for the briefest of moments. "I've no idea."

"A passport," Woodend told him. "But later it had another use. Somebody drew a sketch map on it – a sketch map which showed where to drop off all those stolen cigarettes we found in the ghost train."

"That's of no interest to me," Clough said. "I told you, I kept well clear of Robbie's rackets."

"Yes, you did say that," Woodend agreed. "But you were lyin' through your teeth. Harold Dawson is prepared to swear that you and he were both involved in the blackmailing of Hideaway customers. So is Gerry Fairbright – an' he should know, because he was of them."

Terry Clough's shoulders slumped. "All right, I admit it," he said. "But you don't know what Robbie Peterson was like. He'd have killed me if I hadn't helped him."

Woodend leant back in his chair. "When Robbie left Liverpool, he had every intention of going straight," he told Clough. "An' do you know somethin'? That's exactly what he did."

"I've no idea what you're talkin' about," Clough protested.

"Harold Dawson told me Robbie was too smart to be *seen* to be involved in the blackmail. Gerry Fairbright told me Robbie had just decided to up the amount of money he paid out every week. Neither of those things was true. All the people involved in the various rackets thought they were workin' for Robbie, but they weren't. They were workin' for *you*. You only said Robbie was behind it because while they might think of double crossin' a nobody like Terry Clough, it would never enter their heads to do the same to a hard case like Robbie Peterson."

"Who told you all this?" Clough demanded.

"Clem Green," Woodend said. "You made the mistake of tellin' him and his brother what the real situation was. An' I think I know *why* you did it. Everybody else involved in the rackets saw you only as Robbie's dogsbody, and while that was very useful, it was also gallin' not to have the respect you felt you deserved. You had to have *somebody* who knew you were the real boss, and you chose the Greens."

"Robbie was an idiot," Clough said. "There's a fortune to be made around here if only you've got the sense to see it."

"Robbie didn't want a fortune," Woodend told him. "The club and the attractions were bringin' in enough to keep him more than happy. I don't even know why you wanted one – unless you thought that you're bein' rich would impress your wife."

Terry Clough jerked as if he'd been given an electric shock. "I could have taken her places," he said. "Maybe even abroad. We could have had the best of everythin'."

Woodend shook his head sadly. "You really don't know Jenny at all, do you? Or maybe it's a case of thinkin' the way you do because it's too unpleasant to think any other way. But let's get back to the envelope."

"What about it?"

"I'll tell you what I think happened," Woodend said. "You were sittin' in this office and the phone rang. You picked it up and it was one of your mates from across the Pennines wantin' to fix up another drop. Only it was to be at a different place this time, and he needed to explain how to get there. You picked up the first piece of paper which came to hand, which happened to be this envelope. Careless of Robbie to leave it around, wasn't it?"

"I don't see why," Clough said sullenly. "It was only a used envelope. It wasn't even addressed to him."

"No," Woodend agreed. "It was addressed to Alex Conway. That's why the name sounded familiar when I mentioned it to you. Anyway, you drew the map – the police boffins should have no difficulty provin' it's your handwriting – but then you were careless, too. You lost the envelope. Have you any idea *where* you lost it?"

"No," Clough admitted. "It was just that when I came to look for it, I couldn't find it."

"Well, wherever it was, *Robbie* finds it," Woodend continued. "And given his dodgy background, he knows immediately what it's for. I imagine all this happens last Friday night, just before he's due to do his act in the club. So what does he do with the envelope? He sticks it in the back of the filing cabinet, intendin' to confront you with it later. But that never happens, does it? Because an hour later, he's dead."

Terry Clough jumped to his feet. "You're accusin' me of killin' him, aren't you?" he screamed.

Woodend shook his head. "No, I'm not accusin' you, so why don't you just calm down? You couldn't have murdered Robbie. You an' your brother were down by the lake at the time, havin' an argument over women. But even without a murder charge, you're in plenty of trouble, lad."

Terry Clough looked down the floor. "So what happens now?" he mumbled, almost to himself.

"Now you join your friends the Green brothers in Maltham nick," Woodend told him.

197

Twenty

The police car which brought Michael Clough to The Hideaway arrived only ten minutes after the one taking his brother into custody had left. The two detectives watched through the window as Clough got out of the car and, taking his time, walked towards the office.

"He doesn't seem very concerned that we've called him in," Rutter commented.

"Aye, there's nothin' defensive about yon bugger," Woodend agreed. "But that's the big difference between him an' his brother. Terry's quite rightly suspicious of authority, but Michael *likes* it – because it gives him somethin' to rail against. If we weren't what we are – the establishment – he couldn't be what he is – the rebel."

When he reached the open doorway, Clough stopped and knocked on the jamb, but the mocking expression on his face showed he was doing it more out of irony that politeness.

"Come in an' take a seat, Mr Clough," Woodend said. "We've got a fair bit to get through."

As soon as the young teacher had sat down, Woodend slid the passport application form across the desk to him. "You'll not deny that's your signature, will you?" he asked, jabbing with his finger at a point halfway down the form.

"No, it's mine all right," Clough agreed.

"An' you knew when you were fillin' it in that the person who was applyin' for the passport wasn't really Alex Conway?"

Michael Clough laughed. "Of course I did."

Woodend turned the form around and examined the photograph which was stapled to it. "That wig and false moustache aren't bad," he admitted. "The heavy glasses probably helped

198

as well. They certainly fooled us for a while. But then neither of us had ever met Robbie Peterson in the flesh. If we had, I expect we'd have seen the resemblance right away."

"It wasn't meant to fool anyone who knew him," Clough said haughtily. "It wasn't a disguise."

"I *know* it wasn't a disguise," Woodend replied. "The wig an' the glasses were more like actors' props – they were helpin' him to become a different person."

"I'm underrating you again," Michael Clough said apologetically.

"It was my sergeant who came up with the original idea. All I did was think it through to its logical conclusion," Woodend told him. "The way I see it, when Robbie was in Liverpool, he thought all he had to do to start a new life was get out of the rackets an' move somewhere else. Am I right?"

"You know you are."

"But it didn't work out like that, did it? It wasn't just that he brought his family with him – he brought his reputation as well. The villains in this area knew all about him – so did the police. And though the vicar an' the 'decent' families around Swann's Lake might not have known about his criminal activities, they could see immediately that he was not their sort of person. So there was no seat on the parish council for Robbie, an' no invitations to genteel tea parties for him and Doris."

"I told him it wouldn't work," Michael Clough said, "but he just wouldn't listen."

"No, he had to find out the hard way," Woodend agreed. "And he learned a valuable lesson from it. Robbie Peterson would always be constrained by the past, but Alex Conway, because he *had* no past, could be whatever he wanted to be."

"How did you find out about it?" Michael Clough asked.

"We compared his handwriting from one of the invoices with the handwriting on the passport application form," Rutter said. "We're neither of us experts, but it's a close enough match."

"We'd have found out before if Robbie hadn't been wearing shoes with elevator heels," Woodend said.

Clough looked perplexed. "I'm not sure I understand."

"No, you wouldn't, not havin' been in on the investigation,"

Woodend said dryly. " 'Conway's' neighbour, a sweet old bird called Miss Tufton, told my sergeant that she saw Robbie Peterson enterin' 'Conway's' flat once. She only got a brief glimpse of him, but it was enough for to her to identify him from a photograph. The conclusion we drew from that was that Robbie and 'Conway' were in some sort of racket together. If it hadn't been for the differences in their heights, we might have come to another conclusion – that what Miss Tufton had, in fact, seen was 'Conway' without his disguise."

"Will I face charges?" Michael Clough asked.

"For makin' a false declaration on the passport form? No, there doesn't seem to be a lot of point now that Robbie's dead." Ignoring Clough's reproaching glances, Woodend lit up a Capstan Full Strength. "So you're still goin' to marry Annie, are you?" he asked.

Clough nodded. "Yes I am."

"How long have you known about her dealin' in illegal drugs?"

"Not long," Clough admitted. "I learned about it from one of the boys at my school. His older brother had friends who were Annie's customers. He was worried his brother might become an addict, and so he came to me."

"Sensible lad," Woodend said.

"I'd talked her out of it, you know. Actually, it wasn't too hard – she'd already half-decided to give it up herself. The night she was arrested was going to be her last time."

Woodend looked him straight in the eye. "Do you love Annie, Mr Clough?" he asked.

Michael Clough seemed embarrassed by the question. "I think she loves me," he said. "I'm the only man who's treated her decently in years."

"That wasn't what I asked, an' you know it," Woodend said.

"She's got a lot of fine qualities," Clough replied. "I'm sure I'll *learn* to love her in time."

"And what about Jenny? Where does that leave her?"

"So you knew about that?"

"Not at first," Woodend admitted, "but there were so many little things which only made sense if that was the case. Like the night Robbie was killed, for example. You and your brother were down at the lake, talkin'. And what exactly were you talkin' *about*? It was about Jenny, wasn't it?"

"That's right," Clough admitted. "Terry had suspected something was going on between us for quite some time, but on Friday night he asked me straight out if it was true."

"An' what did you tell him?"

"That Jenny was going to divorce him and marry me."

"And that's when he hit you?"

"Yes. I didn't fight back. I felt I owed him at least one swing at me."

"There were other things that put me on the right track as well," Woodend continued. "Do you remember when I was interviewin' you about your movements on Friday night?"

"Of course I do."

"I couldn't see why you'd abandoned your committee meetin' to come to The Hideaway. You didn't seem like that kind of man. So what I suggested was that you'd come to meet the Peterson girl – and you reacted like I'd hit you in the face with a wet fish."

"Well, it was a bit of a shock," Michael Clough confessed.

"Of course it was," Woodend agreed. "And for a while, I thought it was because you were havin' a secret affair with Annie. But you weren't. What had happened was that we were talkin' about *different people*. My wife was a Howard before we got married. In London, she's called Joan Woodend, because the neighbours don't know any different. But around Preston she's Joan Howard, even now. There's only one Peterson girl to me – Annie. But to people who've been brought up around the family, there are two. For them, Jenny will be Jenny Peterson until the day she dies. And that's who you thought I meant – you thought I'd found out about your affair with Jenny."

"And *then* you knew it all?" Michael said, with just a trace of amused irony in his voice.

But Woodend found nothing amusing in the situation, because now that he knew that Conway was really Peterson – now that the veil had been lifted from his eyes and he was no longer chasing a criminal with a grievance – he had finally pieced together what had happened the night Robbie Peterson met his death.

"No," he said in answer to Michael's question. "Even then I didn't work it out. It was the scene between Jenny and Annie yesterday that finally did it. What could cause two sisters to fight with such ferocity? It could only be a man. An' if I needed anythin' else, there was the look on your brother's face when *he* worked out what the fight was about. Terry wanted to make a lot of money fast, so he could get Jenny away from here. Away from you! But after the fight he realised there was no longer a problem. Jenny couldn't have you because you'd chosen Annie instead."

"You're right," Michael Clough admitted.

"But it's still Jenny you love, isn't it?" Woodend demanded roughly.

"Oh yes," Clough said sadly. "It's still Jenny I love."

"Then why are you abandonin' her now?"

"Jenny's got Terry," Michael Clough said. "He might not be the ideal husband, but he loves her and he's capable of change – especially now Robbie's gone. Annie's got nobody. She needs me."

"You're way off the mark, lad," Woodend said.

"You don't think Annie needs me?"

"I *know* Jenny needs you more. She won't have Terry to stand by her – Terry will be goin' down for quite some time.

"Going down?" Michael repeated, incredulously.

"The problem about always tryin' to see the good side of people is that you don't see the bad side even when it's starin' you in the face. Your brother's both brighter and a lot more crooked then you'd ever have guessed."

"Oh God, my darling Jenny," Clough groaned.

"Aye, your darlin' Jenny," Woodend agreed dourly. "I think it's about time we had a word with her."

Annie Peterson, out on police bail, began counting the flowers on the living-room wall-paper for the sixth or seventh time and – again for the sixth or seventh time – lost her concentration less than halfway up the wall.

She lit a cigarette, then shredded the empty packet it had come from. Her life was a mess, she thought bitterly. And not only hers – the lives of everybody she touched were messes, too. It was easy to blame Robbie – she'd been doing that for years – but it was time to take some responsibility herself.

She thought back to her last conversation she'd had with her sister – the conversation which had ended with them fighting like two wild cats in the yard in front of The Hideaway. The words played in her head. Harsh. Accusing.

'Don't take Michael away from me,' Jenny had pleaded. *'I've suffered so much—'*

'Suffered!' Annie had replied heatedly. *'You don't know the meaning of the word. You got to stay at home. I was Robbie's experiment in social climbing.'* She'd laughed without humour. *'What a joke that was! Who did he ever hope to fool?'*

'He tried to do the best for all of us. It wasn't his fault he got it wrong.'

'Well it certainly wasn't mine,' Annabel had retorted. *'And now I've got the chance of being happy at last, I'm not going to let you stand in my way.'*

Yes, that was what she'd said. But even at the time there'd been at least a part of her which had realised it wasn't true. Michael and Jenny belonged together, and nothing good could ever come from splitting them up. And once she had admitted that to herself, it was obvious to her what *she* had to do.

"Mrs Clough isn't in the house," Rutter told his boss, through the open office door.

Woodend looked up from the report he was writing. "Then maybe she's in the club," he said abstractly.

"She isn't there, either."

Woodend sighed. "So ask Doris where she is. Really, Bob, I should have thought a detective sergeant was perfectly capable of—"

"Mrs Peterson doesn't know either," Rutter interrupted. "Says she hasn't seen her for a couple of hours."

The pen dropped out of Woodend's hand, and he was suddenly

giving his sergeant all his attention. "Are you sayin' she's disappeared?" he demanded.

Rutter laughed. "I wouldn't put it as melodramatically as that, sir."

"Wouldn't you?" Woodend asked, picking up the phone. "Well, I soddin' well would!" He dialled 999 rapidly. "Operator, put me through to Maltham Police." He covered the mouthpiece. "I should have anticipated this, Bob. I should have bloody known."

"Known what?" the puzzled Sergeant asked.

But by then the Chief Inspector had been put through. "This is Woodend . . . yes, Scotland Yard. Get me Inspector Chatterton as quickly as you can." There were several seconds pause before Woodend said, "Chatterton? . . . Jenny Clough's gone missin' . . . That's what I said. . . . I want her found as soon as possible. Put all your available men on the job. An' draft in as many as you can lay your hands on from other divisions. I want a search like there's never been in this area before. An' send a man round to Annie Peterson's. I want her picked up and bringin' down to The Hideaway."

Rutter listened with growing incredulity. When Inspector Chatteron had offered men to help in the murder inquiry, Cloggin'-it Charlie had said he couldn't use them, he reminded himself. Now Woodend seemed to be attempting to mobilise the whole of the Cheshire police force over a matter which couldn't be called anything more than trivial. Of course, there was some cause for concern when the daughter of a murdered man went missing, he admitted to himself – especially when that daughter looked as upset as Jenny Clough had been doing recently. But did an absence of a couple of hours really justify such a hullabaloo? And what business was it of Woodend's anyway?

The Chief Inspector put the phone down and the Sergeant saw that his face was ashen. Woodend reached for his cigarettes, lit one and inhaled deeply. What *was* the matter with him? Rutter wondered.

"I should have had her in here before I talked to Michael Clough," Woodend said, "but I didn't think there was any hurry. To tell the truth, I was probably deliberately puttin' it off. I can see now it was a big mistake – but it's too bloody late. God knows where she's gone, or what she's done."

Rutter sat down opposite his boss. "I've a few questions I'd like to ask about the investigation, sir," he said tactfully.

"The investigation?" Woodend repeated, as if he had no idea what Rutter was talking about.

Rutter suppressed a sigh. Woodend seemed to have completely lost his sense of balance – and the Sergeant had no idea why. Could it be that Jenny Clough had turned his head, just as Liz Poole had in the Salton case? Well, they said there was no fool like an old fool. But somebody had to snap him out of it – and quickly.

"I realise you're worried about Mrs Clough," he said, "but now we know that Conway can't be our killer—"

"The murder!" Woodend said, as if the pin had just dropped. "You're still worryin' your head about the murder, aren't you?"

"It is why we're here, sir," Rutter reminded him.

Woodend let out a deep sigh and looked at his protégé with disappointment in his eyes. "Bloody hell, lad, it's obvious who killed Robbie Peterson," he said. "An' after what happened to Maria, you should be in a better position than most people to work that out. There were only three—"

The phone rang, and Woodend wrenched it off its cradle. "Yes," he said. "Yes . . . yes . . . I see. Are you sure? . . . Well, tell your lads about her as well." He put down the phone and turned his attention back to Rutter. "That was Inspector Chatterton," he said grimly. "He's just had a report in from the man he sent to pick up Annie. Seems that she's disappeared an' all."

Twenty-One

The fairground was long since deserted, its flashing lights replaced by the pale glow of the moon, the gentle slap-slapping of the waves against the shore the only noise now that the hurdy-gurdy had been closed down for the night.

"I wonder where the hell they've gone," Woodend said worriedly, as he looked across the lake. "I'd give half my pension to know that right now."

"They'll be back," Rutter said. "Doris says Jenny's taken nothing with her, and Inspector Chatterton told me Annie's suitcase is still on top of her wardrobe."

"Oh, I never thought either of them was doing a runner," Woodend told him. "I just wish I knew where they were."

Rutter lit one of his cork-tipped cigarettes and held it up in front of him, like a firefly in the night. "Do you think the two of them are together?"

Woodend shook his head. "They're havin' enough difficulty handlin' their own misery, without dealin' with anyone else's."

A fork of lightning cut across the sky, soaking both the funfair and the lake in its eerie light. For a few seconds, the air sizzled softly, then was filled with the explosive anger of a loud clap of thunder.

"When I was a kid back in Lancashire, we used to believe that if we counted slowly after a flash of lightnin', then whatever number we'd reached by the time we heard the thunder was how many miles away the storm was," Woodend said.

"Actually there's a pretty solid scientific basis for that," Rutter told him. "You see, light travels faster than sound and—"

"Oh, to hell with science," Woodend said. "The way I see it is, when you're a kid it's very comforting to know what's comin', even if you don't know *why* it's comin'. The problem with us grown-ups is we forget the 'what' an' think too much about the 'how' and 'why'. That's what gets us into so much trouble."

A few drops of rain spattered on Rutter's shoulder. "I think we'd better get back to The Red Lion before the storm really arrives, sir," he said.

"What time is it?" Woodend asked.

Rutter took out his torch and shone it on his watch. "It's two-fifteen, sir. That probably explains why I'm so bloody tired."

Woodend didn't seem to notice the sarcasm. "Jenny's somewhere near here," he said, almost to himself. "She's *got* to be somewhere near here."

"You're wrong," Rutter said. "If she'd been within a couple of miles of Swann's Lake, the local bobbies would have found her."

"She wouldn't go far from home," Woodend mused, as if he hadn't heard his sergeant. "Home means security – an' Jenny's never been one to strike out on her own."

The rain was falling harder now, and starting to create small puddles in the indented clay beneath their feet.

Rutter felt a couple of drops of water wriggle their way past his shirt collar and slide down the back of his neck. "I really think we should make a move, sir," he said.

A second sheet of lightning, even brighter that the first, filled the night sky, exposing in its harsh glare the lakeside attractions – the roundabout, now shrouded in green canvas; the coconut shy, firmly shuttered; the ghost train, squat and menacing . . .

"Follow me . . ." Woodend said, as if he'd had a sudden inspiration.

"Where are we going?" Rutter asked.

". . . an' get your torch out again, because we're goin' to need it."

Woodend strode rapidly past the rifle range and hoop-la stall. When he reached the ghost train, he mounted the platform, then stepped straight down onto the track. He pushed against one of the swing doors with his hand, and felt it give.

"She'd have her own key," he said over his shoulder. "Or if she didn't, she'd know where to lay her hands on one."

He pushed the door open wide enough to step through the gap and held it there while Rutter followed him. The Sergeant ran the beam of his torch over the walls, spotlighting papier maché ghouls and crude plaster tarantulas.

From somewhere beyond the first bend in the track came a noise which sounded like a wooden crate hitting the metal rails.

"She's in here!" Woodend exclaimed. "I bloody knew she was in here. Christ, I hope we're not too late."

He was already running as he spoke. Twice, he stubbed his toes against the sleepers. Three times he almost lost his balance and only saved himself by slamming into the walls. Behind him, Rutter held the torch as steady as he could – and tried to avoid falling flat on his face.

They turned one bend and there was nothing ahead of them but more yards of empty track. Gasping for breath, they turned the second, and still there was no sign of Jenny Clough. It was only when they had rounded the third that they saw the body swinging from the steel beam.

Woodend grabbed Jenny around the waist and lifted her higher into the air. "My clasp knife!" he shouted to Rutter, as Jenny pummelled his head. "Get my bloody clasp knife! It's in my jacket pocket."

The Sergeant reached into his boss's pocket and pulled out the old-fashioned knife.

"Now cut through the noose," Woodend said. "An' for God's sake be quick about it."

Rutter found the box which Jenny Clough had stood on – the one they had heard falling as they entered the tunnel – and righted it. As he climbed onto it, Jenny lashed out with her left arm, knocking him to the ground.

"Get behind her," Woodend gasped, as he struggled to maintain his grip on the wriggling, kicking woman.

Rutter moved the box, mounted it again, and opened the clasp knife. Jenny was trying to speak – to scream – but her words came out as no more than a loud gurgle.

"Don't struggle, Jenny, luv," Woodend begged. "Please don't struggle."

Rutter tried to hold his torch with one hand and cut through the swinging rope with the other. But it wasn't working! It wasn't bloody working! He needed both hands to do a proper job. He dropped the torch and groped in the darkness for the rope. When he'd found it, he began to slice, hoping he didn't take his own hand off in the process. He could feel beads of sweat forming on his forehead. Christ, the rope was thick. Thick – and as hard as granite.

"Hurry up, lad," Woodend grunted. "I'm not sure how much longer I can hold her."

The rope finally gave. With that parting, Jenny Clough's resistance collapsed, and she went from being a writhing, clawing she-cat into nothing more than a dead weight. Woodend lowered her gently to the ground, but kept a firm hold on her. "Are you all right, lass?" he asked into the darkness.

"I left it too late, didn't I?" Jenny Clough croaked.

The sun was shining brightly across the interview room at Maltham police station. It was hard to believe that only a few hours earlier the thunder and lightning had been hurling their anger towards the earth. Woodend and Rutter sat side by side at one end of the table, and seated opposite them was the pale, dark-haired woman with the rope burns around her neck.

"The police doctor says it's all right for you to talk to us," Woodend told Jenny Clough, "but if you don't feel up to it, lass, you've only to say."

"I made the noose the moment I went into the tunnel," Jenny replied. "Then I just sat there for hours, looking at it. It was only when I heard the doors open that climbed on the box and slipped the rope over my neck."

"We know all that," Woodend said softly.

"Why did I wait so long?" Jenny asked, with anguish in her voice.

"It's always very hard to take that final step," Woodend said. "Wouldn't you rather talk about somethin' else?"

"Like what?"

"Tell me about your father."

"Nothing ever really worked out for Dad," Jenny said.

Sally Spencer

"Mum didn't love him. My sister didn't love him. But I did! *I* loved him."

"I know you did."

"Nobody but me appreciated what a hard time he'd had when he was growin' up. Nobody but me even noticed he was tryin' to put the past behind him." A tear formed in the corner of her eye and she brushed it away with her finger. "I would have done anythin' for him. I married Terry because that was what he wanted, and when he came to Swann's Lake, I came too – because I knew he'd have been lonely without me."

"An' then you fell in love with Michael Clough," Woodend said.

Jenny laughed. "Yes, that was ironic, wasn't it? I'd known him all my life – he was practically the boy-next-door – and suddenly I was hopelessly in love with him. And for the first time in my life, I understood what real happiness was." Her face clouded. "But you can't build a wall with your happiness, can you? You can't shut out the rest of the world with it."

"No," Woodend agreed. "You can't."

"There was still my dad, you see. I was sure that if I went off with Michael it would break his heart, because the way he'd see it, if I loved Michael so much, it must mean that I loved *him* less than I used to." She reached up with her hand and brushed a strand of hair out of her eyes. "But that wasn't the only thing that worried me. I was terrified Dad might be able to talk me out of it. Or talk Michael out of it. He'd already got rid of one man I wanted to marry – back in Liverpool – an' if history repeated itself, only much worse this time, I knew I'd wither up an' die."

Ah yes, the man in Liverpool. What exactly had Sid Dowd said about him? That he'd been a good-looking lad, but it was Robbie's money, not Jenny, that he'd been after. That Peterson had given the lad a stern warning and a hundred pounds – but if that hadn't worked, he wouldn't have hesitated over finding a more violent solution to his problem. Would the new Robbie Peterson – the one who had become Alex Conway – have acted in a different manner? There was no way of knowing now.

Woodend turned his attention back to Jenny Clough. "Tell me about what happened on Friday night," he said.

210

"I'd decided to tell Dad all about Michael and me before anybody else had the chance," Jenny said. "I knew he'd gone to the office, but when I got there, it was in darkness. I clicked the switch, but the light still wouldn't come on. And then I heard him snorin', and before I knew what I was doin', I was pickin' up the hammer and the nail." She stopped and looked into her palms, as if they contained a mirror through which she could see her own soul. "I'm a monster, aren't I?" she asked.

"No, lass, you're not," Woodend told her.

And he believed it. She was a loving worm who had finally turned. She was a slave to duty who had eventually found the burden too hard to bear. But she was not a monster.

"For what it's worth, I don't think you're a monster either," Bob Rutter said softly. "Would you like to tell us the rest of it now."

"There's no more to tell," Jenny said simply. "I killed him. It seemed the best way at the time. He wouldn't suffer, and I'd be savin' us both from a great deal of pain in the future. Only, it didn't work out like that, did it? I killed my lovely dad so I could marry Michael, an' now he doesn't want me any more. So it's all been for nothin'. Funny the way things turn out, isn't it?"

There was so often a pattern to these things, Woodend thought. The last murderer he had arrested in Cheshire had said exactly the same thing. "Funny the way things turn out, isn't it?" And because he was also trapped in that pattern – that process – he answered now just as he had done then. "Funny? Aye, it's bloody hilarious."

"You'll be at the trial, won't you?" Jenny asked.

"I'll have to be," Woodend told her. "They'll be wantin' to hear my evidence."

"When you're in the witness box, givin' your evidence, you will look at me, won't you? You won't just stare at the wall, as if I wasn't there?"

"Oh, I'll look at you," Woodend promised. "An' if I think I can get away with it, I might even risk a quick smile."

Annabel Peterson looked a mess. Her clothes were rumpled and soiled, her hair was bedraggled and her shoulders sagged. There

Sally Spencer

were large bags under her eyes. Woodend had no idea how long she had been standing outside her father's office, waiting for him to return from Maltham, but he was willing to bet it had been a long time.

The Chief Inspector got out of the Wolsey and walked across the yard to where the girl was standing. "You wanted to have a word with me, Annie?" he asked.

Annabel nodded. "If you wouldn't mind. I know it's not part of your job to listen to me any more, but I've got things to get off my chest and I can't think of anyone else to turn to."

"I'm a good listener," Woodend told her.

Annie clenched her hands into tight, frustrated fists. "It's so difficult to know where to begin."

"Why don't you start with where you were last night?"

"I went to Liverpool," Annie said. "I went back to our old house. Don't ask me why. I just did."

"Maybe you wanted to recapture your childhood," Woodend suggested. "The time before you were sent to boarding school."

"Maybe," she agreed. "But if that's what it was, I didn't have much success. The street I grew up in isn't even there any more. It's been bulldozed to make way for a new development. I had to laugh. There didn't seem anything else to do. How's Jenny?"

"She's about as well as can be expected under the circumstances," Woodend said.

Tears came to Annie's eyes. "It's all my fault," she sobbed. "If I hadn't been going to take Michael away from Jenny, she'd never have tried to kill herself."

"She'd still have killed Robbie," Woodend said. "That had nothin' to do with you an' Michael."

"Maybe that wouldn't have happened either if I'd been a better sister," Annabel said. "If I'd offered her my support instead of just resenting her for being the one who got to stay at home."

Her body was racked with sobs. Woodend put his arms around her, and she buried her head in his shoulder. "You can't go takin' all the responsibility on yourself," he said. "There's far too many 'ifs' in the world for that. If Robbie had let Jenny make her own mistakes instead of tryin' to protect her from undesirable men

212

by marrying her off to Terry, she might have been able to cope better. If Michael had followed his heart instead of his sense of duty, he'd have stuck with Jenny and tried to find another way to help you. If Terry had made a better job of bein' a husband, Jenny might never have fallen for his brother. If . . . if . . . if . . . It never bloody stops. And *if* you dwell on it, it'll drive you mad."

Annabel eased herself out of his grip and took a couple of steps back. "Thank you for that," she said emotionally.

Woodend shook his head. "It's only common sense, lass," he said. "What will you do now? Marry Michael and settle down to life as a teacher's wife?"

"No," Annie told. "I really was in love with him, you know. Perhaps I still am. But it's no good – after what's happened, I could never be happy with him again."

"So what *will* you do?"

"If I manage to stay out of gaol . . ." she forced a smile to her face, ". . . there's that 'if' word again . . . then I'll come back home. My mother's going to need my support in all sorts of ways – and there'll be plenty of work to do around the club. And then there's Jenny. With Robbie dead, and Terry in gaol, I'm all she's got."

"You and Michael."

Annie laughed, with bitter irony. "That's right, you can always rely on Michael to sort out other people's problems for them, can't you? Well, not this one. You think I feel guilty? You should see him. He's so eaten up with his own guilt he's no good for anything at the moment." She sighed. "Men *talk* tough, but when it comes down to it, it's usual the women who have to *be* tough."

Woodend nodded. "I'll not contradict you there, lass," he said.

The three policemen were in the buffet at Maltham Railway Station, drinking lukewarm tea and munching on rock cakes which tasted as if they had been made out of real rock. Rutter was leaving for London immediately. Woodend would stay behind to clear up the paperwork. Inspector Chatterton had just come along for the ride.

"I was hooked on the idea of a professional killer," Woodend was explaining to Chatterton. "I tried to keep an open mind – I always do – but there was somethin' about the killin' that suggested the cold, professional approach. It wasn't, of course – if there was any coldness, it was the coldness of desperation. But as long as I had my fixation, I couldn't see the simple truth. The light had failed, the room was in darkness. Gower tried to cross it and fell over – because he didn't know the layout. And why didn't Gower put his torch on? It would have been seen by anybody crossin' from the club to go to the toilets. And that was true of whoever used a torch! Only someone who knew the room well could have got to the desk without goin' sprawlin' over the coffee table Doris had just bought. And only three people *did* know it that well." He counted them off on his fingers. "Terry, Doris and Jenny."

I should have worked it out for myself the moment Maria told me what it was like to be blind, Rutter thought. She had difficulty getting around in a flat she'd lived in for two years in the darkness. It would have been impossible for anyone else. And Robbie Peterson's office was exactly the same.

"I follow your reasoning, sir," Chatterton said. "But how could you be so sure it wasn't one of the other two – Terry or Doris – who did the killing?"

"Terry had an alibi," Woodend reminded him. "He was down by the lake, givin' his brother a black eye."

"And Doris?"

"Most of the time, Doris couldn't stand her husband. But that had been true for years. Why should she suddenly, last Friday, take it into her head to kill him? No, it had to be the result of an extraordinary event, and it was Jenny, not Doris, who'd had her life upset."

"Even so, I don't think, under the same circumstances, I'd have been as sure as you seemed to be when we talked last night," Chatterton said.

"There was somethin' else," Woodend admitted. "The first time I spoke to Jenny in Robbie's office, she seemed distressed, but reasonably calm. It was the same the second time, when she brought me them beans on toast. But the third time was different.

She was all right for the first few seconds, then she suddenly went hysterical, and after that she wouldn't go in there at all. She said the place reminded her too much of her dad. But surely the house – which had in it the furniture Robbie used in life, includin' his favourite chair – would have had much more effect on her than an office filled with police furniture?"

"It *was* where her dad actually met his death," Chatterton pointed out.

"True," Woodend agreed. "But we still come back to the original question. Why wasn't she bothered the first two times? What had changed between them an' her third visit?"

Chatterton closed his eyes and tried to think, but it was no good. "I don't know, sir."

"What did you bring me?" Woodend asked, a trifle impatiently.

"A couple of desks, a—"

"After that. After we'd got all the office furniture."

Suddenly Chatterton understood. "I brought you a duplicate of the hammer which killed Robbie," he said.

"Exactly," Woodend agreed. "I thought it might help me reach into the killer's mind if I got the feel of it. Well, it did no such thing. So I put it in the rack. Now to most people it would have looked completely inconspicuous – just blendin' in with the other tools. You'd be more likely to notice that there was a gap than that there was a full complement of tools. But if you'd taken a hammer from the same position on the rack only a few nights earlier – and used it to kill your father – you'd notice it all right. That's what Jenny did – and that's why she suddenly broke down."

The buffet windows rattled, as a huge steam locomotive pulled into the station. Woodend rose to his feet. "I expect you'll want to say your goodbyes to Inspector Chatterton now, Sergeant," he said, as he headed towards the door.

Rutter shook hands with the Inspector, then followed his boss out onto the platform. Woodend already had one of the doors held open. The Sergeant climbed into the train, then pulled down the window.

"I hope Maria's operation is a success," Woodend said. "But

if things do turn out badly, you know you can always rely on me and Joan for a bit of emotional support."

"Thanks, sir," Rutter replied.

"And about that other matter," Woodend continued. "Don't leave the Force. We need lads like you."

"Is that right?" Rutter asked bitterly. "Or do you need people like Superintendent Jackson, who'll do anything in their power to protect their men from paying for the actions?"

"We need people like *you*," Woodend said firmly. "But since you've brought up Jackson, let me ask you a question. If he'd been on this case, how do you think he'd have handled Jenny's interrogation?"

"Since she wasn't one of his 'lads', he'd have gone at her like a bull in a china shop," Rutter said. "She'd have been a wet rag within five minutes."

"And would you have gone about it in the same way?"

"You know I wouldn't."

"Why not?"

"Because I can't condone what she did, but at least I have some kind of sympathy for her. I can understand the pressures she was under, and I can see that in her place – as wrong as it was – I might have done the same thing."

Woodend nodded. "She asked us if she was a monster, an' we said no. But over the next few months she's goin' to be surrounded by people who think that's *exactly* what she is. Don't you think it'll help her a bit – when all she gets to see is uniforms and grim, unyielding faces – to know that there are at least a couple of bobbies who'll shed the occasional tear for her?"

"That's not much of a consolation for a woman on a murder charge, is it?" Rutter asked.

"No," Woodend agreed. "But, by God, it's better than nothin'."

The guard waved his flag and blew his whistle. The iron monster hissed steam and chugged out of the station. Woodend stood motionless on the platform and watched it until it was out of sight.

Epilogue

It was a mild November morning, but there no feeling of crisp air and warm sunshine inside the Church of St James the Minor. Woodend shifted uneasily in his pew. He didn't like churches which smelled of incense – didn't like churches which were so grand and vaulting that the sound of your footsteps echoed around the roof. And he didn't like wearing his best clothes, either – his starched shirt collar was almost cutting his neck in two.

He changed position again. "Behave yourself, Charlie," his wife hissed. "Everybody's lookin' at you."

Woodend grinned, and glanced around him. *Nobody* was looking at him. All eyes were focussed, just as they should have been, on the front of the church. The Chief Inspector directed his own gaze in the same direction. Bob Rutter looked splendid in his morning coat – absolutely splendid.

I'm just about old enough for him to be my son, Woodend thought. If it hadn't been for the War, maybe he and Joan *would* have had a son of Bob's age. But there *had* been a war, and Rutter *wasn't* his son. Instead, he had a daughter who he loved with all his heart.

He reached into his pocket and fished out the article which had appeared in the previous evening's paper. He'd already read it three or four times, but since he'd used up so many favours bringing about the event it reported, he thought he'd earned the right to look at it again. The headline read:

Disciplinary Body Reports
The Police Disciplinary Board, hearing the charges against Constable Charles Philips (26) has ruled that the constable

217

behaved in an unreasonable and reckless manner during a demonstration outside the Spanish Embassy last August. Several witnesses have testified to seeing him hit an unarmed protestor over the head with his truncheon. The protestor, named as Miss Maria Jiménez, suffered serious injuries. Criminal proceedings are expected to follow.

Woodend folded the article and put it back in his pocket. Yes, he'd had to work hard to get that result. But it had been worth it, because justice had finally been served – not to mention the fact that it had convinced Sergeant Rutter to withdraw his resignation.

The organist struck up the bridal march and the congregation turned to look at the back of the church. The bride was dressed in a flowing white gown and was accompanied by her father, a distinguished, grey-haired man who bore himself like an aristocrat. Together they walked gracefully down the aisle towards the altar.

"Doesn't she look lovely, Charlie," Joan whispered.

"Aye, she does," Woodend admitted. "A real picture."

And he was not the only one who thought it. Bob Rutter had turned his head, and the Chief Inspector could see the expression of blissful happiness on his face.

The bride and her father swept past the Woodends' pew. "She's been practising this bit for days," Joan Woodend said.

"She must have been."

"And just look at her now. She's positively glidin'. If you didn't know, you'd never guess that she was blind, would you?"

"No," Woodend agreed. "No, you wouldn't."

Lightning Source UK Ltd.
Milton Keynes UK
UKOW05f0645290617

304314UK00001B/35/P